JAY TINSIANO & JAY NEWTON

Red Horse

Acknowledgement

We want to extend huge thanks to everyone who helped craft this book. Your contribution helped us make Red Horse the best story we possibly could.

Jim Newton
Diane Velasquez
Dorene A. Johnson USN (Ret)
Lynn Hallbrooks
Lee Jones
Mr Maff

We would also like to give out a shout out to the following for their support.

Ronald Carr
Jane Davies
Adam Chilvers

Join the Jay Tinsiano Reader Group

Free Thriller Starter Library
Books and stories
Previews and Sneak Peeks
Exclusive material

To join the VIP Jay Tinsiano reading group, head to:

www.jaytinsiano.com/newsletter

Prologue

April 26th, 1945.
Deputy Mayor's Office. Leipzig, Germany.

US Army intelligence officer Wes Helms ran a finger down the edge of the manila folder to sharpen the crease. He opened it up, revealing the first page of his "Operation Paperclip" file. An operation run by the Office of Strategic Services, or OSS. His top target had been Dr Wernher Reisser, the head of the secret Nazi weapons programmes. Doctor Reisser had been overseeing some of Germany's biggest technological breakthroughs, including the design and build of the V2 rockets that had been terrorising citizens in London since the beginning of the year.

The Western Allies' intelligence agencies had all been tracking Hitler's secret programmes since the beginning of the war. Now the war was almost over, and the race was on to secure these valuable Nazi assets, but also a record of the personnel involved. Helms was determined that it would be the US that got the booty.

Helms had arrived in Nordhausen a few weeks earlier, just after the US 3rd Armored Division and 104th Infantry Division had liberated the city. They had also found the horrors of the Boelcke Kaserne work camp, which had made more than one soldier retch from the conditions discovered there.

Thousands of workers, Polish, French, Slavic and many others had been forced to work on the V2 programme. The US soldiers found piles of bodies when they arrived, too many to count, and only a handful of survivors.

Helms had been given a quick tour by a Major. Although the scenes initially repulsed him, he felt impressed by the German efficiency of the operation. After, he inspected the V2 facilities and began overseeing the US army as they prepared to take the remaining rocket parts and equipment back to the States. The information from the top Nazi rocket scientist Dr Von Braun led them to a mine shaft where they found related documents for the project.

They had to move fast as the area was due to become part of the Russian zone, and those in the know of Operation Paperclip intended to leave as little as possible for the Russians.

Now, Helms had been lured to Leipzig following in the slipstream of the US advance. The news came that one of his top targets, Wernher Reisser, was there to escape the Soviets and had given himself up to the Americans.

A guard brought in Reisser, a tall, lean man with a gaunt look as though the skin had been stretched over his skull, and he looked much older than his thirty-two years.

"Dr Reisser, please sit down."

The man did so, nervously adjusting his grey cloth suit and settling into the chair. Inexpensive attire thought Helms. A suit that perhaps a low-level official might wear. This was a man hoping to keep a low profile. It was not a great time to be a Nazi, after all.

"We've verified who you are finally," said Helms with a thin smile, looking up from Reisser's identification papers. "Let me begin with a question. Are you happy to be on our side of the line, or would you have preferred to be talking to the Russians?"

Reisser barely suppressed a chortle, waving a dismissive hand.

"I hope you don't think I would ever have any desire to work for Stalin? If that's what you're implying, then you're well wide of the mark."

Helms leaned back and smiled again more genuine this time.

"Just asking the question. I'm interested."

Helms pushed over his pack of Lucky Strikes that Reisser had been glancing at and gestured for him to help himself.

"We should have joined forces and fought the Russians," said Reisser, lighting up and inhaling with satisfaction. "Germany always wanted to seek peace with the West. Hitler told me that when I received the Knight's Cross in Berlin. Churchill didn't want to know. But the Fuhrer always thought it was possible."

Reisser paused and added, "Stalin is your real enemy, Mr Helms. The Russians are your enemy now."

"Did you hear? The US 1st met and shook hands with the Red Army at the Elbe yesterday," he said with satisfaction.

Reisser pursed his lips slightly. "Yes, I overheard the guards mention it. Trust me, that's a friendship that will be short-lived."

Helms sighed and picked up the phone.

"Private, can you get more coffee in here?"

He replaced the receiver and focused on the files again.

"The Red Army will soon have control of this area. Is there anything else you can give us, Doctor? Before it all falls into Stalin's hands?" Helms asked.

Reisser considered the question for a moment. "The bases

still have a lot of equipment. The documents on how to use that equipment and the rest of the personnel are another matter. I would like assurances."

Helms jotted down a note on the file.

"We want to have everything, Dr Reisser. This is not a negotiation."

Reisser leaned back, unbuttoning his suit, and grinned.

"Yes, there is something. Something that your intelligence and Government have little idea about, and I'm not talking about the V2 project. This is something different." He looked at Helms. "Again, I would like assurances."

"You realise high-level Nazis are going to be hung after their trials. There was another concentration camp found this week. The world is appalled and horrified at the Nazi regime."

"I know nothing about that," Reisser said quickly.

"Maybe so, but that hardly gives you much to bargain with."

Reisser glared at Helms.

"Do you want the programme? Do you want the superior German technology and expertise that will take the American war machine to the next level? That is the question you should be concerned with, Colonel Helms."

Helms leaned back in his chair and stared out of the window across the ghostly bombed-out shells of buildings. Leipzig had taken the brunt of repeated Allied bombing campaigns in the previous months before the US army entered the city, leaving it a virtual wasteland. The suicide rate across Germany had spiralled out of control as the inevitable collapse of the Nazi regime came to a head.

Helms stroked the wooden desk. Indeed, the Major, who had been the former resident of this very room, had killed himself in it only days before.

There was a rapid knock at the door, and an orderly brought in a tin jug of coffee before leaving.

Helms offered another cigarette, lit them and then poured coffee for them both.

"It's not the best coffee but all we could find around here," he said.

Helms took a gulp and took a pull on the Lucky Strike.

"I can arrange your safe passage, Reisser, and new identity and accommodations. I have the authority to do almost anything I please. So, tell me about your secrets."

Reisser smiled, tilting his head slightly at Helms.

"Very well, where are your maps of the country?"

****

The Sergeant came into the major's office with the rolled-up maps and handed them over to Helms. "Get me, Captain Richards. Ask him to come here immediately," ordered Helms.

The Sergeant saluted. "Yes, Sir!"

Helms stood up and unrolled the first map and flattened it on the large oak desk, helped by Reisser, who focused his eyes on the Sowie mountain region in Southern Germany near the border with the Czech Republic.

He pointed a bony finger at the map.

"This area here," Reisser said, circling an area in Southern Germany near the Czechoslovakian border, "there is a vast network of underground bases and factories that have been working on the Fuhrer's most secret projects. Which, of course, I was in charge of until three days ago."

"There are over two hundred thousand square metres of tunnels, sixty kilometres of roads, bridges and one hundred kilometres of pipeline," he continued.

"Built under the mountains?" asked Helms.

"Yes, and there are others in Germany, but I don't know the exact locations. My orders were to help construct and run the entire 'Riese.'"

"Riese?"

"It means 'Giant.' The name for the whole complex."

"Is it completed?"

Reisser shook his head. "No. There are countless tunnels, and some areas are unfinished. Some have caved in."

Helms rubbed his short greying curly hair and leaned over the map.

"I want to see it or at least get an idea, a taste of it. What was the situation there when you left?"

"The whole complex was under the command of an SS unit. They guarded all of them, but they were pulling out at the same time I was leaving so I believe them to be empty."

He paused before continuing. "But I cannot discount that there might still be some SS or even WerWolf units in the area."

Helms nodded. He knew all about the WerWolf SS divisions. A force of fanatics, well-armed and highly trained, who were ready to cause chaos even after the defeat of Germany. But recently, there had been no clear evidence they were any real threat. His real worry was the approaching Russians. They weren't that far away, and he would need to move fast before the whole area was overrun.

He couldn't forget his primary mission, the V2 programme in Noshausan. Someone else could handle that, he thought. He knew plenty of competent and trusted Colonels in the US Army in that area who were more than capable of carrying off all the equipment and documents.

"So, these facilities have been abandoned by the SS? Then they should be empty?"

"As I said, that is what I saw at Książ Castle with my own eyes. Everyone was pulling out, and as far as I'm aware, it was the same for the whole area."

"Thank you, Doctor. You can return to your quarters. But be ready for a little trip."

Reisser went to leave.

"And Doctor," Helms added. Reisser turned around to face him.

"If you're not truthful with me, I'll personally shoot you in the back of the head."

***

Two German army trucks emblazoned with Red Cross insignia followed a winding forest road set deep in lower Silesia. Tall canopies of fir trees obstructed the blue sky. Helms and Reisser were sitting in the front of the second truck. The very best soldiers had been picked from the 272 Regiment of the 69th Infantry Division, who had helped take Leipzig only days before. All of them wore civilian clothing but were heavily armed. They also had brought along an army photographer to record anything of interest.

Everyone had been briefed that this was a covert operation. If they were captured in that area by Germans, Russians or Polish alike, they would almost certainly be treated as spies. Wearing US army uniforms would be hard to explain to Soviet troops so far from the Allied lines. It was a tense time between the Allies as the defeat of Germany grew closer.

Helms had complete authority and decided to keep the

operation low-key, making them all wear civilian clothing but with army-issued kit and weapons.

Leipzig airfield, now occupied by the 60th Armored Infantry Battalion, had mostly been bombed by the Allied forces or burned out by the retreating Germans. Helms was looking at the option of having to drive the 270 km or give up the idea of trying to get to see project "Riese" altogether. However, a few calls to military command and he was able to get the use of a C-47 Skytrain, a widely used US transport plane flown down from Nuremberg. The high importance of this mission in the eyes of the US Government gave him plenty of clout.

Helms placed Colonel Wilson in charge of military planning to be based in Leipzig.

After five kilometres, the forest began to thin out and opened up into a plateau of grassy meadows; the grey mounds of the Owl Mountains dominated the horizon to their left.

Helms took out a silver box of cigarettes and offered one to Reisser.

"Beautiful views, aren't they?" Reisser said.

"Absolutely. Shame they're going to be in Russian hands soon."

Reisser looked at him with a frown, pausing the lighting of his cigarette.

"Are the Americans not going to advance any further?"

"They'll be no American occupation of the lower Silesia. According to the 'occupation directive 1067', the US army will be required to withdraw back to pre-defined lines and hand the area over to the Soviets. The top priority is getting as much information about the V2 programme in Nordhausen and whatever you're showing me now. These territories are soon to be in Soviet control."

Reisser lit his cigarette at last and blew a column of smoke into the passing wind.

"We'd better hurry then."

After another hour's drive Reisser directed the convoy towards the Owl mountains that dominated the skyline, and the vehicles slowly made their way upwards on a track surrounded by woodland.

"The Sorna complex is ten kilometres ahead. I suggest we be careful from this point on," Reisser said. Helms nodded and leaned forward to ask the driver to pull over. He beeped his horn three times and stopped. The truck ahead came to a halt a few metres ahead. Helms walked up and spoke briefly to the Captain in the front, who then got out and banged on the side.

"Take a break," he shouted to the soldiers inside.

A column of relieved US marines clambered out to smoke and stretch their legs. A couple ran into the woods to relieve themselves. Reisser joined the captain and Helms as they stood behind the truck.

"Captain Richards. Reisser tells us the complex is ten kilometres up this road."

Helms looked to Reisser, indicating him to elaborate.

"Originally, it was guarded by the SS units. I honestly do not know if there are any still around."

The captain, a heavyset man with rugged features, looked from Reisser to Helms, concern creasing his face.

"You didn't mention taking on any SS units—Sir."

"They shouldn't be there. I'm certain there were orders for them to pull out at least a month ago. At least that's what I heard," Reisser said.

"But you're not certain?" asked the Captain.

Dr Reisser shook his head.

The Captain sighed and looked around at his men. "Great," he muttered.

Helms took the Captain aside.

"Captain. This is of the highest priority to the US Army and Washington. Do you understand?" Helms, despite his shorter height, fixed the Captain with a furrowed stare.

"Yes, Sir. I just like to know what we're up against."

The US vehicles moved closer to the compound and, on finding no resistance, pulled off the road once again. Two groups of three soldiers made their way on foot through the trees towards a round pill box set on a hill just ahead of them. They crawled around it, and two gave the signal to the others that it was empty.

Ahead was a clearing, with a large cave-like entrance, ten metres high and just as wide, set into the side of the mountain. Two more German pillboxes stood on either side. Cautiously, the two groups of marines approached. When they were certain the entrance area was free of the enemy, they signalled Reisser, Helms and the rest of the convoy to drive up.

The groups of figures entered the cave-like entrance, finding it still lit by a series of lights by cables attached to the stone walls and followed the tunnel along for around twenty metres. The man-made structure was formidable. They passed abandoned MG42 machine gun posts and other defences before the area opened up into a high archway of reinforced steel and concrete that reached up into the darkness.

They continued walking through the elaborate, tunnelled complex that never seemed to end. Finally, they came to a long platform built from concrete and set into the side of the rock with rails running along into another tunnel ahead of them.

"How big is this place?" asked the captain.

"About thirty-five square kilometres, in total. It connects to a vast network of tunnels and areas, living quarters, and communications. There are also around five more levels below us, but much more was planned."

"And the exact purpose?" asked Helms.

"It was set up to serve many different functions. Advanced weapons research, a possible hiding place for top officials and other experimental programmes."

They moved along a new set of tunnels that were square with thick power cables, around a foot in width, running along the walls.

"This looks like enough power to run a city," said Helms, catching a glimpse of the German smiling in the little light.

"The power station is ahead," Reisser said.

They reached a set of steel doors that opened up into a vast industrial space, lit by spotlights around the stark walls. Helms looked up in amazement. It looked to him as if the height of the space could be as high as the Washington Monument. Several cranes hung overhead, still and silent, their claws hanging like dead hands in a state of rigor mortis. Away to their right side, a train track disappeared into another dark tunnel mouth. Above them, an arched ceiling, around three hundred metres high, stretched into what seemed like a deathly black sky. Pulleys hung loosely from rails that crisscrossed overhead.

Helms could only imagine the activity that would have happened here. Probably only weeks or days before. Now, it was akin to a ghost town. Abandoned and discarded.

In the central area, a circular silo constructed from steel reached up into the roof; the curved metal disappeared into the rock above them.

All around them were massive machines, engines from aircraft, and parts from what looked to Helms like rockets. Helms recognised an aircraft engine, although it was like nothing he had seen before.

"Jesus," Helms muttered, looking around in amazement. "What is this? A manufacturing plant?"

"This is the central testing area and the construction site for advanced military prototypes. Just one of the Reich's top-secret projects," replied Reisser. Helms could detect a hint of pride in his tone as the German strolled ahead, waving an arm across the floor.

"The track is for bringing in heavy materials from the Eastern side of the mountains. The engine is part of the new Luftwaffe aircraft," Reisser hesitated and corrected himself, "—was—for a new Messerschmitt; the 163. It's rocket-powered."

"Rocket-powered?" Helms had walked over to it, rubbing his hand over the smooth steel.

"Yes, indeed, like the V2s. Capable of reaching one thousand kilometres per hour. All work on the 262 engine systems took place here. I dare say if the Allies had delayed the invasion, even by a few months, you might have been looking at a different outcome of the war."

Helms gave a short laugh. "You sound disappointed."

Reisser sighed. "Only in that the capabilities of all this might not be realised."

"I wouldn't worry about that, Doctor."

Helms turned to the soldiers who had taken up positions around the space.

"Where's the photographer?"

One of the soldiers jogged across and saluted Helms. "Private Damato, Sir."

The private then gestured to the photographer and pointed at the engine. "Get shooting, some pictures—get everything!"

The photographer quickly walked across. "Yes, sir!" He adjusted his large camera, and a simultaneous series of clicks and eruptions of light echoed at their backs.

Reisser turned and threw both arms into the air at the strange black circular silo that stood in the centre of the space as if worshipping a great god. "And this! This is a testing space for 'anti-gravity propulsion.' If we'd had a few more years, well, the mind can only imagine."

Helms joined Reisser at his side, looking up at the sleek tube. "What do you mean by that?"

Reisser paused, savouring the moment.

"This was for creating a place or machine that is free from the force of gravity. Can you imagine? But this is a whole other project. The last device was taken away months ago."

Helms nodded, clearly impressed as he took it all in, if not fully understanding what he was looking at. He felt excitement rising within himself like a child discovering a fantastic new box of toys. Toys no other kid had access to or had seen. The significance of what this German engineer was showing him almost made him tremble. What it could mean; Helms was almost shaking at the thought of a million possibilities. This was gold in the real sense of the word.

"Did you have much success?"

"It was close—with more time—perhaps—?"

"You have the details of all these projects?" asked Helms.

"I can get some of the project documents, certainly," Reisser replied.

"Good. And it was you who designed and built this facility? The architect?"

Reisser smiled. "That's right."

Helms nodded. A faint whisper of an idea, a vision forming.

"This way!" Reisser walked across the train track towards a set of double steel doors tucked away in the far wall.

"Something else you might be interested in..." he added, pushing open the doors.

Helms followed, the camera flashing behind him. The other soldiers had split up and moved cautiously to the other tunnels and doorways that made up the maze they were in, keeping alert.

Reisser flicked on some lights inside the room and turned to Helms, who saw a line of six dummies covered in a dark leathery material and heavy vests covering the chest area. The room was long.

"A shooting range," Reisser said, answering his unasked question. "But the material on the dummies is prototype bullet-resistant material, up to 8mm for certain."

They walked up to the dummies, and Helms felt material, nodding slowly.

"A stronger than steel fibre," Reisser added. Helms turned his head. "Private Damato!"

The private and the photographer came into the room and breezed up to them.

"Get this lot," ordered Helms with a sweep of his hand.

"Alright. What else have we got time for?" Helms asked, turning to Reisser.

They walked back into the main area, Reisser leading them across the far side of the space to a larger tunnel than they had entered. Their shadows moved with them, arching across the walls and pipes that spanned across the ceiling and arrived at another set of large doors that lay half open, leading to another tunnel.

They were at the beginning of a train track that stretched out ahead of them.

Their footsteps echoed through the tunnel as water streamed down the walls and dripped from the ceiling, collecting around in pools on the ground.

The soldiers stayed alert, uttering commands to each other. Two men stayed back behind Helms and Reisser, covering their rear while the others and Captain Richards formed the core central group. Up ahead, two marines led the way.

"What is up here, Doctor?"

Reisser sighed, looking around behind him.

"You'll see."

They followed the curve of the tunnel that ended abruptly with a concrete wall. Set in the wall was a steel door, slightly ajar.

"Rogers, take a look. Be cautious," ordered the Captain. He nodded his head at two other marines who took position on either side of the door. One of the men swung open the door quickly. Private Rodgers moved into space, weapon raised.

The other two followed him in, in combat-ready mode.

After a few minutes, Rodgers came out and walked up to Captain Richards, Helms and Reisser as they stood away from the door.

"You better come and see this," he said, his eyes wide with shock.

The three men followed Rodgers through the door into another big space. A strong smell of decomposition hit the back of their throats, and they all immediately put their hands covering their mouths. Inside, the light was dimmer than the tunnels, but there were enough striped lights to see the cages. Rows and rows of them spread out across the room like blocks in a city.

Rodgers and the other soldiers were standing around with handkerchiefs tied over their faces.

"Flashlight?" ordered Richards.

One of the men produced one from his backpack.

Helms grabbed it and pointed the light at the nearest cage. Dead children. No older than five or six. Five of them.

He looked closer.

All shot in the head.

He moved along the row and saw the same thing.

"What the hell?" someone gasped.

Helms had seen the reports of concentration camps that were being unearthed across Europe, but why would they keep their victims down here?

He continued walking. Behind him, someone had produced more torchlights and was checking the other rows in the grid.

"Hey, over here!" One of the marines. "We got some live ones."

Helms and the others who had spread out converged on the spot.

When he got there, Helms looked down at the faces of two boys staring up at him.

Dirty faces.

Dead eyes as if any life had been squeezed out of them like pips from a lemon.

They stared at the soldiers, some covering their eyes at the light. Their cage had dirty blankets spread over the floor, and the children were virtually naked apart from dirty pyjama bottoms.

Next to the cage was a clipboard resting in a wooden holder. Helms picked it up and held a torch to it. He scanned down a column of three-digit numbers with information written next to each name.

"Sir?"

Helms looked up. Captain Richards was staring at him.

"Yes?" Helms replied.

"The children... shall we get them out of there? Give them water?"

Helms looked down at the children, the subjects.

"Yes," he said finally. "We'll need them."

His eyes immediately fell back on the clipboard and the subject information. Columns of three-digit numbers and other information that looked coded. He flipped through pages of information that he didn't yet understand, yet something told him it was important.

Richards turned to the private.

"Give 'em some water, for Christ's sake," he ordered.

One of the soldiers forced open the cage door and bent down on his knees.

"Hey, don't be afraid. Don't be afraid—" he said to one of the children.

He offered his water bottle to a boy who stared back vacantly.

"Look, it's OK, kid." The private took a sip of the water showing it was safe, and handed it through the gap. The child took a long look at the water bottle and slowly took it from the soldier.

Helms took Reisser aside, and they walked away from the other men.

"What is this place, and what has been going on?"

Reisser stared off into the distance.

"A unique programme. It started with Josef Mengele's human experiments programme. However, this is a step further to physiological control. To control young minds, mould them to the Fuhrer's will and use them as exceptional killers or servants for the regime."

Helms stared at Reisser.

"Mind control?"

"Yes, mind control. Years of work. It started long before the war."

Helms nodded slowly.

"Do you know where Mengele is now?" he asked. Reisser shook his head.

"No, I don't. He was based at the Auschwitz camp, but I doubt he will be there now."

Helms knew the Soviets had liberated the camp back in January. He was either long gone or in Russian hands.

Helms turned and walked over to the Captain. The men were helping the children out of the cage and giving them water and rations.

"Captain. We've been here long enough. I cannot risk our capture. Gather up all the clipboards."

"Yes sir," Richards replied. "The children? Sir?"

Helms looked down and noticed three numbers tattooed into one of the boy's arms; 192. He looked back at the clipboard. The number was there in the column, along with ten others.

His eyes, somehow lacking pity but full of intrigue, fell on the boys who were looking back at him.

"Yes, bring them too."

Chapter 1

04:36 AM, Present day.
Tehran, Iran.

Haleema slowly opened her eyes as the familiar calls of the dawn Fajr prayer drifted through her bedroom window. The haunting call had been her alarm clock ever since she had moved to the apartment five years before. Through the slatted blinds, the light from the street lamps six storeys below gave the room a yellow tinge.

She hadn't been able to get the images out of her head and was sure they had played in her dreams, although she couldn't remember clearly.

Grainy silent video footage of the young Mexican boy, not even in his teens, stepping into the building and proceeding to shoot anyone that got in his way, starting with the security guard. The way the boy carried himself with purpose was calm and efficient. He was chillingly accurate with the targets as if he had been training for years.

There seemed a desperate determination to perform in his mannerisms as if something personal was at stake as he jumped the turnstile at the security desk. He then cornered the chief executive of Cryostone, Harold Walters, as he desperately rapped the elevator button.

The boy reached the elevator doors and pointed his weapon inside.

How many shots did he fire?

She wondered who else had been inside. Who had died that day? The camera angle didn't show it, just the report from the young man's firearm, pumping bullets mercilessly into unseen victims.

Walters, she found out, had been killed. She had pulled the small news item up on a local Colorado website. Having searched using Goya, the global search engine, she found nothing.

She lay in bed replaying the scene in her head for a moment longer. Without much enthusiasm, she sat up, swung her feet to the ground and padded over to the bathroom, the Fajr prayers following her across the open-plan studio. She showered and dried her short black hair in the mirror, looking at herself with brown eyes set against pale skin. Haleema thought herself striking but not beautiful, with an almost boyish look.

Twenty minutes later, she was sitting in front of her 40-inch screen, logging onto Icarus via the VPN. She watched the video again. The motion of death taking place in silence, the time ticking by on the bottom left.

Five times.

He had fired five times.

She dropped the video file link into a private message to Nightowl and typed out an accompanying note:

Something I think you'll be interested in. I found it while at work. Haven't had much time to research all the details but let me know if you want me to dig.

Sirus

Haleema then encrypted the message itself and hit send.

Chapter 2

6.10 PM
Natanz Uranium enrichment plant, Iran.

Ostad Karim Sheraz checked his clipboard papers one more time, making sure his tasks were all ticked off before he left for his long-awaited week's break. Errors were not tolerated in the delicate world of Iranian nuclear physics, and he desperately wanted to have time with the family without worrying about his job and whether something had been missed. He moved slowly along the walkway that led to the main reactor control room, carefully checking for any red lights that might indicate any problems in the system flow paths. He was happy to see only a line of green ones.

The procedures were a lot more stringent following the Stuxnet attack in 2007. The virus, almost certainly created by the US or Israel, had somehow found its way into the facility, which had no external internet connection. Karim and many others knew it was most probably through a third-party software supplier to the plant who had no doubt acted as an unwitting trojan horse.

That virus had destroyed around a thousand fuel-refining centrifuges that had to be quickly replaced. The attack had severely slowed down Iran's nuclear programme, but it had not completely killed it.

One of the control room operators waved a hand from behind the glass that led to the exit and disappeared around the corner. Karim looked around, rechecking the list, making sure the many field operators that took care of the plant maintenance were on top of their tasks. Finally satisfied that everything was covered, Karim headed to the senior supervisor's office, where Garshasp Shah, the senior technical manager, rifled through an old filing cabinet.

"Garshasp! You old devil, unless there's anything else, I think it's time for me to drive into the sunset and leave this hole," said Karim, flashing him a cheeky grin.

Garshasp pulled out a paper folder and tossed it casually onto the desk as he snorted a laugh.

"No, Karim. I think you're safe to take off in that old donkey cart of a car you drive."

"At least that donkey cart will get me away from this place," Karim said with mock satisfaction as he removed his white coat and hung it along with the others.

"So, everything has been powered down until I'm back. Just make sure that the temperature stays level."

Garshasp nodded. "Don't worry; you have a good time. What are you planning to do?"

Karim shrugged as he headed for the door. "See my wife. Perhaps my sons will be around. Hopefully, I can work on the olive and fruit groves. I still need to finish a wall to keep the goats out. Catch up with friends at the square and browse the markets. You know, just relax and forget about this place!"

He held up his arm as he left. "See you next week, Garshasp."

"See you, Karim. Don't work too hard."

Karim took the stairs instead of the oversized lift. He was fast approaching fifty and felt it. Climbing the rusting stairwell to the ground level was probably the only exercise he did anymore. Whether any of his sons or Haleema would bother to visit was another question, but at least he didn't have to work at the facility. He silently thanked Allah, pulling out his security swipe card. The body scanner bleeped as usual as Karim walked through and picked up his wallet and keys from the X-ray carousel.

"Good evening Mr Sheraz," said a young security man who was checking a screen on the other side. Karim nodded and stepped out into the bracing night air and glanced briefly at the vast Karkas mountain chain that rose almost four thousand metres beyond the facility walls.

He walked over to his modest blue Peugeot 206, climbed inside and rubbed his hands briefly before starting up the engine.

Karim drove along a small road, past a row of sand-coloured buildings, and pulled up at the security box. Behind it stood a thirty-metre-high electric fence that surrounded the facility with guard towers dotted along the line. The guard sitting in-side glanced at his card, and the barrier lifted up automatically to let him through onto a lone road. After a few metres, he passed through another ring of security and then turned west for the long drive home, the Karkas mountains filling the view in his rear mirror.

Glancing at his watch, Karim mentally prepared for a long stretch behind the wheel. Getting home to Shiraz was too far to drive in one go, so he usually stopped at a little hotel for the night. It was a few hours' drive, and then he would set off early in the morning and hopefully be back in time for a tasty evening meal. One of the hardest parts of his job was being away from his wife and family. He missed them all, but he needed to put food on their table. A few more years and the family debts would be paid off, and he could consider retiring for good.

Working and living in the secret nuclear facility for extended periods of time was beginning to take its toll on the ageing scientist. It was too far from his hometown, and pressure from the Iranian authorities had been intensifying by the week. His passion for science had long since evaporated, and now he just thought about his groves of olives and oranges that he tenderly cultivated. It was nothing much, just a way to spend time, to escape.

Karim headed across the barren landscape, passing through small villages and towns as the sky on the horizon faded from an intense pinkish hue to a darkened purple and then blackness fell. Karim fiddled with the radio dial. The melodic sound of the Santoor filled the car. He listened to a Persian music station for an hour before changing over to the official Iranian news. Of course, he didn't take every word as gospel, but part of him worried deep down about his future and what was happening in his country.

Reports told of Iranian revolutionary guards fighting another UIS insurgency in Jiroft and Sirjan. That was getting closer and closer to Shiraz, thought Karim, turning up the volume. The news anchor finished by stating victory in Jiroft was imminent. Karim scoffed at the idea that there had been some easy victory. Propaganda. No doubt it was the reverse. The news finished, and he turned off the radio.

As he approached the outskirts of Najafabad, his stop-off town, Karim sighed as a farmer with a herd of sheep blocked the road, crossing from one side to another. Slowing down to a standstill, Karim tapped the horn. The old man held up his stick, acknowledging him, but the sheep did not move any faster.

Perhaps getting to the hotel before midnight was too ambitious.

He noticed a black Toyota pickup appearing in the rearview mirror on the shimmering crest of the hill behind him. His thoughts drifted as he waited for the sheep to clear the road. His sons were seemingly getting more radical in their thinking and outspoken about the government. They should keep their views to themselves, or they'd end up in one of the secret police prisons where no one ever got to leave. And Haleema. So smart and making use of her skills with technology. He hoped he could see them all soon. It had been so long.

The sheep were finally all across, and Karim moved off again, noting the vehicle behind looked brand new, which was unusual in these parts. Ahead, the first buildings of Najafabad; concrete boxes, whitewashed and appearing pinkish in the evening light. The dying sun jettisoned long shadows across the street, and locals went about their business, shutting up market stalls and talking amongst themselves. A group of men hung around a makeshift table at a tea stand, smoking and talking. A woman in a full burqa looked at him with bright green eyes and then quickly turned away as he slowed to make the turn for his hotel.

Karim had a strange, uneasy feeling yet couldn't grasp what his senses were telling him.

As he pulled into the narrow road, he immediately hit the brakes, swearing under his breath at the sight of a van blocking the road. Karim honked the horn and drummed his fingers on the steering wheel for a few moments. Further down the street on the corner was the hotel car park. Deciding it would be quicker to drive around the block, he put the gearstick into reverse. Turning his head, he saw the new Toyota pickup pulling up and boxing him in. Immediately he realised it was a trap, even before the gunmen appeared out of the Toyota.

Panicking, he slammed onto the gas pedal, and his car lurched back towards the gunmen, who were running towards him, scarves covering their faces, weapons drawn.

A shadow appeared in the side mirror.

He shouted out and recoiled as the window smashed, covering him with shards of glass.

A hand reached in and turned off his engine, disappearing as quickly with the keys. The door opened, and he felt intense pressure on his temple.

A gun.

"Slowly get out of the car," said a deep voice with calm confidence.

Karim felt his palms covered in sweat. His eyes were wide with fear. He looked to the side of his assailant and noticed an ammunition belt on the man's waist. Karim froze; his muscles wouldn't function.

Were they secret police? Who else could it be?

"Out!" The voice was louder, and before he could respond, a hand grabbed his shoulder, wrenching him from the car. There was a sudden blast of pain behind his head, and his vision tunnelled.

In a split second, his world darkened.

Chapter 3

Secret location, Tehran, Iran.

Haleema Sheraz tapped the keyboard function to kill the screen, swung around in her chair and stood up, yawning. She looked down at the row of desks where her colleagues all focused on their screens, working on their various tasks. Some chose to sit on bean bags in the corner with their laptops or lounge in a hammock that had been set up across one of the spaces.

The election had been the main topic of conversation. The news had just come through that the ruling party had won outright. The progressive opposition leader, Mehdi Yazdi, had not been heard from since.

Of course, it was no secret that he never had a chance of winning. It just would not be allowed. It was no surprise to Haleema, and as the conversation and murmurs died down, everyone focused on their work.

The Cyber Army was not officially part of the Iranian Government, but everyone who worked there knew where the funding came from. It comprised a group of IT specialists and professional hackers. Their primary task was simply to wage cyber warfare against the West's governments and corporations and hack "enemy sites".

Her particular project was a malware exploit virus that was near completion. She had been tasked with focusing on hacking into corporations working within the military-industrial complex in the United States.

The Iranian authorities had been pressuring her bosses to get results faster, as if hacking and decrypting was just something you needed to "sweat over", and then it would happen. Their work was so complicated the mullahs would hardly comprehend it. Haleema smiled to herself as she logged off, imagining the looks on their faces as she explained it was "over their heads".

It was home time, and she needed a change of scene; the long hours staring at the monitors took their toll. As she grabbed her handbag and said goodbye to a few remaining colleagues, her eyes briefly passed across the stencilled image of the supreme leader, Ali Khamenei, that dominated the wall.

Her friend Ko looked up from his laptop and gave her a wave. To look at him anyone would think he was another one of those affluent kids from Elahieh, but he was one of the best code-breakers she knew.

She had endured a difficult few years since returning to Iran following her studies in England. Fitting back into Iranian society, with its rigid morality laws and demand for absolute service to the state, had been difficult, to say the least. Yet through her programming skills, she had come to the attention of her current employers. To do what she loved doing and get paid, she lowered her expectations after university and became a hacker, indirectly for the government.

The stuffy, windowless bunkered office, set on the basement floors of the Ministry, was a relief to escape from. Haleema buttoned up her dark green manteaux, adjusted her hijab and breathed in the night air. She glanced at her watch, not too late but late enough: 9.33 pm.

Across the quiet four-lane road, a gust of wind blew sheets of newspaper along the carriageway; a taxi slowed on the far side, picking up two men before speeding off. Haleema tutted, annoyed she had missed it and walked along the closed storefronts that lined the main road. Sunbleached posters, half ripped, of the ruling council members of Iran were plastered on the boarded-up derelict storefronts.

Years ago, the streets would have been bustling with life, but as the war with UIS intensified, no one wanted to take any chances. That, along with the fact that Tehran's morality police had raided and forced the closure of dozens of cafes, the mainstay sanctuary of young Tehranis', intellectuals and students tended to clear the streets.

Although it wasn't strictly illegal to be out after 9 pm, it had become a self-fulfilling act, as though anyone found on the streets was judged somehow, if only in questioning stares.

Haleema had recently moved nearer to her work to cut down on the commute and buy her more time for other activities. She wondered whether to drop by her friend's house. There was always something going on at Ali J's, whether it was playing illegal Western music or messing around on his latest game console. All the usual trendy Iranian "in crowd" would probably already be there, sneakily drinking alcohol and breaking a dozen other laws as well.

This young generation of Iranians only wanted to live life on their terms and avoid the crazy laws and authoritarian regimes as much as possible.

Haleema's phone vibrated. She slipped the device out of her

bag and smiled as she read the message from her friend, Dalir. Maybe it would be another late night. A bus pulled up, and she made a run for it, jumping on just before it departed again, and sitting down hastily before checking the news feed on her phone. The situation near her hometown was worsening. The United Islamic State, or Daesh, as they hated being called, seemed to be gaining a firmer stronghold in the south as well as the eastern provinces bordering Afghanistan.

Her family home in Shiraz, where her parents and brothers lived, was right on the knife edge of danger if they made any more gains. Apparently, support for foreign radicals from Iraq and Syria bolstered the Daesh, making them a real threat to the current government.

Haleema didn't know what to think. On the one hand, she had no time for the regime that paid her, a group of backward-thinking old men. Yet UIS seemed to be a much scarier prospect from the stories she had heard of forced slavery, beheadings and massacres. It was easy to see how a whole generation was being isolated when they had to choose between one or the other.

Two more stops went past before Haleema jumped off the bus. She headed through a landscaped garden that led to a series of concrete tenement blocks and walked around it to the rear of the building. There was a myriad of sounds; children laughing, an argument, the distorted tones from a television all drifting between the buildings.

She came to a courtyard, across which was a stand-alone building backed up by a high brick wall. There was a deep repetitive noise, indistinguishable from the other sounds. She pressed a buzzer quickly three times and waited. After a few moments, the door creaked open, and a face peeked out from the darkness inside. The thudding noise more recognisable as a bass line drifting out into the open.

"Hey, Ali. You gonna let me in before you alert the whole city of your den?"

Ali stepped aside to let her in with a nod, and she descended a metal staircase that led into a large basement filled with around twenty young Iranians. A group stood around a pair of record decks at the end of the room, nodding their heads to the beat, drinking beers and smoking.

She glanced around the graffiti-covered walls that her friend Dahir had sprayed up, inspired by the street artists from America and the UK, except the cartoonesque characters were young hip Iranians clad in baseball caps, trainers and oversized T-shirts.

"Dahir!" she shouted. A figure from the group waved a skinny arm, and Dahir made his way over to her.

"Haleema!" He smiled broadly, evidently pleased to see her, and gave her a peck on both cheeks. "So, how are you doing? Still slaving for the supreme leader?"

Haleema waved a dismissive hand and took Dahir's beer. She took a swig and looked around pensively.

"It's a living—for now."

She smiled warmly at him and affectionately ran a hand across his shoulder. "And you? Still seeing that girl? What's her name?"

Dahir shook his head and took back the beer. "No, I'm not sure. She didn't call me." He glanced across the room and smiled at another young guy who had drifted over towards them.

"Omar. You know Haleema?"

They both smiled and shook hands. "No, I don't think so..."

She felt a vibration and fished around in her bag, picking out her phone. She saw from the caller ID it was her mother calling. How could she answer with this music? She placed the phone back in her bag. Omar and Dahir both looked at her questioningly.

Haleema shrugged.

"My mother. I'll have to call her back later."

Dahir leaned over to her. "Something I need to tell you. About why it didn't work out with that girl." Haleema slowly nodded her head, her eyes dropping to Dahir's and Omar's hands that were clasped tightly together.

"Oh..." She raised her eyebrows and nodded again.

"Don't you approve?"

Haleema laughed and gave them both a hug. "Yes, of course, I approve. Whatever makes you happy, Dahir." Her face became more serious. "Please, though, be careful—the authorities."

Dahir gave her shoulder a gentle rub. "Don't you worry, Hal..."

She swung her attention to Omar. "So Omar. Tell me more about yourself."

***

Haleema stepped out of the taxi, swaying slightly. Maybe she'd had one too many beers. She made her way up the concrete steps leading to her apartment block; her small flat was on the third floor.

"Lights," she said, and the main room was illuminated with a warm glow from the ceiling lights. She slipped her coat and shoes off, leaving them neatly by the door. Her modest apartment was clean and well kept, the simple furnishing carefully chosen to her tastes. The lounge area had a coffee table made from wooden crate bottoms that she had sprayed white. A long sofa ran parallel, facing a large television screen that had wires strewn across to a laptop balanced on the coffee table. On one side, a blind obscured a window, and there was a group of plants that complemented the white walls.

She went to the kitchen area in the corner and switched on the kettle, throwing her bag down onto the floor.

"Play Dahir's mix, number 13," she said out loud. A moment later, the audio system began to play a steady rhythmic tune, a homegrown hip-hop mix Dahir had given her. After brewing a mint tea, she slumped down onto the sofa, curling her feet up, cupping the tea in her hands, relieved to be home. She thought about Dahir and his revelation that evening and smiled to herself as she placed the cup on the table. The music filled the room, and Haleema's eyes grew heavy, the long day finally catching up with her.

***

Haleema jolted awake with a sense of unease, her eyes wide. She hadn't returned her mother's call!

She wheeled her legs off the sofa and rooted around for her bag. Finding her phone, she immediately dialled her mother's number and listened to the ringtone. Yellow streams of light fought to get through the half-shut blinds.

How could it be morning already?

Haleema promised herself more early nights and headed to the bathroom, the phone still at her ear.

"Haleema?" The answer was immediate and frantic.

"Sorry, Ma, I was with friends, and then I got home and fell asleep..."

To Haleema's surprise, her mother did not berate her and continued talking. "Your father hasn't arrived. He was supposed to be back yesterday, but he hasn't turned up. Something bad has happened. I know it, Haleema!"

Chapter 4

"Calm down. I'm sure there is a simple explanation."

"I don't know, but your father would call if he was held up and his phone is switched off."

Haleema frowned as she studied her tired face in the mirror.

"I'm sure he just got held up at work or something? You know how things can be there with what he does."

"Yes, but he always phones and lets me know."

Haleema nodded to herself and moved into the bathroom. It was true. He would always call.

"OK, ma. I'll check it out and phone his work."

Her mother whispered her thanks, and they ended the call. Haleema checked her watch and sighed. She was certain it was a waste of time but decided to make the calls. Firstly, she tried his phone. Her mother was right—the line was dead.

Perhaps it was still online through the iPhone app finder? She had added some family members' phones to her account.

Haleema moved back into the living area and slumped down onto the sofa with her iPad, and logged into her cloud account. She tapped through to "find device" to check for her father's phone, holding her breath as she did so.

She read the sentence twice:

The device cannot be located.

With a sigh, Haleema closed the application.

She would have to try his work and see if they knew anything. It took forty minutes before Haleema got through to his department and found herself speaking with her father's subordinate, Garshasp Shah.

"Your father left the facility on Thursday evening, Haleema," he said.

"Are you sure?" Haleema failed to hide the concern in her voice.

"Yes, I saw him go myself. What is wrong... what is happening?"

"Oh, nothing to worry about. I'm sure everything is fine. Thank you for confirming." Haleema cut the call short before the man could respond.

She felt a numb feeling in her chest and a sense of unease.

The next step was the hotel he stayed at in Najafabad. She tapped the maps app and zoomed in on the province where he always stopped over on the way home.

What was the name of that place?

He had mentioned it once. After a minute of searching, she discovered the town only had one hotel, and she proceeded to ring it.

Yes, Karim Sheraz had booked in advance, but no, he had not turned up. She hung up and rubbed her eyes. Did he go somewhere else? To a friend's house? Why was his phone dead and offline?

She stood up, grabbed bottled water from her fridge and paced around her apartment before tapping her mother's number once more.

"So I tried his work, and they told me he left on Thursday evening." Haleema tried to sound calm as if everything was fine.

"So he may have stopped off at a friend's place—do you have..." she continued.

"Haleema, the hotel. Did he get there?" her mother asked, her voice shaking.

Haleema sighed and closed her eyes. "Apparently, he didn't check-in. I think he stayed at a friend's place instead."

"No! He would have told me."

"Ma, please. Do you have some numbers? Anyone he might know on that route." She could sense her mother shaking her head. "No, there's no one..." then a pause, "Actually, wait..."

Haleema listened to her mother rummaging around.

"There's the Farbod family? Could he have seen them?" she asked quickly, a tone of hope returning to her voice.

"Let me have the number," Haleema said, and she quickly scribbled it down with a pencil. "I'll get back to you."

Haleema dialled the number, and there was a long pause before anyone answered. Several minutes later, Haleema ended the call with a sickening feeling in her stomach. Karim had not visited or contacted them.

Haleema swore out loud and fired up her laptop. She tracked her father's possible journey from Natanz to Najafabad via her map app and stared at the red line. If he never checked into the hotel, then something must have happened between Natanz and Najafabad?

It was no good. Although it was the last thing she wanted to do—open herself up to possible interrogation—she would have to notify the police. Her father was definitely missing.

Chapter 5

Monday. 9.14 AM.
Tehran, Iran.

Haleema pressed one eye against the spyhole in the door. Behind it was a middle-aged, portly man with white hair, mopping his brow with a handkerchief as if he had just finished running or something. She was expecting the police but still wanted to be sure.

"Who is it?"

"Detective Papak Rahbar from the Criminal Investigation Police of NAJA." He held up his ID to the peephole.

It was a good start, she thought. She was expecting a low-level uniform, not a detective. She checked the ID and opened the door.

"Haleema Sheraz?"

"Yes, please come in," she said, standing to one side and opening the door.

He walked in. His eyes were immediately drawn to a large piece of street art on the wall that depicted a ghostly silhouette of the Tehran skyline. Haleema expected him to comment, but he said nothing and sat himself down on her sofa without asking.

"So, my father..."

He turned his head slightly. "Do you have any tea?"

Haleema paused, then inhaled sharply. "Sure thing, detective. How do you take it?" she asked.

"I prefer Assam," he said in a flat tone. "White, no sugar, thank you."

Haleema was about to say something but just smiled to herself and walked over to the kitchenette. This man was obviously an elder generation, with all the traditional and rigid views that came with it, but he was the only link to finding her father. She needed him on her side.

Haleema brought back a pot, two cups and a small bottle of milk, placing them on the table.

"Thank you," he said and pulled out a tablet device and appeared to swipe through his notes.

"Right, Haleema, I'm going to record our conversation for the case notes."

Haleema nodded, and he began speaking. "This is Detective Papak Rahbar with Haleema Sheraz at 10.30 AM on the 12th of March."

"So your father is Ostrad Karim Sheraz, with a high-ranking undisclosed position at the Natanz facility?"

"Yes, that's right," she replied.

Rahbar continued reading through his notes. "His colleagues report that he left work as usual on Thursday evening at 6.35 pm, or around that time. He seemed reasonable, in high spirits and looking forward to his leave. He made no phone calls, and the last trace of him we have is CCTV footage of him driving his blue Peugeot 206 out of the Natanz facility."

"That's correct," asserted Haleema.

"And his usual habit was to stop off in Najafabad to break

up the journey?"

"Yes," she replied curtly.

"What about his car?" Haleema asked, pouring his tea before sitting down opposite one of her worn armchairs.

"There's no sign as yet, I'm afraid."

He glanced at his notes.

"Have you received any contact from anyone?" he asked. "Any demands?" the detective added, looking up at her.

"No, no. I already said on the phone."

"And he never talked about UIS?"

"I'm sorry?" she asked, taken aback.

"The United Islamic State. Did he ever talk about them?"

"What are you implying? What has this to do with any-thing?"

Papak sighed and leaned over to sip his tea.

"Miss Sheraz. We have to look into every possibility, and one is that he could have defected to them."

Haleema sat up straight, fixing the detective with a serious look. "Well, that is impossible. He had nothing but contempt for them. We all know what a bunch of animals they are."

Rahbar raised an eyebrow and leaned back with his tea and saucer. "Yes, but some people often can say one thing and believe another."

Haleema shook her head. "Not possible. If they were involved, they would have to have kidnapped him. There is no way my father would join their cause."

"Well, I do hope that is the case. As you can appreciate, there's very little evidence to go on at the moment. If he has been kidnapped, we'd expect you to get a ransom demand relatively soon. In the meantime, we will continue to try to locate his car in the hope that it sheds some light on the situation."

Haleema held her hands out in an imploring gesture. "So what? You're telling me my father has completely disappeared off the face of the earth, and there is nothing more you can do?"

Rahbar put down his tea with a loud clink.

"Look, Ms. Sheraz, I am sorry, but at the moment, there is very little more I can do. We will keep the file open and hope that some new evidence comes to light. We have filed a missing person report, and your father's name and photo have been sent to all our departments, even the border agencies. We will do our best to try to locate him, but with no evidence, I hope you can appreciate that it is like looking for a needle in a haystack."

The detective was already rising from his seat.

"Thank you for your statement, Miss Sheraz. I'll be in touch."

Haleema nodded silently, staring at her tea, then looked up at Rahbar.

"Please. Just do all you can."

Rahbar nodded and left the apartment without another word.

Chapter 6

Undisclosed location, Tehran, Iran.

Massood Rajavil swiped his entry card and stepped through the steel door. He descended the metal steps, his polished leather shoes clicking with each step, the lights automatically flickering on at his movement. The stairwell hugged the circular brick wall that spiralled down to the first sub-level.

A grim-faced guard at the bottom of the subterranean silo saluted him and then continued staring impassively ahead. Massood stepped into a wide corridor, white walls and steel doors spread into the distance. Moans and sobs echoed from behind those doors. He screwed his face up in disgust, not because he felt sorry for their pain and suffering, for these people were the vermin of society, but just because it fed his contempt for them.

They were rats that deserved no dignity.

Milad Ghorbani came out of one of the cells, his white shirt splattered in blood and gave him a nod. He was a short man, overweight and seemed to Massood to be always perspiring.

"Well?"

"He acknowledges that he knows Husseini."

"That he knows him? Well, we know that, don't we? We

need Husseini's whereabouts. What methods have you used?"

Ghorbani looked forlorn. "I already applied level one technique. Should I progress to level two?"

Massood tutted, pushed past him and stopped at the cell doorway. Inside, a naked man in his early twenties was hanging upside down, strung up to the ceiling by his ankles. His body was covered in bruises, cuts, and burns. Ghorbani had certainly been putting in the overtime.

Lighting a cigarette, Massood stepped into the room, walking around the defenceless man like a shark circling a shoal of baitfish. He stopped in front of him and blew smoke in the young man's face. Coughing, the man tried to open his eyes, now just small slits surrounded by puffy purple bruises.

Massood grinned savagely.

"Where is Husseini?"

The man did not answer, coughing again as more smoke blew across his nostrils and mouth.

Massood strolled to a table at the side of the room. He picked up an apron, sliding his head and arms through the protective cloth and tying it at the back. He took two latex gloves from a box and casually walked over to an open toolbox while putting them on. He paused for a moment before plucking out a pair of wire cutters. He seemed to contemplate them for a second, taking another drag of his cigarette before tossing them back in the box. The puffy, bruised eyes of the young man watched him, slowly filling with fear as Massood pulled a cordless power drill from the box.

"Once again, for the last time. Tell me where he is." Massood was grinning again, but his voice was coldly calm. He revved the drill and stepped towards his prisoner.

The young man's eyes darted to the drill, and he nodded furiously despite the crippling pain he was enduring. A croaking gurgle came from his throat before his voice returned.

"Please, stop. I will tell you—I will tell..."

His voice cracked again, and he closed his eyes.

Massood stopped the drill.

"Good, good, now where is he?"

The young man spoke for a minute, revealing what he knew in halting gasps.

Massood nodded.

"Thank you. That's all I needed to know. Easy, wasn't it?"

Then he restarted the drill.

The man's screams echoed through the entire floor, and the drill lowered as if changing down a gear before stopping suddenly—a sound of liquid splattering on the concrete ground. Screams turn to gargled chokes before petering out to silence. Massood stepped out of the room and nodded to Ghorbani.

"Dispose of the body," he said quietly and then walked past him back up the circular steps, his footfall echoing in the silence.

Chapter 7

Madrid International Airport, Spain.

Joe Bowen drained the last of his beer and glanced up at the departures board. The array of yellow dots told him he had another 30 minutes before they displayed the gate number. He hated airports, especially the melodrama of the security. Take off your shoes, spin around and, "Let me check your toothpaste, Sir. Now, walk through this body scanner that does god knows what to your body."

Then he'd have to go through it all again when he got the internal flight in the US.

His eyes drifted to the television screen where the news displayed a group of distraught families. They stood dressed in black at the memorial of the first anniversary of the Madrid train bombing a year ago today.

That was it, of course.

Security was needed for these terrorist atrocities—to protect us.

Except Joe knew that particular Madrid attack was a crock. The story that made the news was nowhere near what had happened. Officially, those responsible had not been caught and punished. Joe knew that was bull. He smiled to himself with some satisfaction that he had dealt with those responsible. The deep state agents, the ones they called Jamall and Zara, were both dead. Zara by his hand, and Jamall burned up by Hugo Reese.

It was ironic he couldn't tell a single soul. He wanted to tell the families: We got them, don't worry. Were they terrorists? Yeah, kind of, but not the type the media talk about. These are worse because they act on behalf of governments, secretive agencies and the state. And guess what? You probably supplement them with your taxes.

Joe felt himself getting riled up again and looked around the busy bar. Holidaymakers and business people were heading in all directions. The huge curved window looked out onto one of the runways, and he caught sight of a Boeing 737 taking off, lifting its tubular bulk off the tarmac and heading to god knows where. He slipped his phone down to his lap, logged into Icarus, the Liberatus encrypted chat feeds and read the message from Sirus before watching the CCTV footage she had sent.

Some kid, a boy, Asian or maybe Latino, the face wasn't clear. He entered the smart office reception wearing a hoodie, jeans, and trainers and walked towards the security desk, pulling out a handgun from his pocket.

Joe watched the footage as the boy shot the security guard in the forehead, leapt the barrier and proceeded to run towards the elevator, firing at another two men and hitting one of them in the head. The boy reached the elevator doors and fired inside.

Joe noted from the date it was over fifteen years old. Then he tapped the screen as the camera caught the boy head-on to pause the video and extended his fingertips on the display to zoom in.

Now he knew why Sirus had sent it.

Jamall.

Joe smiled to himself as he pocketed the phone.

Top work, Sirus.

According to her, none of this came up in any media stories. Only a local news website had initially carried a story, but it had been deleted.

Weird.

And highly suspicious.

He made a mental note to dig into the Cryostone corporation. What was the connection there? Hadn't there been a missing flight involving Cryostone employees that had disappeared in the Indian Ocean?

He had heard of the company, of course, from his Royal Marine days. The British army used plenty of their tech, but it was mostly for the special forces, according to some of his mates in the SAS—the hi-tech stuff; robotics, nano drones, the stuff of edgy sci-fi movies.

He replayed the footage in his mind. The boy was like a machine. Definitely highly trained, even at that age. Joe could tell.

And then a memory of his old friend flashed into his mind. Jake Howle was smiling and winking at him, slapping him on the arm.

Dammit. I lost you, mate, and I'm sorry.

Now that had been a bad day.

A "fubar" day.

Joe remembered the dry fields, surrounded by deep ditches and tree lines shimmering in the ninety-degree heat. He was watching two Afghan men through binoculars who appeared to be looking over at their patrol with interest from behind a compound wall. Then he saw one of the men put a mobile phone to his ear and disappear from view.

Joe turned to the six men lined along the ditch, all dressed in the standard sand-coloured desert rig of the commando, huge backpacks on their backs.

Their patrol was the second of the day, and because they were so undermanned, they had to do at least two runs just to give the watching insurgents the impression they were many more of them in the base.

The route the patrols took had to vary every single time, zigzagging through fields, and around other villages in an unpredictable pattern to keep the enemy guessing. The problem was it made them last longer, increasing the danger, and there were no direct routes back to base when shit hit the fan.

Which it often did.

"They're definitely dicking us. One's got a phone," said Miller.

"Dicking" was a term for Taliban scouts spying on them.

"Get Abu to keep an ear out for any i-comm chatter," Joe said, looking at his friend, Lance Corporal Jake Howle. Grabbing his radio, Jake proceeded to radio the translator back at checkpoint Toki.

K company of Royal Marines 42 commando, stationed at the old farmstead named "Toki", were taking the patrols around a 100-kilometre zone that had been touted as one of the most dangerous places in the world at that time. The area was laden with IEDs planted by the Taliban that turned patrols into a game of "Afghan roulette", as the Marines called it. These mines had maimed over twenty men from their troop and killed another five. Just the day before, two young lads had copped it, hit by an IED. One of them had been due to return to "Butlins" in a week, "Butlins" being slang for Camp Bastion, the main British Army base. Luckily their troop had fought off the attack that followed, but the situation had gone seriously "fubar", which meant "fucked up beyond all recognition".

Joe was hoping it wouldn't be another "fubar" day. But he was out of luck.

"Where's the wanker, now?" one of the marines asked.

"Could be anywhere in that compound," answered another, stating the obvious.

"Jesus!"

It was Company Sergeant Major Miller who was also keeping an eye on the compound wall through his binos. "Sergeant, ten metres, jagged wall, right of the wall, lone tree, object hanging in a tree."

Joe moved his sights to the location and saw it, unable to believe his eyes.

"What the..."

A body part. A leg, in their own familiar desert uniform, was hanging from one of the tree branches.

The others looked over.

"Fucking bastards!"

"The IED that got Keith and Laz yesterday, it must've been them."

Joe closed his eyes for a second, hoping he was imagining it. When he reopened them, the sight was still there.

When the IED had gone off the day before, they managed to retrieve the bodies but had come under fire and were forced to retreat quickly. Unfortunately, that meant some of those body parts had been left behind.

Now, the Taliban were taunting them.

"Are we going in, then, Sarnt?" asked Miller, almost demanding it.

Joe pulled the binos away and looked at Miller and then the others, their faces all masked with disgust. He could tell they were chomping for a fight, but he also suspected they were under enormous psychological strain. Who wouldn't be?

"It's a trap," Joe said, looking back at the wall.

There was a familiar double bleep of the radio that Howle was using, and he listened for a moment before muttering, "Roger, over."

Howle looked at Joe.

"Al says they're planning something big, gonna hit us with something, but then they changed freqs."

Joe nodded. The chatter confirmed they were Taliban, not civvies. "Thought so." And to the others, he said, "If you see them again, engage."

There was a rapid clicking of loading weapons as the men spontaneously aimed at the wall. Joe reached for his own radio.

"Hello Zero, this is Foxtrot Three Zero, LOCSTAT, over."

A voice came back, "Zero, send over." Joe paused to check his location on the military grid reference system, "Foxtrot Three Zero, 41RNQ 95468 30031," he repeated as protocol, "41RNQ 95468 30031, Roger, Over."

Then he added, "Foxtrot Three Zero, we've also sighted body parts and two dickers at the wall. We will engage. Please advise on any other action, over."

There was a pause, and then Captain Boyd's voice came over the radio. "Foxtrot 3 Zero, this is Zero Alpha; hold your position. Command wants that compound intact today."

Although Joe wanted to hit the enemy as much as any other

man there, he didn't like changes to the mission brief. Each patrol had a mission briefing, even if it was just building relations with the local community or being visible in the area.

Now it sounded very much like their current patrol mission was changing fast.

"Hold that position," the Captain repeated, "I'm sending a backup patrol. It'll take a while to saddle up and get there."

Howle looked up at Joe, his face looking surprised. "i-comm chatter picking up a group of five, flanking us from the east. No other details!"

"Shit!" Joe heard himself say.

Not good, not good.

***

Joe checked the departures. Still no gate number. His phone began vibrating in his jacket pocket. Not many had this number.

He looked at the screen.

Hanna.

"Hey, hon."

"Hi, how's it going? I just thought I'd phone before you got on the plane."

Joe smiled.

"Well, thanks. I'm hanging off the wing right now. Bloody breezy up here!"

Hanna laughed easily.

"Just stay off the booze. It's supposed to have double the effect on your body when you're in the air," she said, her German accent barely noticeable.

"Is that right? Excellent, I'm gonna have a great time then."

She laughed again, and Joe saw his departure gate number flash up.

"I'm glad you phoned, Hanna. Nice to hear your voice."

"Yours isn't too bad."

"Yeah, well, I'm working on it." Joe picked up his carry-on bag and joined a stream of people all heading for their gate.

"Listen," Hanna said. "There's a break in my contract. I mean, they're reassessing something, so I have some free time. I was thinking... I could come over and see you in the States."

"Oh," said Joe surprised. "When?"

"Maybe a few days. I'll have to check."

"OK, that'll be great. I mean, you don't mind? It's gonna be mainly me working. Seeing the—" Joe stopped himself. "Listen, hon, gotta go. I'm boarding. I'll call you over there."

"That's OK. Safe journey, love you."

"Love you, see you soon, hon."

Joe disconnected and walked briskly along a long, stark corridor, looking forward to getting onboard and on with his work, hoping the memories of Afghanistan would disappear fast.

Chapter 8

Tehran, Iran.

After avoiding the lifts again on the way out, Inspector Rahbar got back into an ageing white Toyota and looked around. The tree-lined streets were offering a break of greenery in the ever-growing concrete city. It was one of those upcoming neighbourhoods where young and affluent Iranians hung out in cafes with their laptops. Those same youths leant towards the Western ways and away from their actual rulers. Could they be blamed? Rahbar didn't choose to judge as long as they didn't break the law. And upholding the law was what put food on his family's table.

He lit his third cigarette of the morning and brushed his finger along his tablet screen, looking at the notes once again. Not just another missing person. The tenth high-value government asset had disappeared. Another case for the pile. It appeared to be a simple case of the UIS, some strategy they were employing of attacking the government on every front. Could they convince these many key people to join their ranks voluntarily, or was there foul work at play? Still, there was no evidence of kidnapping, not one eyewitness in any of the cases. So, where on earth were they getting their intelligence data? These scientists did not exactly have their CVs online. It was a carefully guarded government secret. Rahbar flicked his cigarette butt out of the window and started the engine. It was most likely a military matter, but these days all the tools of government, including the police, were being rapidly turned to face the threat of the radical fanatics.

Rahbar drove back towards his station, mulling over his thoughts as the sweltering afternoon heat seemed to shimmer across the skyline, obscuring it in a foggy haze. A roar of a motorbike interrupted his thoughts, forcing him to focus on the road.

Haleema was obviously smart, but how different her life seemed compared to his own sister's, whose place in society had been restricted by their parents' more traditional views. Not that his sister was unhappy. Far from it. She had been merely limited in the choices she could make for her own life. The newer generation indeed seemed to be less repressed than his upbringing under the early Revolution. His father had toiled his whole life in a factory, making machine parts until his body couldn't take it anymore, and he was forced into early retirement. His mother worked in the garment industry and still did. Papak Rahbar worked hard to avoid a similar fate, joining the police at seventeen and dedicated the previous twenty years to progress to the rank of Inspector.

His thoughts quickly moved to the case and her father. She had been insistent that he must have been abducted, but there was no evidence to go on. It was difficult to know where to proceed with the little information they had now.

After fighting through the bad traffic in district ten, he finally pulled into the police station on Sattar Khan Street in the north of the city. He made his way through the hot, busy corridors to his office and slumped down behind his desk. Firing up his computer, he checked his work log and saw, with an inward groan, that in his absence, it had hugely expanded. He docked his tablet to his computer, transferring the new additions to the notes in the file marked "Karim Sheraz".

Best he could do for now. There was very little budget funding allocated to his department since the country's problem with UIS had begun to heat up, so he needed to be realistic about what he could achieve with cases that looked like there was no chance of solving.

His phone rang, and he picked it up.

"Inspector Rahbar speaking."

"Inspector, it's Massood. Come to my office and report about the Sheraz case." The line went dead, and Papak picked up his tablet and headed out into the busy corridor. The station was a hive of activity, as always in the ageing building. A row of glass-clad offices revealed mostly men in sweat-soaked shirts at their computers, fans rotating in a hopeless battle against the heat.

Rapping his knuckles on the door, Rahbar stood and waited for his boss to answer.

"Come!"

Rahbar walked in and stood quietly as Massood finished a phone call. The office was dominated by a large oak desk; behind it on the wall was a photograph of Massood shaking hands with a high-level member of the Council of Guardians. The faces of the Council member fixed with a big smile in contrast to Massood, who stared at the camera, looking unimpressed.

The Chief of Police in Iran's capital spoke in sharp hissing commands, berating someone on the other end of the phone before quickly ending the call. He indicated for Papak to sit with a jerk of the head and tapped his screen with long bony fingers briefly before settling his pale green eyes back onto Rahbar.

"So, the disappearance of Osted Karim Sheraz," Massood began quietly. "Naturally, he's a high-level asset for our government which is why we need to go over this case in person."

Rahbar nodded his understanding and outlined the details of Karim's disappearance as well as a summary of the interview with his daughter. Massood clasped his bony hands together, his face impassive, giving no indication of his thoughts.

"It's possible Sheraz was kidnapped," Massood said finally, "however, what evidence is there? It sounds like he was drawn to the UIS, perhaps trying to appease Allah for allowing his daughter to sink into disrepute. Perhaps they'll offer him salvation?" Massood's green eyes studied Rahbar, who smiled unsurely, unable to understand the lack of interest.

Undoubtedly, this was a high priority. Rahbar thought, on the verge of saying something about that, and decided against it.

"I've put a missing report together and sent out his information to the other police departments and the border agencies, see if anything comes up," Rahbar said.

Massood slapped a hand on the table and stood up, indicating the meeting was over. "Yes, don't waste too much time on it. Keep me informed if any new information surfaces and there is something to work on."

Chapter 9

Tennessee, USA.

Joe Bowen turned the rental car off Highway 75 near Marietta, finally free of the traffic chaos of Atlanta. It had been a tiring drive through the city from the airport with all the snarled-up traffic, and he was looking forward to getting a coffee break. It would be good to catch up with his brother Zak, not that they had much in common; they weren't exactly two peas in a pod. Still, it was kind of him to go out of his way to meet, thought Joe.

Perhaps he'd let slip some gossip or info from his secretive CIA world. Unlikely of course, he was too good, too brainwashed to his cause. But then Joe himself had once put on a uniform for queen and country. Time and knowledge change you, sometimes.

The news anchor on the radio had been droning on about the upcoming presidential elections and then switched to the situation in Iran with the rising insurgency of UIS. Another 40,000 US troops were being deployed to Iraq as the war across the border continued to get worse.

Joe parked, switched off the ignition and stepped out of the vehicle. The air was crisp, and he glanced up at the deep blue sky, broken up only by the odd wispy cloud. He strolled across the parking lot towards the glass-fronted shopping mall and the cafe. It was an international coffee chain, and Joe smarted at Zak's choice.

Trust him to pick this place over some smaller outfit, a quaint local homegrown business where the coffee was probably actually bought directly from the farmer. But no, let's hand our money to a tax-dodging corporate octopus and drink their "mud".

He spotted his brother in a booth and gave him a quick wave. Zak had a white shirt on, rolled up at the sleeves like some corporate sharpshooter. He'd aged a bit too, but then how many years had it been? Joe gestured to ask if he wanted anything to drink, and after Zak indicated he did not, Joe ordered a straight black coffee, large.

The barista, an attractive girl with her hair cut short, beamed a smile at him as she took his card.

"Your beverage will be ready in one moment at the collection point, sir. Have a nice day now."

Joe walked along the counter. Funny how they knew all about customer service this side of the pond. The land of smiles made you feel important. Maybe that's how they kept the system going. Treat people nice, make them spend their hard-earned cash on shit they don't need, and make them feel like the centre of the universe, fed by the silver platter.

A young dude, his face pitted with acne like those still at college, hurried through his orders. Finally, after a series of spillages, he handed Joe a mug and smiled with unbridled enthusiasm.

"Here's your coffee, sir. Have a nice day!"

That phrase again. They probably didn't even know the

meaning of it anymore.

Zak stood up as he approached, and they hugged, slapping each other on the back.

"Well, well, Joe. Great to see you. Welcome to the land of the free!" said Zak, brimming with enthusiasm.

"You've got a bit of an accent, there," said Joe. Zak let out a snort.

"It's been, what? Three years since I've seen you. You expect the Queen's English?"

"Yep. I expect you to remember where you came from," Joe said, grinning.

They both sat down in the booth, Joe leaning back against the red leather while Zak cradled his cappuccino, leaning forward slightly as he studied Joe.

"You've aged."

"So have you..."

"And you're a long way from Europe, Joe. How is it over there, still in Spain, by the way? Are you still doing the community thing, building your world-saving tribe, or was it a recycling cult? I can never remember."

Joe ignored the hint of sarcasm and blew on his hot coffee.

"It's great," he retorted. "Feels good to be doing something worthwhile rather than being a killing machine for the government. More your expertise, perhaps?"

Zak held up his hands in mock surrender. "Whoa!—I thought we were just having a pleasant coffee here."

"We are, Zak, we are. Whatever made you think otherwise?" Joe took a sip and grimaced. "Although the coffee leaves a lot to be desired," he added.

Zak stared at Joe with a frown and then tasted his beverage. "I like the coffee here—"

"The burnt aftertaste, you mean—"

Zak tutted. "There's no burned aftertaste—you're just being a whining Brit."

They both smiled at that, and Joe leaned back against the cushioned seat.

"So what brings you back to the States? You mentioned seeing friends or something?" asked Zak.

"Yeah—seeing friends in Atlanta and Nashville," Joe lied. "How's your family?" he asked quickly, changing the subject. "Still living the American dream, a house in the burbs, with a family of servants cooking and cleaning?"

Zak drained his mug and placed it in the middle of the table. "Works for me, just fine."

There was a brief silence as the men looked off past each other at the other customers, continually coming and going into the cafe.

"Is mum going back to Ireland, do you think?" asked Zak, breaking the lull.

Joe slowly shook his head. "I don't know—have you not spoken to the old man recently?"

Zak looked regretful and looked down into his mug. "It's been busy. I'll call him... call them both." He looked up. "Zoe's doing well at Zeos still, though, right? With all the financial markets. She's doing great, by the sounds of it?"

Joe nodded, still staring off into the distance. "Yep—she's swimming with the sharks, all right."

Joe's brown eyes switched back to Zak.

"And how're your dark deeds coming along? The web you guys spin—making plans from your Colorado hideout?"

"Can't talk about any of that shit as you well know."

Joe tutted. "I'm not talking about details or secrets. I just wanted to know when world war three was gonna kick off?"

"How do you mean, Joe? The Iranian situation? Watch the news. It's all there—"

Joe snorted with derision. "News? Won't learn anything there. The news is controlled. Nothing goes out without approval."

Zak laughed. "Come on, Joe, that's BS. This is the most democratic country in the world. Do you think news items have to be signed off by some guy sitting in a cupboard?"

"They're going after alternative news outlets... shutting them down, making it impossible for them to operate. 'Lib News' is under siege because they're offering an alternative view of what's going on. You know, real journalism, like it used to be. Not some corp-owned mouthpiece for the state. Does that sound like a democracy?" said Joe, clearly annoyed. "Look at the Iraqi 'weapons of mass destruction' lie. Most of the mainstream media just went with it," he added.

Zak leaned forward and narrowed his eyes.

"Why are you here, exactly?"

"Doing the buddy tour, brother—seeing ma friends," Joe said in a Southern states accent now. Joe could see he was pushing Zak's buttons just like he used to.

"Stop fucking around."

Joe finished his coffee and made to stand up. "I gotta go. Zak. We're flesh and blood. Remember that. And remember, you're answerable to the people on this planet."

Joe stood up and held out his arms, looking down at an incredulous-looking Zak. Joe returned an easy smile as if to say there were no hard feelings, "Let's meet up again. Have some dinner next time. I promise I won't bait you," he added.

Zak slowly stood up and gave his brother a quick embrace.

"Sure, Joe. I have to go back to Colorado soon though, so don't leave it too long."

Joe nodded, slapped Zak on the shoulder and walked away towards the exit.

Chapter 10

After his meeting with Zak, Joe continued along Highway 75 to Chattanooga, then headed northwest across the vast green landscapes, sparkling lakes and lush forests of Tennessee.

Joe pushed harder on the gas as his vehicle ascended the hill road that snaked through the pine forest and eventually came out on the southern part of the Cumberland plateau. He came to a hairpin bend and kept his eyes peeled for the side track while easing his foot up off the accelerator to cruising speed. He noticed a gate blocking a side road and pulled over. He stepped out of the vehicle and looked around. It was quiet except for the sound of the birds. On the gate was a sign reading: "No Trespassing: Private property". The muddy ground around the gate turned into a track that stretched, twisting and turning until it disappeared through a group of trees. Looking down at his feet, Joe could see wheel marks in the mud—a large vehicle, like a truck by the look of it. There was a subtle sign of white paint on the steel gate as something had passed by too close. He looked up at a small tree adjacent to the gate, a glint in the branches catching his eye—a surveillance camera.

Joe nodded to himself. This must be it.

Joe made a mental note to ask whether there was any motion

detection equipment that wasn't so easily spotted.

He went to the gate handle, where a combination lock clamped it shut and unravelled the six-digit combination messaged to him earlier. He drove in and re-locked the gate before turning into the thick woods, the light fading for the bunched canopies. After ten minutes, the forest seemed to thin, and he noticed two treehouses high up in the branches before a large clearing. Good spotting positions, he guessed.

The north side of the clearing backed onto a cliff, covered in pine trees taking root wherever they could. In the centre of the opening, he could see several small buildings that jutted out from a two-storey house. Opposite, a large farm shed cast a long shadow across the track. Joe drove slowly further into the opening, revealing more buildings under construction further back where a team of builders was hard at work. A rumble carried through his open window from machinery he couldn't see. Joe pulled into a parking area outside the first house and switched off the engine.

He got out and looked up at the steep hill on the opposite side; it would act as a protective barrier for the community. Nestled along the bottom was a row of old buildings that looked like they had recently been refurbished. The track split up and ended in a group of large tents that were pitched on an elongated patch of grass. Several figures milled around outside what looked like a makeshift refreshment area; several trestle tables around which were a line of butane gas bottles feeding cooking equipment and a long camping table.

"Hola, vato."

Joe turned to see Hugo Reese appearing from the doorway of the house, rubbing his hands with a cloth. The two men embraced.

Hugo looked weather-beaten, as if he had been toiling in fields for years, his T-shirt hugging a well-sculptured frame. He was unshaven but looked well and flashed Joe a grin.

"Well, well, who's been busy?" asked Joe, slapping Hugo on his arm.

Hugo laughed. "I saw you on the cam feed, checking out the gate. You want a drink before I show you around?"

"Sure—coffee would be great. Thanks, Hugo. By the way, have you set up any other cams, more hidden ones? Or motion detection for the entrance points?"

Hugo waved a dismissive hand. "Ahh, not yet. I'm getting there." Then he gestured towards one of the large tents. "We're still tryin' to set up the plumbing in the main house, so it filters from the spring, so we'll grab a coffee over there. So, how was your journey, bruh?"

"Long," replied Joe. "But it gave me a chance to get some work done on the flight."

"—and the girls? How they doin'?"

Joe smiled knowingly, "You mean Gianna? She's great, living at the place in Andalucia, doing her thing."

"And Hanna—I meant her as well," Hugo said sheepishly.

Joe laughed now. "OK, I just thought you had a soft spot for Gianna."

"G's a fine woman—that's all I'm sayin', vato." Hugo was smiling, looking away.

"Well, Hanna is coming over the next day or so. She's got a work window, some free time."

"Sweet," Hugo replied.

Joe sighed. "So, are we on schedule here?"

Hugo gave a half-shrug.

"I dunno, it's going as well as can be, but there are always issues. I don't have enough people here right now."

"Keep pushing it as hard as you can," said Joe, "We want to be ready for whatever's coming. It's hard to say what or when it will be, but you can be sure there are games afoot."

"Yeah, I hear you on that, Joe."

Joe turned briefly to glance behind him towards the main road he had driven in by.

"Those spotting posts in the trees. Nice touch but a little too close to the compound. Maybe get some further back."

Hugo nodded as they arrived outside the tent, where two men sat on camp chairs, nursing enamel mugs of coffee.

"Got any more of that?" asked Hugo.

On seeing Joe and Hugo, both men slowly stood up. A man with a clean bald head in his forties, dressed in a chequered shirt and body warmer, stared at Joe without saying anything. The other guy, slightly thinner and taller, wearing an NYC baseball cap, white T-shirt and combat trousers, held out his hand first.

Joe already knew who they both were.

"Joe Bowen? Hugo talked a lot about you. Happy to meet you, buddy," the guy in the cap said. Joe smiled and shook hands. "I'm Josh Pierce, by the way, sorry—" he added.

"Good to meet you, mate."

Joe remembered his file: most of his career had been with the 4th Battalion, 6th Infantry Regiment of the US Army and had left a few years earlier, finishing at the rank of Corporal.

Joe turned to the big bald guy who studied him with sharp green eyes.

"This is Marty," said Hugo.

Joe recalled his impressive details. This guy was an ex-ranger. His former regiment had a reputation for being a lethal, agile and flexible force specialising in joint special operations missions. Marty Faulkner had been a grenadier in the 1st Ranger Battalion based at Hunter Army Airfield, Georgia but had been thrown out for fighting with one of his fellow soldiers. There had apparently been other incidents too, but Joe didn't know much about them.

Not a great start.

Joe wondered what had made him throw away a promising military career like that.

"How's it going, Marty?"

"I'm good," he replied and slowly shook Joe's hand, gripping it tightly.

Joe let go and shook it in mock agony.

"So you're a gripper? Why do people do that?"

Marty smiled for the first time.

"To display power," he said so quietly that Joe had to lean in to hear him.

Joe nodded. "Yeah, it certainly does that."

Josh was already pouring coffee into two mugs. "You guys OK to hold on to the milk and sugar? We ran out."

"Just black for me, anyway," said Joe. They both took the mugs from Josh and thanked him.

"OK, guys, we'll catch up later," said Hugo. Both men continued walking along the side track along the other tents as Falkner and Josh stood and watched them.

A young girl with a blonde mohawk, piercings, and tattoos came out of one of the tents carrying a plastic box and smiled at them.

"Lena! This is Joe."

"How are you finding it?" asked Joe. She beamed a smile at him. "Yeah, it's good, going well. There's a lot to do, though.

A helluva lot to do!"

Joe raised his eyebrow at Hugo.

"Thanks for your honesty. Where are you from?"

"New York, originally."

"Keep it going, Lena. Looks like you're doing well," said Joe. "Catch you later."

The men moved on, passing the rest of the tents towards the hill.

"She's right, Joe. I'll hold my hand up and say we struggled."

"Don't worry, Hugo. Just show me where we're at right now."

They walked up to a stream that looped down from further up the hill. Where it joined the ground, there was a pool with a two-metre water wheel scooping up water in large wooden buckets. A shaft and bearings connected to a smaller wheel on the side, also spinning quickly, hooked up by a bicycle-style chain to a generator and gearing box.

The whole wheel had been built between two parallel stone walls set discreetly back as if it had always been there.

"Nice water source," said Joe.

"Yep, and we can get good steady power from that. About 260 kWh."

"A good start. We should also look at other options."

"Yeah, for sure."

Joe looked up the hill and pointed into the trees.

"The hill is a good natural barrier and protection. Maybe we can get some solar panels and a few wind turbines at the top. They'd need to be discreet, though. Hidden from above otherwise, it'll be a big flashing beacon advertising our presence."

"Yeah, it's possible—if I had more bodies to help, vato. Me

and Josh also looked into maybe digging into the hill for bunker storage. Would make a good emergency hideout as well—but—"

"—but you need more resources," Joe finished.

"With what we have now, it'll take another five years."

Joe nodded silently. Sipping their coffee, they strolled to the centre of the clearing towards the sizeable corrugated farm shed Joe had seen earlier. There was a line of makeshift wooden pens on the outside with pigs in two of them and goats in the others.

"We're still fixing up the barn inside. Wasn't used for years, but we can keep the animals inside when it's done."

They walked in where two men and a woman were constructing separate areas with timber. One of them started an electric saw as they entered, and Hugo was forced to shout.

"We got the veg patches coming in here as well with LED lights."

The sawing stopped suddenly.

"These three are in charge over here, caring for the animals and crops."

One of the figures waved, but the sawing started again.

"Meet them later; I'll show you the rest."

They walked back past the big tents and put their mugs down in the kitchen area. Faulkner and Josh had left, presumably returning to their work. Another man, with brown cropped hair, unshaven with a craggy face bent slightly as he made tea.

Hugo held his hand out towards him. "This is Hodge from your country." Joe and Hodge shook hands.

"Whereabouts?" asked Joe.

"Fulham, mate. For all I know, it's a smouldering shell by now, I haven't been there for over ten years," Hodge declared.

"Good to meet you," said Joe. "Hopefully, catch up properly later," he added.

"Definitely," Hodge replied and turned back to making his tea.

Joe and Hugo continued towards the main original converted farmhouse.

"So, how's it going in Spain?" Hugo asked.

"Yeah, good. I mean, we're a bit ahead of you. Off-grid power is all in place, but there's still a helluva lot to do. But the group is growing rapidly. Plenty of new faces. We've got more groups in the UK, France, as well as over here."

"That's a lotta organising going on."

"It is. But we're getting good people to manage it all. These things all take time."

"And have we got the time? Do you think shit will hit before we're ready?" Hugo shot Joe an apprehensive look as he spoke.

Joe shook his head. "I dunno. Need more intel. Zak wasn't biting, and I've been trying all other possible contacts, but all wells are dry so far."

They approached the main farmhouse, where Joe's vehicle was parked.

"What about your Dad?"

Joe nodded, more to himself than Hugo. "Yeah, I have to speak with him."

They walked inside to a large cloakroom area and a wide hallway with several doors on either side and a grand staircase at the end that curved around toward the next level. Elaborately decorated wallpaper was half scraped off or peeling, and a loud hammering sound echoed through the house. A workman, covered in dust, appeared from one of the rooms, carrying a load of wood planks. He nodded at them and pushed past.

Joe and Hugo looked in on the ground-level rooms that had been decked out with bunk beds in a dormitory-style. At the rear of the house was a vast kitchen with a large central stove and work surface in the centre. A wood-burning stove sat against one of the walls, and huge pots piled up on a dining table. To their left were large French doors to a side garden where several more workmen were milling around, sawing wood on a woodcutter.

"There is something," Joe said as they turned back and descended narrow steps to a basement.

"—am listening."

"Some things to keep an eye on—"

They came to the large basement space that spanned the entire area of the three thousand square metre house—rows of metal storage shelves stacked with plastic sealed containers. Joe noted medical signs on one row and then food on the next.

"We do have a list of key figures. Cabalists, who, if they were to change their routine—well, it might mean something."

They walked along the endless rows of giant tins of corn, beans and condensed milk.

"You mean if they were to run for the hills?"

"Yep. I think we're getting close, and it might be the trigger warning we need."

Hugo stopped and turned to face Joe, taking him by surprise.

"Joe, man. Y'know I trust you, respect you. After all, you helped me out in Spain—you saved my ass."

Joe leaned against a shelf, waiting without expression, wondering where this was going.

"I'm snowed under, man. Up to my eyeballs in this shit. Do you want me to go running around spying on a bunch of hijos de putas?"

Joe smiled and slapped Hugo on the shoulder. He realised the problem in that instant. All this time he had been subconsciously shoehorning Hugo into this project management role that he had evidently been struggling with.

Perhaps it was time to try something else.

***

Joe turned to Lance Corporal Howle as he told him they were about to be outflanked. He caught sight of a puff of smoke at a tree line in the distance.

"Mortar!"

They barely had time to react. The explosion ripped up the soil in the field just behind their line.

"They've got a beanie on us. By the tree line!" Joe pointed as the marines began opening fire in Joe's direction, the relentless cracking of bullets whizzing across the field.

Another puff of smoke.

An explosion, only twenty metres short, covered them with fragments and soil.

Right now, they would be readjusting their target, homing in on them.

Joe shouted over to Jenkins and Boyce.

"Keep an eye on the compound!"

They nodded and turned back to face their original target. Luckily their troops were in a ditch but much too exposed for Joe's liking.

"Simmonds, where's that machine gun? Get up the ditch with Boyce and lay down suppressing fire," shouted Joe, gesturing with his hand.

At that moment, gunfire erupted from the compound, shredding the branches of the trees above them.

"Fuck!"

Jenkins and Boyce were quickly returning fire.

Howle was shouting into the radio for help.

Then, Joe watched as Howle took a bullet in the head, his body crumpling over against the grass-covered ditch wall.

"No! Jake!" Joe moved through the deep ditch water, his boots sticking to the muddy bottom, slowing his progress. When he finally reached Howle, he could see blood streaming down his face, soaking his neck and the front of his uniform.

"Billy!" Joe shouted. Billy Pitman was the medic, but he was pinned down at the other end of the ditch. Besides, Joe could see Jake was already dead, his eyes staring off over Joe's shoulder.

Joe turned as a new noise to the left of the attacking force attracted his attention. The unmistakable chatter of SA80s firing 3-4 round bursts, but none of the rounds came his way. Immediately a second weapon added its staccato to the first, lower pitched and firing 8-10 round bursts in the same direction that Joe identified as a Light Support Weapon, the mainstay of any Brit army fighting patrol.

"Happy days, Jake... So you had us covered after all," Joe muttered.

The initial attackers turned their attention to the newcomers, and an intense firefight broke out between the two groups. The high-pitched crack of hunting rifles with the occasional mortar round mixed in with the sound of professionally handled military long guns. The boom of a Mills grenade echoed from the ridge, and the mortar position fell silent. One by one, the hunting rifles began to fall to the flanking attack of the patrol. All in all, the fight lasted a mere thirty minutes.

But for Joe, that day had lasted forever. When the backup squad arrived, they were able to overcome the ambush position, and air support dealt with the attackers' compound. But it had been too late for Jake Howle.

A week later, Joe Bowen had left the Marines, mentally scarred and disillusioned. The memory of that tour was never far from his mind.

Fuck "Fubar" days. Joe didn't want any more of them as long as he lived.

Chapter 11

Denver, Colorado.

Zak Bowen was surprised not to be heading to the recently relocated CIA headquarters immediately after his arrival at Denver International Airport. He had received the message to come asap just after his meeting with his brother, Joe. Instead, the driver of the military vehicle had informed him Natan Helms required his presence at Buckley Air Force Base, located less than thirty kilometres from the main airport.

He wondered about that. It seemed insane that the CIA had relocated here, out in the middle of a rural state. New York or Pennsylvania would have made more sense.

What could be cooking now? The thought of what might lay ahead excited him. This was the feeling he had yearned for ever since he had achieved his goal of gaining American citizenship and in through the door of the beating heart of the CIA. Of course, if it hadn't been for Rhonda, now his wife of seven years, then that dream may never have happened. Was it luck? Some kind of divine intervention? Yes, he had always loved her, but the fact Daddy was in the CIA iced the cake just a little.

Once inside the base, he was met by a marine sergeant and

taken through a myriad of hallways and doors before arriving at a reception area outside a boardroom door, where two men in dark suits stood waiting.

"Mr Helms will be with you shortly. Please take a seat, sir," one of the men said. Zak nodded and sat himself down on a leather sofa next to a coffee table. Natan Helms was the grandson of Wes Helms, a man who had held sway in the circles of the elite for decades. Wes Helms had held military and intelligence rank from the time of the First World War and played a significant role in the operation at the end of the Second World War to bring Nazi scientists to America to work for the CIA and help set up NASA. Since then, he had become a prominent figure in successive US administrations.

Natan's father, Hector Helms, had operated in the darker reaches of the intelligence world, and Bowen knew no more about him than that.

Natan himself took the career path to Congress, gravitating towards the centre of the Washington power base and now played a crucial part in the shadow behind public figures. Whenever there was a photo of recent successive Presidents or the gathering of world leaders, Natan would most likely be in the background somewhere, turning away, blurred or half hidden behind someone else.

***

In front of Zak, on the opposite wall, hung a large oil painting. He glanced up at a surreal and frightening scene. The detailed brushwork displayed the riders of the four horses of the apocalypse, grim reapers attempting to control their respective horses in various states of distress, jumping up on their hind legs. On the ground were heaps of corpses, long dead, almost blending into the muddy field. Miles behind in the distance, a modern city burned—the flames reaching high into the black night.

Zak found himself fixated on it, staring at it for what seemed like an age before shaking his head and reaching for his smartphone.

What a bizarre painting to hang up on a military airbase.

"Mr. Helms will see you now."

Zak quickly stood up and walked past the apes and into the office. Inside, two men sitting at a low coffee table stood up.

Helms, thin-faced with combed-back white hair and a healthy tan, walked over to greet Zak. With him, a high-ranking military man, well over six foot and broad, with closely shaved grey hair close to the scalp.

Bowen and Helms shook hands.

"Welcome, Mr. Bowen," said Helms. He turned to the army man. "Let me introduce Major General Dean Wexhall," then, to Zak he gestured to an empty chair. "Please take a seat."

"So we hear good things about you, Zak. 'Dedicated and loyal' are the words that have described you."

Zak nodded. "Thank you, sir. I'm just doing my job." Despite being naturally modest, he felt a great sense of pride hearing those words.

"You'll be representing the agency on this, Zak. It will be a military operation and is the highest level classification of secrecy. You're to fly to HAS22 in Iraq. You'll be working directly with Captain Coleman along with his unit, one of our top covert teams."

"Why aren't we using our existing guys, the Rangers or even the SEALs, for this?"

Helms nodded, indicating it was a fair question.

"Politics. Ghost 13 is a unit recruited from the cream of the special forces to conduct higher-level operations on the global field. The boys at the top level want a different slant on this. We're talking deep, deep under the radar. Don't concern yourself—they are the very best."

Zak bit his lip. The gap between the agencies had never been wider, despite all the post-9/11 noise about closer collaboration. This was just another example of the bureaucrats and pen-pushers meddling in something they didn't understand.

Zak nodded slowly. "If you say so, Sir."

Helms nodded to Major General Wexhall, who held up a device in his hand, switching on a screen on the wall. The blinds simultaneously closed, darkening the room. A world map briefly flashed onto the screen before it zoomed quickly onto Iran.

The Major General began his brief with absolute gravity and authority. "We have a developing situation in Iran. Some of their top nuclear scientists have been disappearing for some time. We believe the UIS is behind it, and this obviously would prove to be a huge concern if they were somehow to get the skilled people to make some kind of nuclear weapon."

Zak looked from Wexhall to Helms as he digested the information.

"Some alarming reports have just come in," said Wexhall. The map was replaced with documents marked "Top Secret" on the screen. "If these prove to be accurate, and our sources are reliable, the UIS has captured two hundred kilograms of enriched uranium. Combined with the expertise they can get from those scientists, then well," Wexhall shook his head in dismay, "you can imagine the possible consequences, right?

Obviously, this info is nowhere near the public domain at this time."

Zak swept a hand over his short-cropped hair. "Jesus!"

Helms raised his eyebrows at Zak as if in absolute agreement. "This problem has our highest priority, and we have got to get things in hand. We want you to head over to Iraq and liaise with Captain Coleman. His team will perform the extraction; you are to oversee the mission and then bring any of the rescued hostages back here to safety. The Iranian government is obviously not able to protect its assets, so we're going to have to do it for them. Intelligence has located at least five of these scientists." Helms looked at the Major General. "Anything you want to add?"

Major General Wexhall shook his head. "No, not now. Let's keep it at that." He turned at Zak. "We'll resume the conversation at HAS22."

The three men stood up.

"I hope you appreciate the gravity of this situation," Helms said to both men. "Let both parties work together and keep me informed, Major General."

Chapter 12

Tehran, Iran.

Massood climbed into the rear of his Mercedes E-Class, the leather seats creaking slightly as he sat down. He took out a gold case, plucking a cigarette from it with long fingers, and lit it. He nodded to his waiting driver, who started the engine and slowly drove out of the police station car park.

It had been a long climb to the top of his game, but the position was secure for now. Born into a family well-placed to benefit from the Iranian revolution and the upheaval it had brought to the country. With high connections to the Ayatollah regime, Massood's family retained their place in the Iranian hierarchy.

His father had been in the Shah's original secret police, SAVAK, and had narrowly escaped the reprisals that had followed after the revolution. But then Ayatollah Khomeini changed his mind and decided to retain the infrastructure, renaming it to SAVAMA before it became the Ministry of Intelligence or VAJA as it is today.

It was ironic, thought Massood, that in those Shah days, the SAVAK had learned all its torture techniques from the CIA. But it ran in the blood of the country. No matter who was in control, there would always be a desire for strength through blood.

It didn't matter if Massood didn't buy the entire concept of the mullahs and what they preached. What mattered was power—and retaining that power.

When Massood had finished his university studies, he took his rightful position in the Tehran police force and, with it, the opportunity to build his empire.

Through force and pain if necessary.

When he was just thirty-two, Massood assumed the role of Police Chief after the sudden and inexplicable death of his predecessor. He had been one of the old guards who had somehow managed to retain his position after the revolution.

There had been much work to do. The regime wanted strict enforcement of their policies with no mercy to be shown towards anyone who opposed them. This meant a steady stream of victims for the gallows that began springing up all around Iran.

It had kept Massood busy.

If the Shah, deposed by the Ayatollahs in 1979, were to regain power tomorrow, Massood knew he would do exactly the same for his regime.

It didn't matter.

As long as he and his family retained the lifestyle they had become accustomed to and the power. That was non-negotiable. Power was Massood's drug.

The balance, however, was tipped as the Daesh was rising, and he would make sure he was on the right side when the switch came.

Besides, as an asset helping tip, the balance was his latest required objective.

Massood rechecked his phone. There was no message yet, but it wouldn't be long.

The Mercedes skirted the Azadi Tower, the colossal monument that stood guard at the gates of Tehran and headed south. Busy people crowded the streets, and traders made their way along the stationary vehicles selling fruit, snacks, and water. Ahead another police roadblock was holding up the traffic. The frequency of events such as these increased as the fear of Daesh attacks intensified.

Only last week, two suicide bombers, posing as a couple of tourists, had infiltrated the capital and blown themselves up in busy markets, killing dozens. Massood had known it was coming. He knew about them all.

Massood leaned forward, pointing a bony finger ahead to the sidewalk.

"There's some space, get up there, and we'll get them to wave us through."

The driver did as ordered, mounting the raised pavement, almost sideswiping a row of fruit carts as he sped past the stationary cars.

The police at the roadblock gave them dirty looks as they rolled to a stop, and one walked towards the vehicle. His expression changed as soon as he realised it was the chief— immediately waving it through.

There was a buzz on Massood's phone. He opened the message, which was a series of letters and typed in a long string of numbers, his key to decrypt.

The text revealed itself on his screen.

Cargo in place for pickup. Current hosts will be replaced, so no invoice required.

Massood nodded, satisfied.

Good, they were taking care of it.

He could relax.

Perhaps he would celebrate later, get some of those young prostitutes he enjoyed occasionally and have a few drinks. The one thing about his real employers, they could supply anything he desired.

Chapter 13

Liberatus Basecamp
Tennessee

From outside, nothing but the chirping of birdsong. Joe slowly opened his eyes and stared absentmindedly at the sunlight slipping through the partially shuttered window, spilling into the en-suite room. Rugs haphazardly covered the floor in an attempt to make it cosy. An old oak wardrobe, one lone wooden chair in the corner and the bed they were sleeping in.

He thought about everything he'd seen here so far. Yesterday he'd been concerned about the schedule and how far behind it was. A thousand little jobs still to be done gnawed at him. Yet now, after a contented sleep, it didn't seem so bad. He rolled over and looked and the beautiful woman lying next to him. Hanna's chest was rhythmically rising and falling as she slept next to him; her warm body curled up, the smooth bare skin of her back partly exposed from the white duvet.

She had got in the night before around midnight, exhausted and jet lagged but happy to see Joe and share a nightcap before demanding bed.

He stroked his hand over her thigh and nestled into her back, lightly placing his arms around her waist, soaking up the warmth. She turned her head slightly. "Hmm, I see you're awake early?" she mumbled, reaching her hand back to caress him.

"You realise it's our dating anniversary tomorrow," he whispered. "Three years," he added, gently kissing her ear.

She paused for a second and turned around to face him, pulling a face of fake shock, her blonde locks spilling around her shoulders and neck.

"Oh wow. Yes, of course, it is—"

"You mean, you forgot?" he teased, pulling her to him, kissing her lips. "You'd better make up for it, then," he added. She giggled lightly, then pressed her lips against his, moaning softly as he caressed her body.

They made love again and then lay staring at the cracked ceiling in the content afterglow of sex, the duvet half strewn onto the floor.

"So, how's it all coming along here?" she asked.

"Yeah, it's getting there, slowly. I've been thinking it might not be Hugo's cup of tea managing the project. So we agreed to get someone else, maybe Lena. She seems smart and organised."

"Oh, right? And what about Hugo?"

"I think he'd be better in the field, maybe."

"Is he in agreement?" She moved her hand up his chest.

"Sure, if the training goes well."

Hanna nestled her head into his chest with a satisfied sigh.

There was a brief silence, then, "Do you think all this prepping for the 'Apocalypse' is worth doing? I mean with the resources, all your energy," she asked.

"Do you think it is?"

She looked up at him and smiled but said nothing.

"When are you going back to the grindstone?" he asked, changing the subject.

She sighed. "I have five days or so here. Still, a bit of work to do, though."

"Damn," he muttered.

"But I'm sure there's time for a little tour around Tennessee." She looked up at him, grinning.

"Oh yeah. I'm sure I can take a day to drive the queen around."

She slapped his chest playfully. "...and breakfast? Are you going to fix me breakfast, Joe, then show me around this... ranch of yours?"

"Hmm, you know how to cook, don't you?" he said, grinning. Hanna grabbed his hand, pushing it back, squeezing it between his fingers. "Cheeky monkey. I'll have eggs benedict, with toast and spinach, please."

She pushed herself off the bed and stood up, flashing him a mock frown, her fully naked body facing him proudly, hands on hips.

"Yes, Joe? Is that clear?"

Joe pushed himself up on the bed, moving one hand behind his head.

"I think I could manage a fried egg. Will that do ya?"

She stuck her tongue out at him before padding over to the bathroom. After a few seconds, she called through. "Hey, there's no water here."

"Bucket, in the corner."

There was a "tut!" from Hanna as Joe rolled onto his side, smirking.

Chapter 14

UIS training camp, 150 kilometres south of Sirjan.

The recruits marched back and forth, kicking up yellow dust from the ground, their boot falling in and out of rhythm. Around twenty of them, clad in black military fatigues, came to a halt in the centre of the training yard. The bearded commander bellowed another order, and there was a haphazard attempt at a straight line as the recruits struggled unsuccessfully to comply. The commander corrected it, shouting and waving his arms at them until the line was presentable. He pushed one young man back and berated him. Amir and Fadin stood together in the lineup, staring directly ahead as the commander unslung his weapon and held it up for them.

"Recruits for the United Islamic cause, I am Yafir Al-Adel. Repeat after me—we swear allegiance."

"We swear allegiance," the recruits shouted in unison.

"....To the prince of the faithful and the caliph of the Muslims."

"To the prince of the faithful and the caliph of the Muslims," they echoed.

"Abu Bakr Mosa!"

"Abu Bakr Mosa!"

The commander slowly walked to a row of metal crates. He lifted the lid of the first one and pulled out a green canvas bag, rolled it up and secured it with three buckles. He placed the roll on top of the next crate and proceeded to open the buckles. Inside the roll were four AK-47s, tied in place and surrounded by padding. The commander pulled off the ties and took out one of the rifles. All eyes were on him. He raised it in the air for all to see.

"The only way to enforce Sharia is with weapons—we will kill infidels and apostates and humiliate them, Insha Allah!"

With that resounding cry still echoing in the air, he brought the weapon down and held it out before them with both hands.

"This is a standard issue Russian AK-47. You will each get to know this weapon inside out!" he bellowed, pacing up and down along the line, eyeing each recruit closely.

"First, we are going to take these weapons apart, clean them and then re-assemble here. Understood?" The commander gestured at a row of makeshift tables made from fruit crates to the side of the training yard

A unified shout of enthusiastic assent erupted from the men.

"Now, pay close attention. You remove the magazine, like so—" Al-Adel removed the magazine, "—and the charging handle must be pulled back to discharge any rounds." The commander did so quickly and expertly.

"Now, remove the cleaning rod located at the front of the rifle below the barrel," he continued, slowly demonstrating stripping the rifle apart.

"Now, to re-assemble, we follow those same steps but in reverse." Picking up the pieces, the commander methodically put the weapon back together, talking through each step, finally slapping the magazine back in and then emphatically cocking the weapon with a flourish.

"You!" the commander pointed directly at Amir and jerked his arm back, gesturing him to come forward. The commander was a small man, his voice raspy yet carrying strength and confidence that made it evident to all why he was a leader.

Amir hesitated as if stuck to the ground beneath him.

Fadin hissed at him. "Go!"

At last, Amir managed to move, walking over to the commander, who handed him the weapon.

"Your AK-47, boy!" the commander demanded.

Amir took the gun in his hands.

"Now, remove the magazine, then pull the charging handle back to discharge any rounds," the commander said. Amir quickly followed his command.

"Now, remove the cleaning rod located at the front of the rifle below the barrel."

Again, Amir's efforts were slow and cumbersome compared to the commander. A moment later, Amir felt the sweat forming on his back as he struggled to follow the procedure.

"Remove the bolt cover—Remove the bolt spring—Pull out the bolt and charging handle."

The orders seemed to speed up, and finally, the commander lost his patience and pushed Amir back into the line.

"You!" He pointed at Fadin and quickly pointed his finger to the spot beside him. Fadin glanced at his brother and stepped up next to the commander. He repeated the instructions, stripping down the weapon, ready for cleaning, and Fadin followed his lead quickly and efficiently.

"Have you all managed to get that, or do I need to show you, *al' balah*, once again?" shouted the commander, using the Arabic word for blockheads to emphasize the scorn in his command. The men nodded their agreement more out of fear of being humiliated than from true understanding.

"Good! Now each of you collect a rifle, find a space at the table, and show me how it's done."

***

Amir loaded the magazine into the rifle, tucking the stock into his shoulder. He held one hand around the pistol grip, finger on the trigger. His other hand held the forend handle near the front sight block.

A few months before, Amir would never have guessed he would get to use a Kalashnikov. He had fired weapons, yes. But those were old rifles that barely worked, and you were lucky if you didn't shoot yourself. These AKs felt like a different beast altogether. Along the line, other recruits began firing their weapons for the first time; a loud cracking noise began to crescendo through the camp.

He focused on the front sight and the target, a cardboard cutout soldier around twenty metres away. His finger tightened on the trigger. There was a rapid peppering sound as the bullets ripped into the cutout, shredding it to pieces. Amir was taken aback by the destructive power he had just unleashed. The barrel of the weapon continued to rise, and a stream of bullets ripped up through the head of the target and above. Amir struggled to keep the rifle in check, and only when the rest of the magazine had been spent did he regain his control of the weapon.

The commander quickly came over as Amir recovered his composure. Amir looked down at the weapon as if it had been possessed by some evil spirit. A few nearby recruits laughed as the commander grabbed the Kalashnikov from him and looked down at Amir in mild contempt.

"Let's try that again. Remember, short bursts, fire three to four rounds only, then release the trigger, resight the rifle and fire again."

The shadows grew longer as the afternoon turned to evening. The recruits finished on the range and made their way to another part of the camp for the continuation of their training. Ahead of them, Fadin and Amir saw a line of shallow trenches with barbed wire rolled over the top. At the far end was a line of sandbags with gaps in between.

Just ten metres short of what looked like a small assault course, the commander ordered them to place their weapons on the ground and kneel in lines of ten before nodding to another instructor who had been waiting for them.

The squat, short man walked along the line, shouting, "You will step onto the battlefield on your own two feet, and when you step off, you will be carried on people's shoulders after your martyrdom." He then ordered the men to tense their stomach muscles. He swung his foot, kicking the first recruit in the stomach, who responded with a loud grunt of pain.

"You must be tough, stronger than you can imagine—" The instructor continued to talk as he kicked each one in the line. Amir's turn came, and he took the blow and immediately threw up in front of himself. The instructor laughed and moved on to Fadin. He tensed his stomach muscles and took the kick with a grunt but stayed upright.

After the last recruit had been kicked, the instructor turned back to them and pointed across the barbed wire.

"You are to crawl under the wire and get to the end, then take out the targets at the end in the shortest possible time." He swung round his AK-47 from his back and checked it briefly. "We will be firing live rounds over your heads, so keep low. Don't forget your weapons. Now go!"

The first line of recruits moved forward, getting down on their stomachs, cradling their weapons in their elbows and crawling forward under the wire as live bullets flew over their heads. Amir and Fadin were next to each other, digging their elbows into the soil, moving as fast as they could. In his peripheral vision, Amir could see the instructor walking casually alongside them and occasionally letting rip with a barrage of gunfire across their heads.

"He'll kill us!" said Amir.

"Just keep moving," Fadin replied, his face a mask of grim determination. They reached the end and scrambled out, taking positions behind the sandbags. They began firing at the card cutouts of soldiers that had targets painted on their helmets. Fadin fired in quick succession, getting a series of excellent hits. Amir struggled with his weapon for a few seconds, then managed to start shooting, his aim way off. He adjusted and managed to hit the shoulder, the rest of the shots not even catching the figure.

After each of them had emptied their magazines at the targets, the instructor ordered them to leave the course to allow the second wave of recruits their turn.

"Well?" asked Fadin as they walked back to the barracks.

"Well, what?"

"Is it everything you hoped for?"

Amir sensed a hint of sarcasm but chose to ignore it. He nodded his head.

"Yes, everything and more. We are making history, brother."

Fadin spat onto the ground and turned to Amir.

"I wonder what kind of history?"

Amir shook his head slightly, sensing Fadin was baiting him, but said nothing.

The sun had turned orange, sinking behind the distant mountains, casting the buildings in a warm pinkish hue.

***

Shiraz, Fars Province.
Three days earlier.

Amir and Fadin stood in the courtyard of their family home, casually chatting while sweeping the dust and leaves that had gathered over the last few days. The kitchen windows were open, and they could smell the delicious aroma of their mother's cooking. Bademjan stew was a family favourite, and the smell of lamb, onions, and turmeric drifted across the yard when they heard a shout.

Hassam came running in from the back gate, waving his arms.

Amir held up his floor sweeper at Hassam as if it was a weapon.

"Halt. You're on Sheraz territory now." He grinned at his childhood friend, who, judging by the sweat on his shirt, had been running for quite some time. Amir's expression changed to a bemused frown. "What are you rushing around for?"

The brothers had both grown up with Hassam since child-hood. They had gone to school together, but it was Amir who was closest with Hassam now, as Fadin had drifted in another direction as they grew older. Hassam looked at them both, brimming with excitement even as he gasped for breath. The thin teenager leaned down, hands on his knees.

"Haven't you heard? Everyone is on the streets. There's a demonstration at Valiasr; everyone is protesting about the election and Yazdi's arrest!" They had all watched the election in the previous few days as the establishment retained power. Then came the arrest of the opposition leader, Mehdi Yazdi, and he had not been heard from since.

"Sounds like trouble," said Fadin, placing a broom against the stone wall. Fadin, the eldest son, had a commanding presence, tall, broad-shouldered, with a hard face that turned to Hassam. He placed his hands on his hips in a manner that suggested a high degree of scepticism.

Hassam looked up at Fadin. His earlier enthusiasm dissipated, replaced by intense seriousness. He stood upright and waved his hand at the street beyond the wall. "They're ignoring the people's will, as always. Everyone is angry. Why don't you come and see for yourself?"

"What difference will it make? It's always the same old story with the elections. They rig it every time and then act surprised at the outcome," Fadin said matter-of-factually.

"How many are there?" asked Amir eagerly, ignoring Fadin's cynical words.

Hassam spoke quickly: "Thousands—and more demonstrations are happening across the country. I heard tens of thousands are marching in Tehran. All of social media is raving about it, but of course, there's nothing on the official news channels. Well? Let's go, Amir, come on!"

He tugged at Amir's arm, and they both turned towards the gate.

"Wait!" Fadin walked up to them. "Maybe you are both

too young to remember 2009 or 2011, the Days of Rage. But it never ends well." He looked at each of the younger men in turn, eyes filled with concern. He paused as if considering something.

"Do you want to go, Amir?" he said, looking at his younger brother.

Amir nodded at him.

"You were down there yourself, Hassam?" Fadin asked

Hassam nodded his head, "Yes, yes... there are freedom flags everywhere. People are chanting. I've never seen anything like it."

Despite the danger, Fadin felt intrigued.

"Alright. Let's go then."

***

As the three men approached, the noise of the protest steadily grew louder. Soon they were working their way through the ever-thickening crowd towards the sounds of chanting and singing.

Hassam had not been exaggerating. It seemed like the whole city had converged on Valiasr Park. The Cable Bridge, connecting the Park with Salman Farsi Blvd east, swayed dangerously over the Khoshk River. The overspill of people had brought all the traffic near the Park to a standstill.

Flags moved to and fro, dotted above the sea of heads like sails of old ships. Banners read: "Where's my vote?" "If you can't win an election, rig it!" As they got nearer the centre, the chants became clear: "Where is Yazdi! Where is Yazdi!" High-pitched whistles and beating drums drifted across from some unseen point. Young men draped in Iranian flags, with scarves across their faces, milled around on the boulevard that bordered the park.

A young man with a beard nudged Amir in the arm and handed him a small printed leaflet. He gave a quick nod before moving off into the throng without saying a word. He stared down at the white text on black, headed by the symbol of UIS, the Daesh. A cheer caused him to look up, and he absently placed the leaflet in his back jeans pocket.

From the other end, nearer the subway station, a distorted megaphone blasted out words of anger, drawing cheers from the people closest to it. At the corners of the park and along the outside, police vans began to park up, the evening sun catching on the helmets as riot police spilt out onto the streets and lined up, interlocked shields at the ready.

The mood bristled with anger and frustration, electrifying the air and affecting everyone. For a while, Fadin, Amir, and Hassam just stood around, watching in awe, taking it all in, almost disbelieving that this was happening in their city. Then, they moved again, along the outside of the main throng, before Amir spotted a girl he knew and kissed her on the cheek.

"This is Laleh," he said, grinning at his brother and Hassam. Fadin nodded knowingly and smiled at her. So this is the girl he likes, he thought.

As they chatted, Fadin spotted more armoured police vehicles moving along the cable bridge overhead. He nudged Amir and pointed at them. "There's trouble. They're trying to surround the protestors."

Just then, from the direction of the distant subway came a series of popping sounds like champagne corks being released. Streams of white vapour flew through the air and into the crowd. There were screams and shouts, and slowly, a single cloud of white smoke formed, drifting slowly with the breeze and through the assembled throng. Then, more puffs of white smoke. A distant cry: "Tear gas!" and the swarm of protesters began to writhe, convulsed by the acrid fumes which engulfed them. As if by some unseen signal, rocks and other heavy objects sailed through the air toward the police line. Heads turned as many protesters looked to see where these missiles were coming from. As if sensing imminent danger, several parts of the crowd attempted to distance themselves from the impending conflict and the police. In contrast, a hundred or so masked youths, some carrying rocks while others wielded glass bottles full of liquid sporting rags stuffed into their necks, began to jog towards the police.

A series of loud cracks, like fireworks in a distant field, punctured the air around them.

"They're shooting at us!" Amir said.

"Come on," Fadin shouted, jerking his hand. Amir grabbed his friend's arm, and they all headed back the way they had come. The crowd seemed to swell and surge as a single mass that threatened to catch up with them. Stampeding feet. Fadin glanced back.

Overhead on the bridge, streams of tear gas canisters began raining down onto the escaping crowd. People clutched their faces, dropping to their knees. The screams were louder, nearer. The whistle of a bullet nearly hit Fadin, ripping up the grass instead.

Amir and Hassam were ahead—more gunfire. Laleh fell to the ground like a limp doll right in front of Fadin, almost tripping him up. He immediately crouched down beside her, seeing a darkening stain of blood appear across her chest and a twisted mask of agony on her face. She lay limp and unmoving.

"Amir!" he shouted. Amir and Hassam stopped and turned. Amir stared back, and his face dropped at the sight of Laleh sprawled over the grass of the park.

Chapter 15

Amir leaned his elbows on his knees, staring at the tiled floor in the hospital waiting room. Fadin and Hassam were sitting on either side of him, watching as the hospital became busier. It would have been risky bringing Laleh to the hospital with a bullet wound inflicted by the police at any time, but especially on the same evening as a violent rally. Hospital authorities were compelled to report any cases where victims of violence had come forward for treatment. The rumours of multiple arrests, and large numbers of others killed or wounded blurred into insignificance for Amir. All he could do was fret about the girl. It had been sheer grace from Allah that his father knew so many people and that one of them was a doctor.

"Amir."

It was this doctor who stood in front of them now, looking down at him with what seemed to Amir like sympathy.

Amir stood up, alert, questions racing across his face.

"How is she?" he spat out before he could continue.

"I need to speak to Laleh's parents first. I'm sorry, Amir."

"Yes, yes, of course. I already phoned them—her parents, they're coming." He paused, then slowly, he said: "Is she alright?"

The doctor glanced at Fadin and Hassam as if thinking of

the right words. "I'm sorry, Amir, I need to speak to relatives first."

He looked at Amir as if to ask for his understanding. Amir nodded slowly, his eyes drifting to the middle distance down the corridor to where they had operated on her. "Of course—thank you, doctor."

Amir slumped back down on the bench, his brother's hand immediately on his shoulder. "He didn't say she—" Fadin began.

"She's dead!" Amir interjected, deep grief welling up in his voice. "I could tell by his eyes, but he needs to inform the family first."

******

Amir had stewed with bitterness all the following day, a taste of bile infecting his throat. He sat in the small courtyard at their home, smoking a cigarette, letting it burn to his fingers, barely aware of the smoke drifting up his arm.

Those bastards, he kept thinking, over and over. Laleh had been his dream girl, someone he'd thought might be his wife one day. It had been fleeting, a few dates, nothing serious, yet the feeling she'd given him, the potential happiness, now that was snuffed out and extinguished. One minute she had been fine, demonstrating her anger at the rigged election results, like him, like them all. Next, shot in the back like a feral dog beneath contempt.

Fadin and Hassam came out of the house and drew up the wooden chairs and muttered sympathies, but they were, to his mind, just empty words. She was gone now.

"How long can we live like this?" he hissed quietly.

"This is the way it has always been," said Fadin, pragmatically, "since the Revolution."

Amir stood up suddenly, a flash of anger on his face and walked away to the far side of the courtyard. "Why does it have to be like this? This fucking government is pissing over our lives—"

There was a silence as no one knew what to say.

Amir fished around for another cigarette and found the leaflet, pushed into his hand at the rally. He turned it over, reading the words carefully as they talked about a dream shared by the Iranian people. A dream of one more Revolution. His simmering anger and sense of impotence had eaten away at him all through the previous night, turning to hope, offering a way of fighting back of getting vengeance.

He turned to Fadin and Hassam, staring at them both, his eyes which were previously full of sorrow for the loss of his love, now filled with steely determination and something else. Hate.

"I think there's a way to fight back."

******

The three men walked through the streets of their neighbourhood. The heat from the sun was slowly waning as day turned into evening. They turned a corner and came to a doorway where a man in black robes stood guard outside.

Hassam spoke first. "We've been invited by the Imam."

The man, tall and imposing, cast his dark eyes over each one of them before speaking.

"What is the code?"

"The Caliph of Iran," said Hassam enthusiastically.

He nodded and moved through the door, parting a set of hanging doors just inside that revealed a dark, musty room which was empty except for a couple of chairs, unturned and broken. There was a faint murmur of voices from behind a door at the far end, and the guard walked up to it and knocked four times rapidly and then opened the door, shooing them all inside.

A group of young men, some of whom the brothers recognised, were sitting cross-legged in rows on a large rug as the imam spoke to them. He paused speaking as Hassam, Amir, and Fadin appeared in the doorway and indicated a space with a brusque wave of the hand. They stooped slightly as they hurriedly took their seats before the mullah continued. He was a tall, thickset man, and despite his loose robes, it was apparent he kept himself in shape.

"—So you see, the West continues to spin the lies and fuels the total war in our whole region for their own interests. Why would they attack Iraq over 9/11 with no evidence? Because it had nothing to do with their devilish false flag event and everything to do with controlling the oil at the behest of their partners of Shayṭān."

He paused and sipped water from his glass, and looked around at the recruits.

"So now we know our leaders have secretly sought a peace deal with the great Shayṭān, America. Yes, that's right. Behind closed doors, they have met our true enemies and made a secret alliance that is completely against the interests of the people of Iran. The Iranian government is behind the Ayatollah and his plans. They are selling us out to Shayṭān and insulting Allah! Remember, the Qur'an tells us: 'Those who believe fight in the way of Allah, and those who disbelieve fight in the way of Shayṭān.' So I ask you, are you ready to fight for your god?"

There was a murmur of agreement and nodding around the room.

"God is powerful and exalted in might, and in combat with the enemies of God, he granted his followers success and empowered them to fulfil their purpose—and if you desire what God has promised, then set out in jihad for his cause. And you should fear not falling in battle, for those who readily fight in the cause of God are those who forsake this world in favour of the Hereafter. Whoever stands up and fights in the cause of God and then gets killed or attains victory will be granted a great recompense."

"But doesn't the Qur'an forbid violence?" ventured one of the young men, gazing with raptured eyes at the imam.

The imam fixed him with a thoughtful gaze, then slowly smiled knowingly.

"Ahh, yes. As you have undoubtedly read, Islam allows war in 'self-defence'. To defend Islam rather than to spread it, to protect those who have been removed from their homes by force because they are Muslims, and to protect the innocent who are being oppressed. However, one can also take a different view. The other verses in the Qur'an, the 'sword verses', have revoked any verses that permit warfare only in defence. Islam is currently under attack from the West. That is why we must defend ourselves."

The Imam answered a few other questions, then finished and concluded the meeting with a call for the audience to pledge themselves to the United Islamic State. A majority of the men joined right there on the spot, fuelled and angered by the revelations of the sell-out by their government to the

Great Satan. No one had heard of this secret deal, and the growing civil war suddenly seemed to make sense to them. Of course, they must fight and rise up. Before, it had looked like another government problem, a distant threat unrelated to their lives. But with each month in the last year, the reports of fighting and grown closer and more real.

Amir looked at his older brother, his face a mask of determination. "What do you think, brother? If what the imam says is true, then we have no choice but to fight, surely?"

"If... what the imam says is true," replied Fadin quietly.

Hassam, sitting on the far side of Amir, leaned over, evidently as keen as Amir.

"What are we waiting for?"

Fadin made to stand up as if to leave. "Come on, Amir. I don't think this is the way."

"But, Fadin?" Amir was looking up at his brother, frowning as if he had been insulted. "You're serious? Look, it's only a matter of time before we are all pulled into this."

"This is all about politics and men with too much power, Amir. Not our concern." He began to walk towards the door. Amir stood up and nodded to Hassam.

Fadin turned at the door to look to see if Amir and Hassam were following him and saw them both joining the crowd to enrol. He walked back over and grabbed Amir by the arm.

"What are you doing, brother? This is not our war. You want to get yourself killed?"

Amir shook his arm free.

"I'll do what I want!"

"You always were a stubborn idiot. Now let's go!" Fadin had raised his voice and became conscious of it. A few faces from the crowd glanced back at them.

"Let's go back and talk about this," he said, quieter now.

Amir didn't move and looked ahead, his face impassive. Hassam looked away, pretending to study a poster on the wall.

"Hassam. You agree to this?"

Hassam turned around with the same look as Amir. "It's the right thing to do, Fadin. Iran needs us."

Fadin gestured to the men chatting loudly with a sweeping hand. "It needs less of this! Look what happened to Syria."

"I thought you would be with me on this, brother," said Amir. He turned away from Fadin and pushed his way through the other recruits, waving a hand towards the mullah. The guard had stepped into the room and was helping organise the men, funnelling the ones that had given over their details to a side entrance.

Fadin watched in horror as his brother did the same, handing over his sheet of paper and moving to the side entrance. He glanced back at Fadin as the big guard pushed him slightly through the door.

"Amir!"

Then he was gone, and Hassam followed behind, moving towards the door.

Fadin swore to himself and ran as fast as he could back home.

His mother was already by the backyard door and sensed immediately something was wrong.

"What is it? Where is Amir?"

He walked up to her and held her gently by the arms, pausing for a moment, looking straight into her eyes.

"We went to a meeting, and he joined up with UIS."

She frowned with puzzlement as if not understanding. "What? Why?"

"I'm sorry. I tried to stop him, but he was determined.

Listen, I have to go back. I just wanted to tell you. Do not worry—" He moved away from her.

"What?" she said, looking confused.

"Do not worry, mother. I will look after him," he repeated.

"Where are you going?" She moved towards him, grabbing at his forearm, but he was already walking back out to the street and began running.

"Fadin!" He heard her shouting his name as he turned the corner. He shut his eyes and tried to block out her shouts but he could still hear her words.

"Fadin! Come back to me, do not go, please!"

He continued running until he could no longer hear her and slowed down, walking in the direction of the meeting place. Fadin had always looked out for his younger brother. He wasn't going to stop now.

Chapter 16

Tehran, Iran.

Haleema slammed the apartment door and tossed her draw-string bag onto the sofa. She was fuming at the attitude of the police. Why were they so reluctant to get their teeth into the investigation? Isn't that what they got paid to do?

Haleema put on the kettle and dropped a peppermint tea bag into her mug. She moved over to the kitchen window that gave her a good view of the busy side street; the last of the commuters were still making their way home.

She dialled her mother's phone and waited for her to pick up.

Down below in the street, a mix of smartly dressed people, women in headscarves and tradesmen moved in different directions like ants. Two men without helmets on a motorbike, a common sight in Iran, raced onto the main road. A truck with a group of workmen in the back, looking exhausted. Then the ringing tone on her phone stopped, and a familiar voice brought her back to the room.

"Mother? It's me. How are you? Any word from him?"

"Hello, Haleema. No, nothing!" she replied. Haleema could hear the distinct lack of hope in her voice.

"What did the police say?" her mother asked.

"They asked questions and said they were 'investigating' and 'not to worry, we'll soon find him'. In other words, they are really not doing a lot," Haleema replied with her exasperation, adding an edge to her voice.

"What are Amir and Fadin doing?"

There was a pause.

"I was going to—"

"What is it?" Haleema asked alarm in her voice.

"They went to join that group, that group—" Her voice faded, and Haleema heard a gentle weeping.

"What group? You don't mean the Daesh?"

Another pause.

"Amir went first, and then Fadin went after him—I tried to stop him, I tried."

This could not be true. Was she to lose her brothers as well as her father? She closed her eyes tight.

"Oh god. It's alright, ma—it's alright. We'll figure this out." Somehow.

She reassured her mother once again and said goodbye.

The feeling of hopelessness overwhelmed Haleema; she felt the walls close in and a sick feeling in the pit of her stomach.

She needed to figure this out. Needed time to think.

The tea wasn't helping. She needed coffee. After putting on the pot, she went into her bedroom and to the desk in the corner that housed a two-screen computer.

"Fyre, alight," she said aloud. The computer automatically booted up on her voice command, and she proceeded to enter a complex password.

The system was designed to recognise her voice only. If the wrong startup word or voice pattern were used, there would just be two more attempts allowed, after which the hard drives would be automatically erased.

She opened up a browser and logged on before quickly checking her VPN was running. The Supreme Council for Cyberspace, known as the SCC, had control over all the internet providers, and that meant eyes would be watching.

Not only that, the SCC had built an entirely separate and more controlled internet commonly named "Halah internet". The real world wide web was still available, but the government had made it very expensive and deliberately choked the loading speeds to try to force users over to Iran's internal version, which was heavily monitored and censored too.

It was only a matter of time before they shut off the wider internet altogether, thought Haleema.

She had also heard a rumour that the Western powers were attempting the same thing, building it in secret to usher in more surveillance and control. It was another task "Nightowl" wanted her to look into. The Liberatus News operation would indeed be interested to know more about that.

Now, though, could she find any clues as to where her father had gone? Perhaps there was a digital trail that would show her the way. His credit card? She went to the Saman bank website, the flower logo and blue branding offering security for financial assets. Had he changed the password? She was always nagging him to change it every so often and make it more difficult to guess.

Tapping the keyboard, Haleema entered the one she had been given by her mother a few months previously. Her mother struggled with modern tech, and she was often asked to help out. So Haleema had always been the "go-to girl" for any technical problems in the family home.

The login worked. Karim had not changed it at all, and Haleema wasn't sure whether to curse or thank him. She clicked on the transactions tab and focused on the various payments. There was a debit card supermarket purchase from the previous Wednesday, just a few days before he fell off the grid.

Other transactions included the usual mundane stuff; household bills, TV subscription, and groceries. The supermarket transaction had been the last, and she noted there had been no payment made to the hotel he would have stayed at.

She closed the bank website tab and logged into her father's iCloud account, and clicked on the find device once again to see if it had updated at all.

Still offline.

She had an ominous feeling it wasn't going to come back online anytime soon and leaned back in her chair to sip the bitter coffee that brought her some comfort.

The phone was the key.

The telecom company records could give her more information. The cell towers would transmit the position of the phone even if the cloud account could not, as well as the history of where it had been. Distance-based positioning and trilateration would locate the phone at its last point of being active. At least that would give a rough idea of his last known whereabouts.

But the only way to get this information was from the telecoms company.

She racked her memory for the network he used.

Was it MTN? Yes, she was sure that was it.

She did a routine search and found their customer-facing website and clicked through to a service engineer's login page.

Shouldn't the police be doing this?

Haleema shook her head. She could hack it herself—she knew she could, even though it would take some time, but how long would it take the police? How many weeks before they bothered to get around to all this?

She fired up a new terminal window on the second screen and typed in a series of commands.

Thinking through the process quickly, Haleema figured she'd need to find a list of employees, refine them and then figure out their email.

She checked the login page to see what data she would need; an email and password.

Next, she turned her attention to the telecoms website and found a short list of high-level employees. She focused on the top five names, especially anyone in the tech department and copied them over to an Excel sheet, then created fields next to each name for a list of possible email addresses based on the company domain name, adding the employees' names in a different order.

She was able to connect to the mail server using a telnet console. Then, once she was able to communicate with the mail server, it was just a case of pinging and checking the transcript, which verified whether the email address existed or not.

Once she had a list of real emails, next was the more difficult part: hacking the password.

The key to successful password cracking was to use multiple iterations, going after the easiest passwords with the first iteration to the most difficult passwords using different techniques for each iteration.

Her computer probably didn't have enough horsepower to

launch a brute-force attack. Besides, it was time-consuming and, for hackers, was always the last resort.

She then booted up a hacking tool called THC-Hydra and began the process. She typed a random word into the password field that returned a list of data from the web form. The "failure string" captured any incorrect passwords, providing it to Hydra and enabling it to move on to the next attempt. The software used what was called a Hybrid password attack that would use a combination of dictionary words, numbers and special characters to find out the correct password.

Haleema let it do its thing and took a break, topping up her coffee and snacking on some fruit. She rubbed her tired eyes and stared out of the window, trying to ignore the constant sick feeling in her stomach.

After a few hours, the computer "chimed", and she quickly walked back to it. One had matched for a manager, and she had access.

She logged in and breathed out in relief.

Once in, the trilateration method gave her the data she needed. She uploaded the coordinates into an online map app. After a few seconds, she was looking at a map, along with a traceroute of her father's phone and also the times at the various points. A red line layered over the map, displayed his or his phone's journey. It went from the Natanz facility and followed Route 7 south towards Isfahan. That would have been him heading to his hotel, she thought.

Her eyes followed the route as she scrolled down the map, where it ended abruptly at Najafabad. The route then showed it diverted along the northern border of the town and then turned right into the eastern part of the city before stopping on the road in an area named Amir Abad.

Haleema stared at the screen. At last, she had somewhere to start.

On the map, Haleema zoomed in on a warehouse complex with a single road leading into it. This was where the coordinates last placed the phone. Four large white-roofed buildings with scrap cars piled up in a yard on the left-hand side. At the rear, there appeared to be large machinery. Haleema couldn't make it out but guessed it was crushing equipment to do with the scrapyard.

She tried to ignore the rising bad feeling and swallowed hard.

***

Haleema made more coffee; it felt like she was finally making headway. She checked the warehouse business addresses. Two of the warehouses were registered as empty; the other two appeared to be legal companies. One was a white goods wholesaler, and the other was a vehicle repair garage with a scrapping yard. Haleema checked their business registration credentials, and all appeared to be in order. The companies have filed their annual accounts.

Next, Haleema clicked back to the map and zoomed in on the roads nearest these warehouses. The northern highway that spiked off Route 7 was a busy inner city road, which must have some camera feeds, she thought. The Iranian government, while openly criticising the West's surveillance state, were taking a leaf out of its book and ramping up its own CCTV culture.

To access those feeds meant breaking into the central government mainframe. Not impossible for her, but time-consuming. Every second she spent on this, she felt her father getting further and further away.

What did they say? The first forty-eight hours after a crime was the most important if you wanted to solve it. Now they were days after his disappearance, and she couldn't afford to waste any time at all.

Think smart, Haleema.

***

Now that she had a time and location of where her father's vehicle had been, it gave her some hope they could find something on the CCTV. And then she thought of her friend, Damir.

It was the Ministry of Roads & Urban Development that controlled the complex public surveillance structure in Iran. However, the actual technical equipment was supplied by a company called Qtech, and as far as Haleema could figure out, public camera footage would go through them first before anything of interest was handed over to the police.

The phone rang, and Damir picked up.

"Hi, got a minute?"

Damir grunted, then cleared his throat.

"Hal, how's it going?"

"I need a huge favour. I don't want to ask, but I need you to do something for me."

***

Haleema was watching the reel of roadside CCTV, the quality was not excellent, but she knew her father's car well. She had carefully watched the footage from one of the more prominent junctions around the time her father should have passed through. But what if he wasn't in his car? There was no way she could pick him out then. She stared at the monitor as endless vehicles sped by in monotone and silence.

Damir, an employee at Qtech, had protested but eventually saw how getting access to the footage would help Haleema and agreed, albeit reluctantly. It was just a case of isolating the timespan of footage that Haleema asked for from the CCTV on the main road in Amir Abad and handing it to her.

After fifteen minutes, she saw something that made her pause. Her father's car! A swell of excitement. She rewound the video and zoomed in on the number plate. It was indeed his. She zoomed in to see if she could make out who was driving, but there was too much reflected light from the windscreen to see clearly who was behind the wheel.

This felt like a big piece of the puzzle!

What did this mean? Her father's car had passed through here, and her father or at least his phone, had as well. There was no way to identify the driver or anyone else in the vehicle, but she finally felt she was making real progress. She watched the clip again: two vans in front and behind. It seemed like they were driving in convoy.

She noted the van's number plates and started searching for them on the transport department's website. Both had been reported as apparent write-offs. What could that mean?

The details explained they had been involved in a crash a year before. So, how could they still be on the road? Unless someone had just used the number plates on new vehicles. Easily done if you owned a scrap yard?

She printed off a batch of screenshots from the footage and leaned back in her chair.

I'm going to find you, Dad. I'm going to find you, even if it kills me.

Chapter 17

Haleema woke up just after five in the morning and forced herself out of bed. She had called into work the previous evening and told them she needed time off due to family circumstances.

She had a quick breakfast of peppermint tea and slices of fruit, grabbed her small backpack and left.

The drive to Najafabad from Tehran took nearly five hours, during which time her mind kept going over the details of what she had found out so far. The CCTV footage and the location of the phone GPS. It all pointed to her father being taken and only one reason for it.

He had been kidnapped.

She reached the industrial section of the town that stood west of Isfahan just before noon and drove past a row of sand-coloured box buildings, which were so prevalent in Iran. On the outskirts of the town lay the mountainous hills. Five hundred kilometres beyond was her hometown, Shiraz.

Haleema felt her throat tighten, thinking of her mother there, alone. There would be friends and family gathering around to support and comfort her, of course. But she had lost her husband and two sons within the same week. Not knowing their fates, whether they were still alive, must be slowly eating away at her mother's resolve, as it was with hers.

Haleema felt a tear run down her cheek and wiped it away. She knew she must go and see her. Once she had checked out this place, she vowed to check in on her mother.

Fadin and Amir.

What would become of them?

Everyone knew the stories despite the government-controlled media playing it down.

The beheadings, the bloodlust and the bizarre laws of the Daesh.

She shook her head. What had made them go and join that?

Up ahead, the warehouse complex came into view, and Haleema slowed down as she took a look down the entrance road. As she passed by, she could see metal gates that looked to be open. A few figures moved around in front of one of the warehouses.

She turned into a side road that ran alongside the complex, protected by a metal fence and parked up by a tree.

What to do?

Brazenly walk through the front? She probably wouldn't get very far that way. Through the gaps in the fence, she could make out the piles of scrap cars at the rear of the warehouses. She walked further towards the rear side and peeped through, scanning the vehicles for her father's blue Peugeot or any sign of the vans she had seen in the CCTV footage.

Seeing nothing that rang a bell, she glanced back at the road and continued walking. The fence became more dilapidated just before it changed direction and ran parallel to the rear of the complex. There was a distant crunching sound followed by what sounded like a bulldozer wrestling with metal.

She spotted a gap, big enough for her to slip through.

Without hesitation, she took another look around and ducked through. Inside she saw a pile of old tyres stacked up that gave her a good hiding place for a moment.

Across the far side of the yard, the car crusher continued to do its work. Alongside it, a massive crane was in the process of grabbing another old vehicle between its metal hooks.

Straight ahead of her was a gap between cars stacked four high and the fence. She checked the coast was clear and went for it, heart beating hard, hands sweaty as she once again scanned the vehicles. There was no problem breaking the rules online, but Haleema rarely did anything wrong in the outside world.

The sound of the crusher hydraulics echoed across the yard as it crumpled another vehicle with ease.

She moved carefully down the entire row, checking each car that could be her father's—nothing! She walked around a burned-out Ford van at the end corner. For a moment, she didn't see it, continuing to scan the scrap heap, then she glanced down and saw a German Shepherd lying in the shade.

It raised its head. Haleema and the dog looked at each other at the same time.

Shit!

The dog immediately growled, baring its vicious-looking teeth and stood up.

Haleema stepped back quickly, suddenly very much regretting her little incursion.

The dog ran at Haleema, then just as quickly, its neck jerked back, and a taut chain sprang from the dusty ground.

Thank Allah!

She stepped back again, but the dog was barking aggressively.

A large man stepped into view, seemingly coming from nowhere. He must have been right around that corner.

"Hey!" he shouted.

"*Khafe sho!*" he hissed at the animal. He walked past it, waving his hand to calm it down, his eyes fixed on Haleema. The dog gave a low guttural noise and cowed its head before curling back up in its spot.

"What are you doing here?" the man demanded.

Haleema immediately beamed a smile, her mind racing.

"Ahh, so sorry I was lost, looking for the office." She brushed a hand through her hair, forcing herself to stay calm.

"My mother's car. It has broken down and needs scrapping. Can you collect it? It's on the main road to Tiran."

The man was still frowning and reached for his pocket. Haleema's eyes darted to his hand as he pulled out a cloth and proceeded to clean his hands. She breathed out slowly.

The expression on his face lightened as he thought of the money he could charge for a collection from Tiran. He nodded and gestured for her to follow him.

Haleema skirted well away from the dog when passing, and they walked into the main yard at the rear of the building. They went past the large crusher that continued to pulverise yet another car and headed towards a portacabin office at the side of the warehouse complex.

Haleema's eyes moved across the other stacked-up cars. Disappointment clawed at her. She would have to tell the man some bullshit and get out of there. This lead had come to nothing.

Just ahead, her eyes settled on the blue Peugeot. The wheels were removed. Her eyes widened as she approached it. The football motif was hanging from the rearview mirror. The familiar scratch above the front wheel arch.

That's it!

The number plate had been removed, but it was his car, no doubt about it.

She had to stop herself from shouting out. Automatically, she took out her phone. Her heart raced. It was confirmed then. Something had happened to him.

A quick look to make sure she couldn't be seen. The man was still ahead of her as they passed by the car. She turned and raised her phone. There was a loud click that caused Haleema's heart to quicken.

The man stopped, turned around and began to move towards her.

"Hey, what are you doing?" he snapped, clearly intent on grabbing her phone. "You're taking pictures, aren't you? Give me that phone! No pictures allowed here!"

Haleema quickly slipped the phone into her front jeans pocket and continued walking, giving him a half-shrug.

"What are you talking about? I just sent a message!"

Behind her, the dog began to bark in the distance.

She tried to move past him, but his strong hands grabbed her shoulder and pushed her back.

"Hey! Get your hands off me!" she shouted, genuinely annoyed.

"Give me your phone." He moved towards her threateningly and tried to grab at her front pocket, but instead, his hand gripped her inner thigh. She began stepping back as he kept walking closer.

"The phone, now!" he hissed, grabbing at her again. She slapped his hand away, turning quickly on her heel and sprinted back the way she had come. She could hear the man start to give chase. As she drew closer to the dog, it snarled and strained at his leash. Haleema took a wide berth away from it and turned the corner, the shouts of the brute closing in behind her. As she cleared the building, she came out at the front of the scrapyard. She saw the front gates and made a beeline for them. Another man came out of a door in the building, intrigued by all the noise. He looked at Haleema, a mild look of confusion on his face before he saw the man chasing her.

"Ervin, grab her!"

Luckily for Haleema, Ervin was slow to react, and with her agile speed, she got past him easily. Now, with two on her tail, Haleema kept her head down and focused on sprinting as fast as she could to the exit. She ran past the portacabin office and through the gates before glancing behind to see how far her pursuers were behind her.

The men had slowed up and stopped, red-faced and apparently not the running types. They had seen that she was off the premises. The brute waved an arm, shouting abuse, while the other had his mobile phone out.

Haleema tore around the corner and jumped back into her car. Her hands were visibly shaking as she fumbled with the key fob.

She breathed out slowly, calming herself and started the engine.

Chapter 18

Baft, Kerman Province, Iran.

The recruits were packed into a large bus that was almost certainly older than any of them and trundled noisily along the road, rocking the passengers with each bump. They wore black militia uniforms with the symbol of UIS, the sickle moon above the earth, sewn into the lapels. Their faces were masked with scarves, heads covered with dark keffiyehs, and AK-47s in hand. Amir could feel the sweat on his palms as he held the weapon tight with the barrel facing upwards. The air was dry; dust seemed to have settled over all the seats and the floor. Apart from the grinding engine and rattles of the old bus, it was deadly quiet. Very few of the men spoke, each man lost in his thoughts. Only one of the leaders and the driver indulged in conversation.

Ahead of them, in a battered white Suzuki pickup truck, their commander, with two other leaders, led the way. Their wheels belched so much dust that it covered the windshield of the bus, and the driver had to use his wipers. They sped through a village, passing the residents who either looked away or bowed their heads. The vehicles left the village and continued on the seemingly never-ending road.

On either side of them, hills and olive groves flashed by, and in the distance, several men gazed at the dry mountain range in the distance.

Fadin was sitting next to his brother and leaned into him.

"It looks like you'll get to fight just as you wished, Amir. Just be careful."

Amir swallowed hard and continued to stare out of the windows.

"Amir, are you feeling alright?"

"Yes, yes, I am fine."

The bus hit a bump, jerking the passengers from side to side. The road seemed to be getting worse.

"Just be careful," added Fadin. "Don't take any unnecessary risks. It only takes one mistake and—"

Amir continued to stare out of the window, his brother's words adding reality to the situation that he had been trying to avoid. The image of him being a freedom fighter was far easier to digest than the reality he now faced. Now he sat on a bus with a tool of death in his arms. Knowing he may soon have to kill another human in the name of his god.

After another hour's drive, the truck and bus came around the bend, where the cliffs on each side formed a gully with rocks lining their crests. They continued for around ten metres and then pulled off the road in front of a cluster of rocks.

"Everybody out!" shouted the driver.

The new soldiers of UIS trooped off the bus and formed a haphazard line while the three commanders discussed amongst themselves. The small commander who had put them through their brief training programme walked up and down, checking his men, shoving a few to straighten the line before speaking, flanked by the others.

"Brothers of Islam, today will be your first blood. We will be taking out a convoy that is supplying the treacherous dogs of Shayṭān!"

He pointed at two recruits.

"You two, go and help with the device."

The two men moved quickly to the pickup truck and began unloading a small crate.

The commander continued: "We have chosen this place as it offers us the best tactical advantage over our enemy. Timing is going to be everything. Security team one will be situated here on the ridge," he said, pointing to the closest group of rocks on the crest. "Once the device has been detonated, your job is to ensure the first armed vehicle is neutralised. Security team two will be situated at that far point over there." He pointed to a cluster of rocks in the distance. "Once the device has gone off, your job will be to take out the rear escort. All the rest of you who make up the main attack force will spread out between teams one and two. Once team two has taken out the rear escort, you will break cover and take control of the convoy vehicles. It is imperative you all remain out of sight until the device goes off and the trap is sprung. The device will be hidden at the end of the gulley, here where the road is the narrowest." He gestured behind him to a bend in the road where the men were preparing the bomb.

"When the convoy approaches, keep calm and remember your training. Do not be afraid, as Allah will be with us."

He paused, looking at the eyes of his recruits as if searching for any doubts or weaknesses, ending with Amir. The dark eyes bore into him for a few seconds, and then he raised his fist and shouted to the whole group.

"For Allah and Islam! To a United Islamic State!"

The recruits hollered and shouted in unison, throwing their fists in the air. The tension lifted, and the men fired up with adrenaline now, followed their leaders up the hill to take their positions. Amir and Fadin were directed to a position near each other. Crouching down to lie hidden just below the ridge, they settled in to wait. Fadin caught Amir's eye, giving him a reassuring nod.

So, this was it. Now, at last, we are doing God's work, thought Amir. He checked his weapon, determined to do well and make up for his shaky start. He looked at his brother.

And to prove myself to him!

Fadin was checking his weapon thoroughly. Once satisfied, he put it down on the ground and pulled out a flask of water, taking a swig.

Why had Fadin joined after trying to stop him? After all that fuss about how he should go home to his mother. Then he had turned up at the training camp saying he had decided that it was a good idea to be on the side of the eventual winners in the civil war.

That seemed reasonable enough, but he knew his brother and changing his mind, once made up, was not something that featured in his DNA. Still, it was great to have him by his side. He felt so much happier for it. And to see his friend, Hassam, who was further along the line, also preparing to break first blood.

They watched the bus and truck being driven away to be hidden out of sight. Two men dusted over the tracks with palm leaves while the other two finished up with the improvised explosive device (IED).

Finally, those men moved towards the rocks and got into their hiding positions, and it fell quiet, except for the sound of buzzards overhead and the wind whistling through the rocks.

Twenty minutes passed, and the distant sound of vehicles piqued the men's attention after the lull in the rising heat. The commanders evenly spread out along the line, giving them to signal with a sign of a fist to standby.

The gentle purring became louder, turning into a grinding uneven growl. They could hear the convoy, but the bend in the road gave them no visual contact until the last moment. An Iranian army truck appeared first and drove towards them at a slow pace. Behind it came a stream of white vans with the red cross insignia emblazoned on the side. As the armoured vehicle drove straight to their position, Amir covered his ears with his hands. He heard the loud explosion he expected, the waves of violent energy rolling up the hillside and the echo bouncing off the cliff face opposite.

Muffled screams pierced the receding deafening caused by the initial explosion.

An Iranian soldier stumbled out of the side of the burning vehicle, clearly disorientated, holding his face.

Another explosion further down the line as the rear army escort got taken out.

Then the familiar sound of an AK-47 peppering the convoy as an attacker started firing volleys of bullets toward the burning vehicles.

The soldier, still clutching his face, hit the ground.

More recruits began firing until the thunderous sound of gunfire dominated the small gully. Security team one, armed with an RPG launcher, shot at the lead vehicle as more surviving soldiers jumped out, trying to escape the burning hell they were trapped in. The explosion took out the entire front cabin, sending body parts across the road.

The convoy of around ten vehicles had come to a halt. Some of the drivers exited their lorries on the opposite side, trying to escape the bullets. Others just dived to the floors of their cabs and prayed.

Amir fired at the burning embers of the first vehicle, but there were no targets left.

A shout came down the lines from the commanders to cease fire and move down the hill. Immediately black figures rose from their hiding places, and the force of attackers streamed down onto the road. The UIS recruits were ordered to capture all the surviving drivers and any others and line them up. Sporadic gunfire continued as a few pockets of resistance were mopped up.

Slowly the survivors were brought forward from their hiding places. Terror etched on their faces, their hands above their heads. Some pleaded for their lives; another just stared at the ground, unwilling to look his captors in the eye. Amir moved around the side of a truck, his weapon raised and found the driver huddled down by the front wheel.

"Hands above your head," rasped Amir. The driver, an older man with grey hair, raised shaking hands.

"Stand up!"

The old man did so but was struggling due to a lack of strength as if his muscles were failing him.

Amir tutted and grabbed his arm to help him up. The driver leaned against the truck door and nodded. "Thank you," he said.

Amir looked into his eyes for a moment, sensing his fear.

Feeling a rising sense of pity, Amir quickly snuffed it out and jerked the barrel of his weapon at the man, "Come on," he growled. They moved toward the others. There were fifteen drivers and aid workers lined up on their knees, hands on heads. Some of the recruits patrolled the line while the commanders directed others to search the vehicles and check for what supplies they contained.

There was an air of jubilation among the fighters. A rabble of voices rose through the gully. The commanders had gathered together and were speaking among themselves. Fadin and Amir's commander walked over to the recruits and summoned them to gather together away from their prisoners.

"Fighters for Islam. Very good. We have secured the supplies. I am proud of you all. We are all doing God's work here, make no mistake, but the mission is not over yet. These men are infidels, running dogs for the corrupt government. We have no use for them."

The small man grabbed one of the recruits' AK-47s, spat onto the dry ground and walked over to the prisoners. He stood in front of them, levelling the weapon at the cowering men and two women.

"Now listen to me," he shouted. "The supplies you have been transporting were for the corrupt government. The very liars who have betrayed our country. Today, those of you who are still alive are very lucky. Those of you who choose the correct path will live. Those of you who resist that path will be sent to hell."

"Today, you must repent your religion! Allah is the light and the way—unless you are Muslim and swear allegiance to the UIS, you will not see the true path. Refuse, and your life will end today."

Several of the drivers looked at each other and then at the commander, who walked to the end of the line and pointed his gun at the first man in the line.

"Will you join us?"

The man nodded his head enthusiastically.

The commander gestured for him to leave the line. He was taken aside by another recruit as the commander moved to the next man. One by one, they joined the huddle of drivers who had agreed to join to save their lives.

Amir and Fadin were casting glances at each other as the selection process played out. Amir watched as the commander reached the older prisoner, the driver he had just pulled out of his truck, tears running down his cheeks.

"Will you follow Allah to salvation?"

"Jesus Christ is my Lord and Saviour. I will not renounce him."

Without hesitation, the commander summoned a recruit over and jabbed a finger at the prisoner. The young recruit hesitated and then walked around the back of the prisoner.

The commander stared down at the prisoner.

"I ask you again. Convert to our cause, the only true religion or die."

The man, seemingly calmer now, simply looked at the ground.

"No. I cannot."

He clasped his heads together and began to pray.

The commander spat at him in disgust and stepped back out of the way, nodding at the recruit behind him. The young recruit took a deep breath and aimed at the back of the head, and fired a single shot.

Amir turned away. The feeling of euphoria from their successful hijacking had changed to one of uneasy sickness.

Another single gunshot.

This time splatter of brains and blood which hit the sand

was in front of the elderly man that Amir had moved from the truck. His body slumped forward, instantly dead, his face a mask of terror.

There was silence, just for a moment, and then the commander walked to the last man and asked him the same question.

Chapter 19

2.35 PM
Isfahan, Isfahan Province, Iran.

Haleema drove away from the scrapyard and into Isfahan. As the immediate danger passed, she felt the adrenaline rush from the near miss coursing through her. Her hands shook slightly, and she needed to get a drink. Spotting a roadside cafe, she quickly pulled the car over. Sitting at plastic tables by the entrance, a group of old men drank coffee and smoked cigarettes in the shade of the canopy. They gave her momentary curious glances before going back to their conversation.

Inside, the cafe had a cosy, rustic look. She imagined that little had changed here in the last twenty years. There were a few well-worn wooden tables and chairs, a small counter with a coffee machine and old-fashioned mechanical cash till. The aromatic smell of cooking spices hit her senses as she approached, making her mouth water. A small man with a weather-beaten face came out from the kitchen and gave her a warm smile. After ordering tea, bottles of water and the lunch special, she settled herself down on a table near the back of the cafe. She decided to call that Inspector Rahbar and email him the evidence she had found immediately.

She typed Rahbar a quick message, added the photo from the scrapyard and added the screenshots from the CCTV and hit "send". Then she flipped through the phone contacts and pulled up his number, and tapped the green icon.

The ringing continued for a while, and she was about to disconnect when his voice came on.

"It's Haleema Sheraz. I've sent you an email with photographic evidence of my father's car in a scrapyard."

There was a pause as Rahbar obviously processed this information. He sighed impatiently.

"Hello, Ms Sheraz. I hope you are well. So," he paused, and Haleema heard typing, "Where was this taken exactly?" he asked after a few moments.

"A vehicle scrapyard in Najafabad."

"Najafabad? That's a long way from Tehran. What took you there?"

"Trying to find my father. Did you see the picture?"

"Yes, it's in front of me. So your evidence is just a photo of a blue Peugeot 206?"

"It was my father's car! His Fajr Sepasi F.C. tag was still hanging on the rearview mirror. That's his soccer team. And there was a scratch by the wheel arch that I know was one he put there. Please, they will have it crushed. Can't you send local police from here?"

"No," Rahbar said emphatically, "I can't just go and order raids based on this." He paused.

Haleema could imagine him casting his critical eyes over her photo.

"So you're going to do nothing?" she asked.

Rahbar sighed. "We are not 'doing nothing,' Ms Sheraz. We

are continuing the investigation. And these photos from the traffic cameras, how exactly did you get them?" he asked, irritated.

"I have a friend who works for the transport department. He was kind enough to find them for me," replied Haleema.

"Your 'evidence' so far is a picture of a car, similar to your father's, at an intersection between two vans. But this image is unclear, so it's hard to make out exactly who is driving. Your photo of another similar car at the scrap yard is without number plates, so it's impossible to make a positive ID. Now if you either had high enough quality photographs so you might be able to recognise the scratches on it, that may be more convincing proof. As it is, I will have to take this to my superiors to see if they consider these photos sufficient evidence to get the go-ahead for a warrant to search this property. And let's just say it is indeed your father's car, with evidence to show that he was abducted. Do you really think it will still be there if we go back? Had you waited for me to come with you, then we may have had some concrete evidence! Now, all we have is some vague photos which could be interpreted in any number of different ways. For example, this could simply be your father driving his car to the scrap yard of his own free will. Perhaps even selling it to them before starting a new life, working with the UIS."

"Have you finished?" Haleema snapped, angry at the superior tone that had crept into Rahbar's voice. "He has not joined the Daesh!" A few faces turned and glanced at her. "He has not joined them," she repeated, more quietly this time.

"Alright, Ms Sheraz. Thank you for the information—"

Haleema cut the call, tapping the red icon and slammed it on the table, shaking her head.

She desperately wanted to scream out loud, the frustration eating her up.

This was going nowhere. It was evident to her now. She needed help from somewhere else, or she would find her father alone.

Chapter 20

16.13 PM
Isfahan, Iran.

After booking into a small hotel close to the historic Naqsh-e Jahan Square, she settled into her small room with the sound of gushing water from the ornate fountains in the Square drifting through the window. Haleema phoned her friend, Damir. She still felt annoyed from the call with Rahbar, yet a steely resolve fuelled her determination.

"Hey, Hal. How are you doing?"

"Hi, Damir. Not so good…"

"Everything alright?"

"My father, I— think he's been kidnapped by the Daesh."

"Kidnapped!? What the hell, Hal! Are you sure?"

"Yes, yes, I'm sure, now. We haven't heard a thing."

"So, he just disappeared without a trace?"

"The last anyone saw of him; he was leaving work as usual on Thursday night. Then I got a call from my mum saying he hadn't arrived home. I did some digging and managed to trace his car to a scrapyard at Najafabad. I told the police, but they didn't wanna do shit. So I went there myself to take a look."

"You went on your own! You are something, Hal. Did you

find anything?"

"I managed to get a little look around before some ape got suspicious. Saw his car and took a photo. I told the police, but they're not helping. In fact, they're barely interested. They say without signs of a struggle; it looks like he's probably gone on his own accord. But that's just not like him at all, but they were just not convinced."

There was a pause as Dahir took in the information.

"God, I'm sorry. The police aren't doing anything?"

"They're going through the motions. The inspector I talked to is suggesting he's joined them."

"Joined the Daesh? That's..." Dahir sighed. "Haleema," he added.

"What?"

"If they have him, if that is what has happened, then there might be a way to find out. I never told you this but one of my relatives was taken by the Daesh, six months ago,"

"What, really? I'm sorry, Dahir— "

"It's OK. The family got her back. The point is there is someone who might be able to help you. I want to help. I can check the flights and come down."

"No, no. It's alright."

"Please, Hal. I could do with a break from Tehran. Let me see what I can do. Let me do some calling, and then I'll send you a link to the person who helped us."

***

An hour later, Haleema was looking at a man in his early fifties through a video chat link. Wavy grey hair sprouted out from under his hat, and he sported a neat moustache. His eyes told a story of tragedy, yet they still burned with the determination to do right.

Omid Husseini, looking off camera, explained that his family had been lost to the Daesh. Their souls had long departed, and bones now merely dust buried in the ground. He could no longer help dead bones, but there were so many other families, women and children that needed his help. He had dealt with hundreds of distraught relatives who had lost members to the brutal rebels, either through resisting and fighting or kidnapping.

That was his cause now.

He looked once again at the camera.

"So, if you want my help. We are ready."

Haleema nodded and swallowed hard.

What did she have to lose?

"I can send a picture of my father... his details," she said quietly, trying to hold down the hope she was now feeling.

Husseini nodded and smiled.

"Yes, send it over, and we'll see what we can do. But remember not to get your hopes up. The chances are small, especially of anything happening quickly."

Haleema nodded and felt tears welling up. She rubbed her eye.

"Yes, yes. I know. Thank you so much, Mr Husseini. I'll hang up and send it right over."

"I'll keep you updated and let you know as soon as I hear anything. Goodbye, and take care Haleema."

He smiled once more before the screen went blank.

Haleema immediately began scrolling through her photo library until she found a good clear one of her father that had been taken recently.

She sent it to Husseini's number along with a simple message.

Here is the information. His name is Ostad Karim Sheraz. Let me know if you can help?

Chapter 21

Tehran, Iran.

Massood put the phone down on Inspector Rahbar and drummed his fingers on the solid oak desk. He was sitting in his spacious study at home. The shelves were packed with rare books that he barely read. Wooden slatted blinds covered the French patio doors, keeping out the bright sunlight.

The cargo deliveries were going well. Seven scientists and physicists had successfully been obtained. He checked the encrypted messaging channel on his mobile. The payment was due for the local thugs who had carried out the dirty work, and they were getting impatient.

Not that he cared. He could have them all arrested or shot at the snap of a finger. It wasn't like he hadn't done it before. There were probably hundreds of those in opposition to the current regime that he had made disappear. But no, he would much prefer it was taken care of in some other way. Less messy, fewer loose ends to deal with.

But that girl was getting too involved and beginning to tread on her toes.

A number of scenarios flashed through his mind, none of them pleasant.

On his screen, he had a view of Rahbar's email inbox and was able to read any of his messages, as well as look around his computer. He had long ago got the techs to install snooping software on all the top-ranking police in Tehran. It was how he kept in power—eliminating his enemies before they got too strong. And then he saw a name in an email to Rahbar that made him sit up sharply.

Haleema Sheraz.

Massood read the email carefully; it gave him some interesting information. He stood up, an immediate plan forming in his mind as he opened the glass doors to the patio. A warm breeze greeted him as he stepped outside and walked to an ornate metal table and chairs. A pot of coffee and a single china cup and saucer awaited him. He sat down, placing his gold cigarette case next to the coffee.

Beyond the patio was a vast extended garden of neatly trimmed bushes, with a patchwork of flowers meticulously maintained by his gardener and a water fountain as the central piece. Further across a vibrant green lawn, his young twin boys were playing catch with their mother.

Beyond the garden were high stone walls topped with electric fencing. He looked across to the small orchard of fig trees that created a wooded area and saw one of his armed guards on his routine perimeter check. Massood checked his Rolex watch and was pleased to note that the armed security was precisely on schedule. He poured coffee and took out a mobile phone from his jacket pocket, one he rarely used and dialled the number he had for the UIS commander, Yafir Al-Adel.

After five rings, a raspy voice answered.

"It's Jack of Spades. I hope you are well. I wanted to let you know I bumped into an old acquaintance of ours," Massood said cheerily.

"Oh, I'm listening," the voice said.

"Our mutual friend, Omid. He very much wanted to invite you to dinner. I cannot make it, unfortunately, but he said you were more than welcome to invite friends."

"That's exciting. I would very much like to see him again. Where is he nowadays?"

"I'll give you the details, but I would very much suggest meeting him sooner rather than later. He may have to leave, and it would be a shame to miss him."

"Yes, good. I look forward to it. Thanks for letting me know," the raspy voice replied.

"Another thing," Massood said quickly. "There's a girl. An old friend who's making her way there. I'll add the details as well."

"Of course, anything to help," the voice replied.

The call ended, and Massood pulled a small piece of paper that was neatly folded in half. He typed out the address that was written on it and a brief message before hitting the send button, then put the phone down and sipped his coffee. He reached into his pocket and pulled out his ornate lighter. He brought the flame up to a corner of the paper. As the little flames started to engulf the paper, he dropped it, watching it slowly burn to ash.

One of the boys noticed him for the first time and waved. Massood waved back and lit a cigarette.

Chapter 22

Isfahan Province, Iran.

Haleema and Damir drove out of Isfahan along Route 62 towards Naein. On either side of them lay the vast emptiness of the shimmering desert. Directly ahead, the rugged hills of Jeshvaghan slowly drew closer as they passed by small forgotten towns and farmsteads. The aircon was providing them with a protective cocoon from the oppressive rising heat surrounding them.

After the conversation with Husseini, Haleema had thought hard and decided to email Inspector Rahbar with a note of what she was doing. Despite his stubbornness, he seemed the only other person who was remotely interested in resolving this mess.

The news came on over the radio, and Haleema reached for the dial to turn it up slightly. The report covered the advancements of the Daesh in the south. An aid convoy near Baft was the latest to fall victim to their attacks. It then called for the people to be vigilant against the Daesh and inform the authorities of any suspicious activity.

"It still seems surreal, like it's all happening somewhere else, but Baft is only six hour's drive from my family home in

Shiraz. What's going to happen to my hometown if they take over there?" Haleema said.

"I'm sure the government will take action against them before it gets that far," responded Damir. "You know what a lot of these southern towns are like, a little backward thinking. I doubt they gave Daesh much resistance."

"Still," he went on, "it makes this whole thing seem a lot more real when it involves places and people you know. And when the government does take action, you know it will be an overt display of power, and won't that make more people join the Daesh?"

"Possibly..." mused Haleema. "But they can't just sit by and watch the country get taken over."

"Well, if they don't put a stop to it soon, it will be an all-out civil war. The movement had been slowly gaining more support. God only knows what my brothers were thinking."

Damir leaned over and switched the radio off, putting on some of his music. A thudding bassline filled the car, and Haleema welcomed the distraction from her thoughts.

The hills arose on either side as they reached a valley. Naein appeared in the distance, the vast blue sky providing a backdrop to the low silhouettes of its buildings. Haleema and Damir didn't speak. Both lost in their own thoughts. Haleema felt increasingly anxious and knew Damir was too.

The house for meeting Omid Husseini was on a side road. It split off the main highway just before the town. The smooth tarmac gave way to a bumpier, less maintained gravelled surface. After several minutes the SatNav indicated their turn was next, and Haleema swung the car off onto a narrow road.

They passed several houses that appeared derelict. The road soon became a simple dirt track, and the wind picked up, blowing dust and sand across their vehicle.

"It's very quiet," said Damir, breaking their silence. Haleema checked the SatNav again. They were very close to their destination.

Looking up, the house came into view. It was a two-storey grey building, standing alone with several vehicles parked outside. She pulled over, switched off the engine and turned to Damir.

"This is my only lead. I hope this man can help."

Damir nodded and leaned over, hugging her.

"Let's find him. Come on."

They got out of the car and walked over to the house. It looked like it was still under construction, with bare breeze blocks exposed and other building materials lying around. A half-built wall surrounded the outside at the front, and a cement mixer lay idle behind it.

Haleema and Damir exchanged glances but continued to the door and knocked. She leaned her ear against it and tried to listen, making out only the faint sound of conversation. Then, she heard footsteps and stepped away from the door. It creaked open, and a young male peered at her suspiciously.

"I'm Haleema Sheraz. I've come to meet Omid Husseini. He's expecting me," Haleema said.

The man looked up the road and then back at Haleema and Damir.

"I'm sorry, it's not possible. You need to leave."

"What? I made an appointment," Haleema retorted a hint of desperation in her voice.

Haleema looked at Damir in exasperation, who gave her a subtle shrug. "We've travelled a long way. I need to find my father, and Omid said he would help." She leaned her hand against the door and craned her neck, peering past him.

"Is Omid here?"

Then the door opened up wide. Another man, stocky with a craggy-lined face dressed in a dark shirt and jeans, appeared behind the younger one and gestured at them.

"You want to see Omid Husseini? Come in," he said.

"Thank you!" Haleema said and walked past the younger one, giving him a look which he avoided. Damir followed as the young man closed the door.

***

The craggy-faced man led them into a dingy hallway. He opened the door to the front room and invited them inside with a sweep of the hand.

"This is the waiting area. We will get you to see Omid as soon as we can."

Haleema and Damir walked into the gloomy room; it, too, looked like it was still under construction. One single light hung from the ceiling, casting a dim orange hue on the walls. The window had been boarded up with wood, but a crack lets in some external light. As her eyes became accustomed, Haleema saw dark shapes and then realised the room was full of people.

Three middle-aged women were sitting on a sofa, and a young girl aged around five asleep on one of their laps. A frail old man and woman clutching what looked like photographs in their hands sat near the window. Opposite them were two younger women, with three boys lying on the bare tiled floor. One of the young boys was crying and was being comforted by his mother. Everyone looked anxious as they looked up at Haleema and Damir.

Haleema nodded at a few who caught her eye and looked around for somewhere to sit. There was a space in one of the corners next to the three women seated on the sofa, and they went over and crouched down, sitting on the floor cross-legged.

Haleema and Damir both looked at each other, Haleema raising an eyebrow, but they said nothing. Then she caught the eye of one of the women on the sofa.

"What are you here for?" Haleema asked, addressing one of the women who sat nearest her.

She waved a hand. "My husband and brother disappeared. Taken by them."

Another woman nodded. "My sister," another said. "Taken by the Daesh. We came here to see Mr Husseini for help."

Haleema nodded slowly as she listened to their stories. All similar, all laced with tragedy and woe.

After ten minutes, the younger man came into the room and gestured for one of the women who had been speaking to Haleema to go through. His eyes darted over to Haleema and Damir as the woman smiled at them and left the room.

"Hey, do you know how long it's going to be?" Haleema asked, irritated. The youth said nothing, merely shrugging his shoulders before leaving and closing the door.

Several minutes later, the three women with the little girl were called, their anticipation of good news evident as they left for their appointment. After half an hour more had passed Haleema and Damir were left alone in the room. Damir moved to a more comfortable chair and played on his phone while Haleema became more agitated, staring hard at the closed door.

Time passed, and they heard nothing except for distant

voices and the occasional car passing by the house. Haleema stood up. Her legs ached, and she was getting increasingly impatient and concerned. She went to the door and tried to open it.

Locked?

She banged on the wooden panel door. Damir came over to her and put a hand on her shoulder as if to calm her down, but she ignored him.

"Hey. Why have you locked this door?" she shouted. There was no response.

She banged again and heard a shuffle outside. The lock clicked, and the door opened. The man with the craggy face stood looking at her as if offended by her complaint.

"Yes, yes. You can come. Our friend is here!" he said, sneering. He walked off down the hallway.

"At last," she said, following the guard. Damir grabbed her again, more forcefully this time.

"Wait a minute, Haleema. I'm not sure about this— something doesn't feel right!"

Haleema turned and looked at her friend.

"I know it all seems odd but isn't this what you were expecting? You said Husseini helped your family, so we know he can be trusted, right? This might be my only chance to find my father. Let's just get this over with quickly, OK?"

She walked briskly on behind the guard who had gone through a door at the rear of the house.

"Haleema!" Damir shouted, then reluctantly followed her.

As she arrived at the back door, a smell hit her. The bright light confused her eyes after the gloomy interior, and she shielded her eyes with her hand as she stepped out into a courtyard.

She squinted as her eyes adjusted. She could just make out the silhouettes of several figures. They stood in a semi-circle, all with weapons pointed at her and Damir.

Down on the ground was a row of bodies. Haleema took in the scene in a split second. All neatly laid out on their backs. Mostly men and a few women too. Their throats were cut, open bloody gashes that attracted swarming flies.

On one man, she recognised the familiar wavy grey hair of Omar Husseini.

Ah Ya Allah!

Haleema began to turn. She felt Damir's hand on her shoulder again.

"Hal, get out of here!" Damir shouted.

A violent crack, and Haleema saw the butt of a rifle hit Damir's skull. She saw his eyes roll as his body fell forward into the dirt.

"Damir!" she screamed. She stepped forward to go to him.

A young thug, no older than twenty, stood by the side of the door. He turned his bloodied rifle around quickly and pointed the barrel at her friend on the ground.

She looked up at him in horror.

"Nooo! Dammirrr!"

The bullet splattered his brain and blood tissue across the concrete ground, the gunshot echoing off the courtyard walls.

A hand grabbed her mouth, and she tried to struggle. More hands gripped her arms, and she felt a sharp pain on the back of her knees. Her legs gave way under her, and then a hood covered her head.

Something struck her skull, a lightning strike of pain shot through her head. She felt her body being pulled back and tasted the metallic blood in her mouth before completely blacking out.

Chapter 23

UIS stronghold at Bam, Kerman Province

Several hundred UIS fighters, all dressed in their black robes, packed the square, the sound of Fajr prayer carried far beyond the mosque's walls. They bowed forward, hands and foreheads pressed to the ground facing Mecca for the last time and resumed a standing position.

The prayers were called to an end by the Imam, and the horde began to leave the square in droves.

Fadin and Amir managed to bump into each other as they went through the arch-shaped gate that led to the main street. Amir gave his brother a friendly slap on the shoulder.

"So, we have to report to the barracks now. I heard a rumour there is something planned."

Fadin nodded and began to scan his eyes along the wall where hundreds of AK-47s had been left outside, along with named backpacks. He spotted his own weapon and picked it up.

The rest of the fighters slowly collected their gear, too and made their way down the street to the main barracks that had, until recently, been the police station in the town. They crowded into the central courtyard and milled around until

Commander Yafir Al-Adel appeared, speaking briefly to one of his subordinates before stepping up onto the makeshift platform on one side of the yard where speakers had been set up in each corner.

Al-Adel was handed a microphone and began to speak.

"Brothers! Today is a great day as we are once again joining the bloody struggle to free our oppressed lands from the apostates for our great caliph.

"We will expand the Caliph's territory and bring Allah's word to more people as we move into Sirjan. We are chosen by Allah and here to do his will. We are happy to serve him, to forego our life of luxuries and be rewarded with an eternity in paradise." The commander raised his fist in the air. "Allahu Akbar!" he shouted.

The crowd followed his lead and threw their fists in the air, a wave of euphoria exploding from the courtyard and shouting as one.

"Ali Akbar!"

After the pep talk, the crowd of fighters was told to report to their immediate superiors and board the buses outside the barracks. The crowd dispersed with one more shout to their commander and began to drift as one to the exit.

The fighters were briefed before boarding a total of six buses. The vehicles then began to move off through the town. They waved their AK-47s from the windows at passers-by, who waved back, cheering them as they passed. On the main road out of the town, the vehicles split directions, with three heading along the 86 and the others on the 71. Fadin and Amir were heading north on 71, and both stared out at the passing countryside.

The murmur of conversations began to die into silence as

the bus travelled at top speed, the engine noise dominating the vehicle interior.

"Do you think we will see our families again?" asked Amir.

"God willing," said Fadin, still facing the dirty window.

"The commander talked about poisoning their wells, attacking their crops—but that contradicts what Muhammad talks about," Fadin turned to Amir, talking softly. "He says to leave water wells and crops alone."

Amir shook his head, "The commander knows what is best; he will lead us on the right path," he said with finality.

Fadin stared into the mid-distance and returned to the window view. They passed a sign that read "Sirjan" and the bus gears began to change down. The endless fields gave way to a few empty block buildings. Fadin caught a glimpse of people rushing inside and shutting the doors.

"I wonder what they are thinking?" asked Amir.

"They're terrified," replied Fadin. "Terrified of us," he said again, as if to himself.

A shout from the front told them to ready themselves, and the men clasped their weapons tighter. The bus pulled over, and they were ordered off. The brothers stepped onto the tarmac road, feeling the scorching heat rising from it. They were several hundred metres from the town and could see it shimmering in the morning heat. Amir could see a few cars that were headed in their direction stop and do a three-point turn before heading back at speed.

Amir estimated there were around forty fighters when all the men had exited the buses. Would it be enough? He wondered.

The men were ordered to move up the road in two columns, marching past the first houses and stores. In the centre of their mass, two men held up the black UIS flag. Leading their way was one of the commanders who began to shout through a megaphone to the buildings in front of them.

"We are here to free you from the oppressive Ayatollah. Muslim brothers and sisters need not fear us—"

He continued to repeat the mantra as they approached the heart of the city. As they got closer, they came to a roundabout; there were several armoured police vehicles across the road. There were also army 4x4s behind them blocking the way, and Amir caught a glimpse of the figures in Iranian guard uniforms assembled behind them.

A hand signal from the lead commander and the two columns of men instantly moved off to either side of the road, crouching down out of any potential frontal firing line. Amir took a position by an abandoned fruit stall and looked down at the small oranges on the dusty ground. The shopkeepers and sellers hadn't even pulled down their shutters. They must have just left at the sight of the black army approaching.

Amir watched his brother, along with a small squad of fighters, peel off and scurry down a side street, looking for a way around the force facing them. One of the commanders had evidently been impressed with Fadin and picked him for more adventurous missions. In normal circumstances, Amir would have been jealous. His older brother always ahead, always winning. Getting the favoured treatment from their father.

In normal circumstances.

But now, Amir felt so scared he didn't care what Fadin did.

The commander pointed his megaphone ahead at the police block.

"You may try to call for backup, but you will see this is just half our force. The other half is now engaging your friends, so sadly for you, there is no backup."

There was no response.

"You have five minutes to lay down your arms, or we will open fire!"

Amir peeked nervously from behind the stall sign, clearly hearing his breath and squinted as the sun rays tipped over a nearby rooftop.

He wondered if he was really cut out for this.

The previous ambush was straightforward, against unarmed men. Here they were faced with armed police and Iranian army soldiers who must be much better trained than they were.

Amir adjusted his stance, shifting his leg. His sweaty palms let the rifle slip, and he grabbed it quickly. His finger slipped on the trigger, and a volley of fire peppered the ground.

For a second, there was complete silence as Amir suddenly realised what had happened. He shirked back behind the stall and looked around as the other fighters stared at him.

Then the silence abruptly ended.

A volley of gunfire came from the barricade, bullets hitting off the shop fronts, shattering glass windows and pinging off metal surfaces. Amir crouched his head as low as he could, feeling the debris spraying over his head. The other fighters opposite and ahead of Amir began firing back, unleashing a hellish vortex of noise.

Taking short breaths, Amir adjusted his weapon and got into a firing position. In a flash, he saw one of the fighters on the opposite side of the road take a hit in his arm. The man screamed and instantly pressed his palm over the wound before spinning around and falling back behind a car.

Amir could just hear their commander shouting above the continuing fire but couldn't understand the words. Ahead the blockade of vehicles was getting a hailstorm of return fire.

Underneath the cars, Amir could make out the body of one of the policemen, lying motionless in a growing pool of blood. Most of the others had retreated, just leaving a handful of soldiers who had taken cover, sporadically returning burst fire from their machine guns.

Bullets pounding into the road kicked up dust, and Amir tasted it in the back of his throat. The air became thick with the smell of gunpowder, and the sun seemed to bake every corner of the growing battleground.

Another shout from the commander, who was waving his arm frantically.

Amir heard him this time.

"Forward! Forward for Allah!"

The dark figures of the Daesh rose from their positions on both sides of the street and streamed forward along the edges. Some stopped and fired off rounds before moving forward again. Amir clutched his weapon. The handle was slippery with sweat, and he had to force himself to get to his feet. Most of the gunfire now seemed to be from the AK-47s of his comrades.

A group of three fighters rushed past him, and he spotted his childhood friend, Hassam, who had joined up on the same day Fadin and Amir had.

"Come on, Amir! What are you waiting for? We've got them on the run!"

Amir nodded and wiped the spittle from his mouth, and began running behind them. The gunfire had died down. Just a few sporadic gunshots rang out ahead of them. As they got closer, Amir caught a glimpse of an Iranian soldier writhing around on the ground behind the vehicles. Two others cowered as they held their hands up in the air, begging for their lives in Farsi.

Two UIS figures rushed around the vehicles. One took out a pistol and fired at the soldier who had been writhing in the dust. They turned to the other prisoners, pointing their weapons and instructing them to lie down in the dirt.

Amir stepped up and stared down at a soldier's body. Half his face had caved in from a bullet, and dark red oozed through his uniform from other wounds. The bodies of those at the blockade were strewn all over the road like piles of rags, bloodied and shredded.

The flies were already swarming, darting to and fro as if wanting to do their part.

A group of fighters appeared with the commander, Fadin, among them. The commander looked down his nose at the prisoners.

Fadin and Amir caught each other's eye and nodded silently.

The commander, Yafir Al-Adel, stepped up and lazily kicked a boot into the side of one corpse. He placed his hands on his hips and looked around at the gathering fighters, who observed him before he waved a finger at Fadin.

"Soldier! Line them up on their knees!"

Fadin stepped forward and grabbed one of the Iranian guards by the collar, pushing him down. He gestured to the other one, who didn't need to be told twice.

"Comrade Amir Sheraz!"

Amir looked up from the corpse at the bark of his name and saw the commander gesturing for him to step forward. He pointed for Amir to take up a position behind the kneeling prisoners.

"Shoot them!" he ordered.

Amir felt his sweaty palms on the gun again; his stomach

churned, legs threatened to give way. He stared back at the commander, trying to regain his composure. Time seemed to slow down in his mind as all eyes of the black-clad figures turned to Amir. He was barely aware of the prisoners whimpering as they begged for their lives.

At that moment, Amir regretted everything, wishing he had listened to his brother all those weeks ago. He swallowed hard, but his throat was dry and acidic.

One of the soldiers began to pray.

Amir met the blazing eyes of the commander, who seemed to be testing or daring him. He strolled around behind the prisoners and raised his rifle to the back of a soldier's head. He felt his palms caked with sweat, his stomach churning.

Amir shook his head.

"No, I cannot," he said.

There was a moment of tense silence, and the commander continued staring at Amir.

Then a smile broke out. He began to laugh. Quietly, at first and then it turned into a roar that surprised everyone watching. No one had heard the commander laugh.

"You are a weak livered boy who must have more guts than sense to defy his superior officer. Do you want to die yourself, boy?"

Amir, flushed of all strength, knew he wasn't going to kill anyone that day, even if it meant dying himself.

He said nothing.

"Commander!" Fadin walked up next to Amir, his weapon ready and stared at Al-Adel.

"I will take care of this," he said.

The commander gestured with his hand at all of them.

"Get on with it. We still have to take the police and council buildings and claim this town today!"

He walked off, followed by the other fighters.

Fadin took out an M9 pistol from his belt and looked at Amir as if to say, "I'm doing this because of you." He raised his arm and fired quickly, killing the first without hesitation. The body slumped forward, and the other turned and looked down at his comrade.

"Please, I have family... my fam—"

A second gunshot rang out. A second body hit the ground.

Fadin turned to his brother.

"You're right, Amir. We must cleanse this country from the corrupt leaders and take power. Isn't that right, Amir?" Fadin walked away without waiting for an answer.

Amir looked down the street. There were bodies and pools of blood scattering the road, along with shattered glass from the trashed stores. The daylight was turning orange as a dust storm approached, and its eerie hue seemed to Amir to cast a premonition of the scenes of apocalyptic destruction yet to come.

Chapter 24

Sirjan, Iran.

Haleema couldn't breathe. Everything was black, and she didn't know if her eyes were open. She tried to get up, but her hands were bound. She screamed out as she fought against her restraints. Her head was still spinning slightly, and she had a pounding headache. Then she remembered the hood.

Haleema took a deep breath and steadied her nerves—panicking now would not help her situation. Recent memories flashed before her. There was intense pain in her jaw, and the taste of blood still lingered in her mouth. The backs of her legs were also in agony. When she tried to move her hands, it was impossible—the rope was cutting into her wrists.

She remembered being grabbed.

The bodies.

Damir.

The pit of her stomach welled up with nausea at the images in her mind.

She had dragged him in to help her—and now—he was dead.

Pushing the dark thoughts away, Haleema tried to calm herself. As her heart rate dropped, she became more aware of her surroundings. Gentle vibrations shook through her, and she could just hear the hum of an engine. How long had she been unconscious?

The heat was stifling. Haleema took deep breaths to try to get some oxygen, but it was hard with her head covered. She tried to call out, but only a hoarse whisper came out of her mouth. The claustrophobic feeling of the confined space and lack of oxygen started to press in as if she were drowning.

The vehicle turned sharply to the left, leaving the smooth road and driving over a rougher track. The journey went on, Haleema losing all sense of time. The stronger vibrations and bumps were numbing her body and mind. The heat and nausea increased. It had to end. Then the vehicle slowed, turned a few times and came to a halt. She heard distant voices and the sound of a door creaking open. Hands grabbed her, and she was pulled out, hitting the floor with a bump. Then they took her by the ankles and dragged her along the floor.

She was taken into a colder environment with a tiled floor. A house? They picked her up and dropped her down on what felt like a bed. She was turned over onto her stomach and felt the rope being removed. Then her hood came off, and she sucked in some much-needed air again and again. She opened her eyes and half turned onto her back, squinting at the light. A man with a dirty T-shirt stood over her and gave her a toothless grin.

"Welcome to paradise!"

He disappeared from view, and she heard a door slam. In the next few moments, a shadow moved across the room, and a female face loomed over. The woman gave her a sympathetic smile. Haleema felt a wet cloth mop her brow. It felt so soothing, and the sudden warmth and humanity made Haleema weep silently at first.

Damir.

"It's alright. We'll get you fixed up. Do you want some water?" a young woman asked.

Haleema could barely speak and simply nodded through choked gasps, her sobs increasing.

Another older woman appeared with a water bottle and gently held it to her mouth, feeding her small gulps until Haleema nodded. She whispered her thanks and closed her eyes.

"You rest for a while," the woman said.

Haleema drifted in and out of sleep. Nightmarish images of Damir's body and the others infiltrated her dreams.

***

The light woke her, streaming through the shutters on the small windows exposing floating dust in the air. The walls were white stone and devoid of any pictures or decoration, only marks and dirt stains.

Haleema stared into the mid-distance, her mind blank and fuzzy. She could feel the bruise swelling on her jaw but blanked out the pain.

None of it mattered anymore.

She would have stayed there on the bed had she not needed the bathroom. One of the women she recognised from her arrival helped her stand up. Haleema felt battered, but she realised it wasn't that bad, and she would recover.

"My name is Kimiya," the younger woman offered as she steered Haleema to the door.

"Haleema," she replied.

They headed down a hallway. For the first time, Haleema

got a sense of where she was being held.

As they walked down the corridor, Haleema caught a glimpse of a large kitchen where dozens of other women, some with children clinging to their legs, were busy preparing food. At the rear of the house, a doorway looked out onto the courtyard, where three more women were scrubbing clothes on wooden racks.

Kimiya smiled and gestured to the small bathroom just inside the back of the house.

"Here it is. I'll wait for you outside."

When Haleema emerged, she crouched down on a stone slab and smiled weakly at Kimiya. Kimiya finished hanging a sheet from the lines crisscrossing the yard and came over to her.

"We need to get you fixed. They'll want you to work soon."

Haleema glanced up at the walls surrounding the courtyard and the barbed wire draped along the top of it.

"What is this place? Where are we?"

"Sirjan," she replied.

"Sirjan? They captured Sirjan?"

Haleema could not believe it. Barely four hours' drive west was Shiraz. Had they captured that as well?

"Shiraz? Did you know if they got there, do you know?"

Kimiya shook her head.

"I don't think so. But it's hard to get any information here. No television, radio or internet access is allowed."

It was what Haleema expected.

"Do you know anyone who has access to a phone—or anything like that?"

"I knew of a woman in Najaf Shahr, in the south of the town, who had one. But she was found out and killed," said Kimiya.

Haleema leaned against the wall, feeling sick all of a sudden.

The reality of having been kidnapped to be a slave for the Daesh weighed heavily on her.

Later that afternoon, the other older woman, Afsoon, showed her the rest of the house. It was to be their new home, Haleema's new prison.

Haleema thought about Omid Husseini. He must have been compromised badly. They evidently tracked him down, sent a snatch squad, captured the house and used his phone to reel in the unsuspecting victims, including herself.

She wondered where the others in Husseini's house had been taken, and her thoughts turned to escape.

***

Over the next few days, Haleema was shown a routine that consisted of continuous washing, scrubbing, and cooking. The house seemed to be part of the UIS logistics division, supporting the fighters by washing and cooking for some of them. She was confined to the house with several of the other women. The room she shared with Kimiya was at the back of the house on the second floor, overlooking the rear courtyard. Whenever she had a spare minute, she was thinking of ways to give her captors the slip. She'd noticed the wall that separated their courtyard from the neighbour's had no barbed wire on top. How she'd get to the wall or what actually to do when she was over was still a problem. She gazed out of her bedroom window looking at the wall and its promise of freedom. Haleema also made a mental note that the neighbour's courtyard had an old door leading to the rear street, easy to get out, but only if she could make it across that open space.

The only time allowed out of the house was a trip to the market with two others and a guard who walked behind them. Haleema, along with the others, had been told to wear a full-length burqa when leaving the house.

The first time they had gone out, Haleema noted their building was set among dozens of other stone houses that stretched up a hill in their district. A few blocks from the house, they walked and came to a main street. The grim-faced inhabitants of the city went about their daily business, but there was a sour atmosphere. Looking down the street to her left, she saw a group of UIS fighters congregated outside a stall drinking and eating. Beyond them, the buildings dwindled, leading to one of the main exits to the city. A large lorry, along with a pickup truck, was parked across the carriageway. Another group of fighters stood around by the vehicles preventing entrance to the town.

They continued across the street and came to a large square and a busy food market.

Haleema focused on her chores, buying the vegetables on her list while subtly taking as much of her surroundings in as possible. Her legs still hurt from her capture, preventing her from walking too fast.

They carried the food back and immediately set about preparing the evening meal. They prepared the vegetables, lamb meat and bags of rice before setting up trestle tables in the backyard for the fighters. Then they spent several hours cooking. A handful of fighters arrived and were greeted by the housemaster who Haleema had not seen before. He was young and cruel looking and only seemed to communicate by shouting at the women when they did something wrong. The fighters and the housemaster sat outside for another few hours, talking and laughing casually as if they were destined to win their war.

By the time they had gone and the women had cleaned up, Haleema was too tired to think about how to escape and crawled onto her dirty mattress set on the floor in one of the rooms.

Kimiya entered and crouched down on her bedding, looking at Haleema.

"Have you ever tried to escape?" she asked Kimiya without opening her eyes.

"Two girls tried last week. They were based at one of the other houses. Apparently, they got as far as Shahrbabak and were obviously hoping to get picked up by someone with a kind heart."

She paused.

"That was their plan, anyway. The Daesh found them in the fields, and they haven't been seen since."

There was silence as Haleema wondered at their fate.

"How long have you been here, Kimiya?"

"Two months. They came to our town. Many left before, but we were too late. Not many people knew they were coming, including us. The police here were rounded up and then shot. Then they brought us here."

"So you know this town?" Haleema leaned on her elbow, looking at the young girl.

"Yes. Some of it."

"Are you able to draw me a map? Mark out where their barracks are, their checkpoints."

The girl looked away and then down at the floor.

"It is very dangerous to try to escape. They will kill without hesitation."

"I know, I understand. I won't put you in any danger, Kimiya. I'd just like to know more about the town layout. Get an understanding of where I am."

The girl nodded and stood up.

"I'll find a pencil and paper."

Fifteen minutes later, Haleema studied the crudely drawn map under candlelight as Kimiya fell asleep. She had asked the girl to mark out where the fighters were housed and any areas where they might also congregate.

Despite her tiredness, she studied it hard, committing every detail to memory before folding the paper up into a tiny square and hiding it inside a hole in her mattress.

***

Over the next few days, Haleema kept her head down, continuing her chores while keeping her eyes open. She knew she needed to heal and be fully fit again before making any escape attempts. There was no way she was going to rot in this place. She just had to get out as soon as possible.

The crossroads on the north end of town was the main route out, but that was evidently blocked day and night. From what Kimiya had shown her on the map, there were other main roads out of the city. As far as she knew, the ones to avoid were any to the south and east. The Daesh were overrunning the entire southern region of the country, and yet the government's official news channels had blatantly played down their victories.

She wondered how far they were from her hometown now. The situation was confusing. Now she was worried about her mother. Was she safe?

How dare her brothers leave her—to join them!

After another full day of continuous chores, Haleema was outside in the yard and saw a convoy of around five pickup trucks filled with Daesh fighters drive past.

She turned to Kimiya, who was taking clothes off the line.

"What is happening?"

"They go off to ambush or fight somewhere. It happens every once in a while."

"So, there will be less of them in the town."

Kimiya shrugged.

"It's hard to know. Usually, they are gone for a few days."

An opportunity had presented itself, and Haleema was determined to take advantage.

"I think I'm going to try and get out of here tonight. You should come with me."

Kimiya was folding the clothes into a pile and looked at Haleema nervously.

"I don't know..."

"You want to stay here? It could be more dangerous in the long run. Don't you want to see your family again?"

"Yes..." Kimiya looked sad for a moment, as if she was thinking about an impossible dream.

"... but I don't know where they are."

"Is there anyone you can go to? If we can get out of the town?"

"Yes," she said. "There is someone."

She looked at Haleema with renewed hope.

"So, what is your plan?" Kimiya's eyes were bright with anticipation.

Chapter 25

3.22 AM
Sirjan, Iran.

A subdued moonlight reflected dimly off the houses that lined the hillside, giving them a ghostly appearance. The town was quiet, just the distant howling of a dog drifting on the breeze.

They had asked the other women if they wanted to go with them, but all had declined.

"The more of us that leave, the higher chance we'll get captured," Afsoon had said. "But you must go!"

Haleema knew it was true, yet she wanted to save them all. Something good had to come out of all this. She was doing it for Damir, for her family.

"I will get you out of here, somehow," Haleema said. Afsoon smiled and nodded, and hugged her. Creeping silently through the house, Haleema checked outside the front through a small window in the bathroom. Below she could see several guards congregating around a fire pit, smoking, laughing and making crude jokes.

She watched them take out a bottle of bourbon and quickly pass it around before hiding it again. Haleema laughed to herself; the pure hypocrisy of these people was a joke. They preached one thing to their followers, but when no one was looking, they would happily flaunt the laws of Islam.

Even though they killed in the name of Islam, they drank alcohol, and Haleema wondered how they could truly call themselves soldiers of Islam. Killing in her religion's name while behaving in private with a self-absorbed contempt for anyone else made them nothing but a gang of thugs.

Pathetic.

Tonight it seemed Kimiya was right. A lot of the men had left town for whatever foul work they were up to. Haleema hoped it didn't involve her hometown. She returned to her room and sat down on her mattress, hoping it would be the last night in this prison. Below their room, the courtyard, where high walls with barbed wire along the top made their plan all the more formidable.

Over the previous days, Haleema and Kimiya had gathered supplies for their journey; water, fruit, nuts, as well as a change of clothes and stashed them in their room. One of the other women had kindly given them a small backpack. According to Kimiya, the Daesh did occasional searches, but it hadn't happened while Haleema had been there. Perhaps, in their arrogance, they imagined the women were too scared to try to escape. They always made extreme examples of anyone who tried and got caught. She had heard a few tales since arriving, not just about the woman running away. Some of the fighters got cold feet as well.

They stayed awake, listening to the usual murmur of voices and laughter coming from the guards at the front of the house. It seemed to go on forever, and Haleema quietly prayed they would finish their booze and slump into slumber sooner rather than later. In Haleema's mind, the contempt for them grew, fuelling her desire to get away and be done with this hellhole.

Haleema was not sure what time it was when they heard the voices grow louder—a slam of the door. The housemaster and a guard must be back inside. Their footfall headed into the front room downstairs, which was an assigned guard room. There was continued talking for a while, and then it went quiet. Haleema estimated, from her recent surveillance, that there would be two in the front room and one in the backyard. There was the much closer sound of the back door closing, followed by the bolt and padlock clicking into place. Then, the creak of a fold-out chair as the guard slumped down onto it, sitting directly below their room.

"I'm scared," whispered Kimiya.

Haleema could see her silhouette on the bed next to her, still as a rock.

"I'm scared too, but we can do this, Kimiya."

"I don't know if I can go through with this. I..."

Haleema cut her off. "What did we talk about?" She instantly regretted her schoolteacher tone. "I mean, you don't want to be here forever, do you?"

There was a pause in the darkness. "No."

"Good."

They lay in silence for a while, and after twenty minutes, when it seemed the whole neighbourhood was sleeping, Haleema slowly got up and went to the door, listening carefully for any noise within the house. It sounded quiet, just the distant snoring of one guard. She walked to the window and slid it up inch by inch, holding her breath and then checked on the guard below. Like every night when she had looked, he had drifted off, his head lolled to one side, a rifle perched across his lap.

Very slowly, she continued to ease the window up as far as it would go. When it was wide open, she turned to Kimiya and nodded that it was time. Kimiya stared back wide-eyed, the dread apparent on her face. Haleema gave her a reassuring smile and patted her on the arm, hoping to shore up her confidence.

"I'll take the backpack and go first," she whispered. "Watch and do as I do when it's your turn. I'll get the back door open, then signal you to follow. Alright?"

Kimiya's eyes darted to the sleeping guard below and back to Haleema before smiling weakly.

Haleema secured the bag around her shoulders, straddling the window frame before hauling out her lower body, facing into the room. She glanced down at the guard intermittently as she arched the metatarsal of her foot against the stone wall until she was hanging. Her feet dangled around half a metre from the top of the narrow wall.

Kimiya held onto her forearms as a gesture of support more than anything, and they caught each other's eye. Determination, hope, and fear combined.

A horrible thought came to her.

Was the wall solid enough? Would it send loose stone down onto the guard?

Too late now. She would struggle to get back even if she wanted to. She nodded at Kimiya, who loosened her grip and looked down at the wall again.

Heart racing, she let go and landed, quickly going into a crouch on both hands. A fearful glance told her the guard had hardly stirred, and she inwardly sighed with relief. Focusing on the neighbour's side, she carefully climbed down, using her feet to balance herself and drop quietly onto the concrete ground. She froze at the sound of her landing and waited for a few moments, looking up at the window.

Kimiya was nowhere to be seen.

Haleema moved to the door set in the stone wall and slowly eased the handle. There was a click. She stopped and listened, then slowly pulled the door back. Although unlocked, the bottom noisily scraped the ground. She waited, listening again for any sound from the guard next door. She returned to the wall and looked up at the window, waving one arm, gesturing for Kimiya to follow on down, although she still couldn't see her.

Come on, Kimiya. Don't bail on me. Where are you?

Haleema looked around at the door. It was right there, beyond it, her freedom.

When she looked back at the window, Kimiya had appeared and was gingerly climbing out. A glance down, for a moment, her face caught in the moonlight—an unmistakable look of abject fear. She paused for a moment, then swung both legs out, scraping her feet down the wall.

Haleema gritted her teeth, screaming inside her head.

Too loud! Way too loud!

Then, with her legs dangling, she dropped and landed awkwardly with a crunch. Haleema watched with one hand over her mouth at Kimiya losing her balance and stumbling back. Sprinkles of light dust floated down onto Haleema. Then, she recovered and leant forward, crouching down on all fours and froze as if captured in a photograph.

There was a moment when neither woman could breathe— a grunt from the guard on the far side of the wall and then silence. Kimiya slowly turned her head to look at Haleema, who moved underneath, her arms held up, desperately gesturing for her to get off the wall fast. Kimiya moved slowly now, edging herself around and scraping her knees onto the stone, and began to find footwells to ease her descent. She climbed lower until she was out of sight from the other courtyard, and Haleema helped her to the ground. They both hugged, the fear and relief reaching its crescendo.

"Come on," Haleema whispered as she made for the door.

Then, the courtyard suddenly basked in a flood of light. Both women froze as if in headlights at the neighbour's ground-floor window.

A glimpse of a figure behind the blind.

A cough from the guard.

Haleema grabbed Kimiya's hand, pulling her through the door and out into the alleyway. Without hesitating, both girls tore down the dusty road, hand in hand.

At the corner, Haleema scanned both sides. It was clear. They crossed the street and carried on moving, keeping to the shadows. As they rounded the next corner, they came to the marketplace. Devoid now of the daytime hustle, the stalls had all been packed away. Crates scattered on the concrete ground while debris and trash blew past them on the gentle night breeze.

Then, Haleema spotted movement.

Two Daesh guards were coming through the marketplace.

Haleema pushed Kimiya back, and they edged into an enclave set in a wall. They crouched down on their haunches to keep as small as possible. The voices grew closer.

Haleema gulped.

If they came down their road, they would be seen for certain.

The sound of footfall came close to the corner, then faded.

After waiting for a minute to be sure they had gone, Haleema crept back to the corner. She peeped around and saw the distant figures moving towards the blockade that crossed the main road that led out of the city.

The pickup truck still blocked the road, and there was an armoured vehicle there as well now. She narrowed her eyes, the moon giving excellent visibility. Haleema could just make out a slight movement through the rear window.

Haleema turned back to Kimiya and whispered.

"There's more in the truck; those two might be swapping shifts with them. We have to be careful. Are you sure there's no other way?"

Kimiya looked at her with wide, fearful eyes and shook her head.

Haleema checked to her left. All was deadly quiet. The town was asleep.

She gestured to Kimiya, and they moved down the road in the opposite direction from the roadblock, staying close to the shuttered stores. The road curved slightly, and soon they were out of sight from the blockade, and Haleema began to scan cars to try to steal. She had no idea how to, but how else were they to get out of here? The option of making their way across the barren rocky landscape of the Iranian rulers on foot was a non-starter. They had to get a vehicle.

"Haleema!"

She turned to see headlights, the beam moving across buildings as it navigated dips in the road.

"In here!" hissed Haleema, pointing towards an upturned refrigerator that had evidently been abandoned. They crept behind it, crouching down as the car approached. It could only be Daesh as the curfew was strict, and few dared break it.

As the engine grew louder, Kimiya tugged at Haleema's elbow. She turned to her with a finger to her lips. As it passed them, Kimiya tugged again.

Haleema felt annoyed. Did she want them to get caught?

"The truck," she whispered. "It is full of pistachios. They grow in this province and sell them in other towns."

Haleema looked at the sacks piled up in the back of the old Ford truck as it slowed down at the crossroads. The vehicle pulled over, and the driver got out and walked into a building.

"You're sure it's leaving the city?" Haleema asked.

"Yes, yes—" Kimiya was already positioned like a sprinter waiting for the gunshot.

"OK. Let's go. Be careful!" said Haleema.

They both sensed the chance and moved quickly across to the vehicle. They climbed into the back and crawled to the rear, carefully pushing the sacks of pistachios aside to hide behind them. Curling into a foetal position to make themselves as small as possible, they waited. Haleema could just see through the wooden slats that ran along the side of the truck.

It seemed like an age before the driver returned. A quiet cough followed by a house door shutting, footsteps, and then the truck door opening and closing. The engine roared to life, and the radio started blasting before the driver quickly turned it down.

They drove for around ten minutes before the vehicle stopped, and they heard voices. He was being checked by Daesh. Haleema saw a black-clad figure walk past the back of the truck while another continued to talk to the driver.

She held her breath, her heart beating hard. If this was it, then at least they had tried.

The guard started to move one of the sacks to the side.

He stabbed at it with his knife, checking the contents, then replaced his blade in a holder across his chest. A burst of laughter from the driver, sharing a joke.

The beating in Haleema's ears drowned out their words.

He would see them! They were right at the back, and if he came up into the truck, it'd only take one glance—

She couldn't look anymore and just closed her eyes.

The sound of a foot on the step-up at the back.

He's coming in.

More laughter, and they heard the searcher shout something back.

"What's that you're saying?"

Then, the voice from the other guard called him back. Haleema opened her eyes again and glimpsed the guard moving around the other side of the truck and back to the checkpoint.

The guards and the driver continued speaking for another few moments, then Haleema heard the slam on the bonnet, and the engine revved to life again. The vehicle moved forward, leaving the dark figures behind, and finally, Haleema allowed herself to breathe again. They both sat upright. Haleema squeezed Kimiya's arm, beaming at each other, the overwhelming relief evident.

Out of the viper's nest, thought Haleema. Now, could they get to safety?

Her determination to get out of this and find her father was now stronger than ever.

They shared water and ate small chunks of bread, listening to the drone of the engine as it headed farther and farther away from Sirjan. After several hours Haleema sensed the gears of the truck change down, and the vehicle slowed. She peeped out through the wooden slats and, in the dawn's early light, caught a glimpse of a woman outside a butcher's store.

"Where do we think we are?" Haleema asked.

Kimiya shuffled over and looked at the passing houses and stores.

"Neyriz, I think, but I'm not sure."

Haleema was suddenly filled with hope. She was close to her hometown of Shiraz, much closer. She made a quick calculation. From what she knew, the Daesh were not in this area. It was a risk, however.

"We should bail out here," said Haleema. "What do you think?"

Kimiya nodded. "Yes, we don't know where he's going."

Haleema grabbed their backpack, and they crawled to the rear of the vehicle and waited. After several minutes the truck stopped, and the driver headed towards a building close by. Haleema saw a group of women, early morning shoppers, standing by a market stall selling clothes who gave them a curious glance before turning their attention back to the bargains on offer. Several of them were dressed normally in hijabs and jeans, attire that was not allowed in Daesh territory. That told them all they needed to know.

Haleema forced open the rear gate and jumped down onto the road. She grabbed Kimiya's arm and helped her down.

"Let's go!"

They walked quickly down a side street where traders were starting to sell their assortments of baskets, clothes, and rugs before disappearing into the growing crowd.

Chapter 26

Shiraz, Fars Province.

Haleema's mother served out the rice and lamb from the pot while Haleema and Kimiya brought in bowls of side dishes containing sangak bread and yoghurt dips. They sat down around the wooden table tucked into a corner in the kitchen.

The feeling of relief when she had hugged her mother and the fact she was home had worn off, replaced by a sense of frustration again. The reality of those empty chairs where her father and brothers should be sitting gnawed away at her. Although her mother was putting on a cheery mask, Haleema knew their absence was affecting her too.

From Neyriz, they had telephoned Haleema's mother to ask a family friend to come and pick them up and waited nervously in a cafe until he arrived. Two hours later, they were back in Shiraz.

"Well, thank Allah you are safe, Haleema," her mother said, gesturing to Kimiya to eat more.

Haleema nodded, toying with her food. She didn't mention her kidnapping. There was no point in adding more worries to her mother's list, and certainly, she couldn't face talking about Damir. His body would still be lying among those others, and suddenly she lost what little appetite she had and downed her fork and spoon.

"You must eat Haleema. Are you not hungry?"

"I'm sorry. It's Dad. I need to follow up with the police, see if there's any progress."

Her mother nodded, the expression changing to one of grim understanding.

"I'm sure they've been working hard to..." Her voice faded as she looked into the middle distance, lost in thought.

"I'll use his computer. Is it still upstairs?"

Her mother nodded and attempted a smile, but Haleema could see her worry.

Haleema looked at Kimiya and grinned. "Hey, I hope you're enjoying your dining experience at the Hotel Sheraz," she said. They all laughed.

"It's a lovely house. A great—hotel," Kimiya replied, mirroring Haleema's grin.

Haleema excused herself and made a herbal tea before walking up to her father's study. On one wall was a map of the world, and underneath a large desk with a computer. To the left, there were shelves from floor to ceiling holding stacks of books. She remembered some of them from her childhood, and snippets of memory came flooding back to her. Typical that he still held onto them.

At least her father had encouraged her to create a life for herself and grow up, allowing her to flourish. Some of the strictness of her friend's families seemed like something out of one of those black comedies she had streamed online. She thanked Allah that she had been born a Sheraz and she wasn't going to be married off to some one-eyed peasant who was no more intelligent than a goat or pig. No, her father had always encouraged her to live on a more independent path. She still remembered the first computer he bought her on her tenth birthday and her mother's disapproval of such a gift for a young girl. Although her relationship with her mother was stable, she had always been her father's girl, and him treating her with the same respect as her brothers, Amir and Fadin.

She fired up the PC and went straight to the Tor browser, and began to download her coding tools. Next, she searched for the phone number of the Sattar Khan police station in Tehran and opened up Skype. Within minutes she was on the line to Papak.

"Haleema, we're working through the leads, but there is still nothing new to share with you."

Haleema exhaled loudly and shook her head. Was it a surprise?

"Listen, I was taken by the Daesh at Naein, and my friend was killed by them. But I guess you're not too concerned by that." She didn't bother to hide the frustration in her voice.

"You were taken? Tell me what happened."

"I was trying to find my father through Omid Husseini, who is now dead. The same men who kidnapped me killed Husseini and his helpers, including my friend. But I guess you're not going to do anything about that?"

There was a pause as if Papak was writing something down. He sighed.

"Haleema, I'm sorry about your bad experience and the loss of your friend. I'll need to question you on this, but you need to leave these investigations to the police authorities. You could be stepping on the edge of the law. Don't forget what happened to those involved in the Green Revolution."

Haleema's throat tightened. The uprising in 2009 over the

disputed election results that had resulted in hundreds of protesters being rounded up and tortured.

"Is that a threat?"

Papak let out a laugh. "You think I am part of that department? No, I am still trying to find your father. I just think you should be careful."

"Well, thank you for your concern," said Haleema bitterly.

"So, it still seems the most likely scenario is that he defected to the UIS. There have been a few similar cases."

"Similar cases? Who?"

"I cannot go into any more details, Ms Sheraz. I'll be in touch if I hear any more news about your father. Good day," said Papak before hanging up the line.

Haleema watched the call connection drop on her screen and bit her lip.

Similar cases?

Before going any further, Haleema downloaded a VPN, or Virtual Private Network, just to be sure her location couldn't be seen. This would ensure her IP was hidden as it would be using several computers scattered around different countries. Any digital breadcrumb trail would then lead into the abyss.

Then she began searching.

The official Iranian internet would have nothing on it. Of course, they wouldn't report any government failings in a million years. The Internet has seen controls since the 2009 protests, but hopefully, there should still be posts somewhere.

She quickly found a few examples of what she was looking for in the forum section of the Liberatus news website. One section automatically posted any news articles that were triggered by specific keywords, in this case, "Iranian scientist."

According to the article sources, there were a series of cases involving around five nuclear scientists who had been reported missing by their families.

She sipped her tea and clicked through to a new article. It was about the case of Partash Ghasemi, a specialist engineer who witnesses claimed had been dragged from his car and put into a van. The police investigation had come to nothing and was still open.

In another case, another scientist left work just as Haleema's father had and was never seen again. Each situation was, in fact, alarmingly similar to her father's fate.

There had to be a connection. The police had to see this! Didn't the fact that nuclear scientists were going missing alarm them, or anyone higher up in government for that matter?

She got up and paced the room, clutching her tea for comfort, and looked across the seemingly endless block buildings of Shiraz, the mountains barely visible in the distance.

What was the Daesh planning with nuclear scientists? A vision of a mushroom cloud rising above her beloved city flashed into her mind, making her physically shudder.

Chapter 27

Haleema sat back in her father's computer chair, the old leather squeaking under her weight. Her mind was racing; how much information did the police have about the missing scientist? What had stopped them from acting? She was curious to try to find out whether Papak had held anything back from her. What were they doing? Not much, she imagined.

Working on her Dad's computer was OK, but she missed her laptop badly. It was all set up with everything she needed and ordered just the way she liked. Hacking the police servers was a tall order and would take time. But there was another possibility. She accessed her code library and pulled up a pre-scripted virus that she had helped develop as part of her role at the Cyber Army. It was a simple phishing hook that could plant a virus on anyone accessing it. To make it work, she needed to be convincing. She thought for a moment.

Best to be anonymous on this one.

She took her time setting up a remote email server to disguise the sending address and began drafting a carefully worded email with an enticing subject line that promised a tip-off. The content of the email was blank, but it wouldn't matter if he opened it. She then attached the virus and hovered her mouse over the "send" button.

"Do your worst," she muttered and clicked.

Using the Tor browser and a VPN, she could browse with reasonable anonymity and delve into the dark web: a vast part of the internet, unindexed by standard search engines and hidden from view.

This area of the internet has been highlighted in the mass media as a place where terrorists, drug and human traffickers and a host of other undesirables connect to do business. It was also the domain of hackers and groups that wanted to resist the authoritarian system and have unmonitored privacy.

Haleema tried not to dwell on what she came across and focused on the dates when the scientists, including her father, had gone missing. Each date pulled her down a wormhole, leading to nothing, and after an hour, she slapped the desk in frustration.

A thread from a message board appeared that made her sit up and take notice. The message board, called Gnostic Board, was ominous enough, but it was the name of the specific thread.

Red_horse0333.

She frowned and hovered her pointer over the link.

Red horse?

Wasn't that one of the horses of the Apocalypse from the bible?

Her memory reverted to nearly a year before to the information that she had helped Joe Bowen aka "Nightowl" with—the business of that Spanish flu virus and the documents they had unearthed from Batchman's iPad.

—codenamed: White Horse.

The connection was tenuous at best, but she was intrigued enough to click on it and read.

The first and last message at the top was dated a few days

before her father had been kidnapped.

JackofSpades934: @AceofHearts391, Your horses are waiting.

Underneath was a picture of a horse in a field grazing.

AceofHearts391: Hope it's a good thoroughbred.

Haleema scrolled down to the previous message that featured another image of a different group of horses, posted by the JackofSpades username, this time with no text.

She read the other messages and more images. She pulled up the dates list of when the other scientists and engineers had all gone missing.

All of them corresponded to the posts within a few days.

She made a note of the thread and clicked around the rest of the message board, which was a simple-looking web page that listed various topics like a forum. The subjects ranged from porn to credit card firesales to assassins for hire, and Haleema skipped through them with mild contempt.

She returned to the Red Horse post heading, staring at it in frustration. Somehow she knew some answers lay in the content of that post, but what?

There was a knock at the door.

"Haleema. I'm taking Kimiya to the market. Do you want to come?"

"No, I'm just in the middle of something."

Her mother opened the door and frowned at her. Haleema clicked her mouse, and the screen changed to a Goya search page.

"Are you OK? You look stressed." She came over behind her and began to massage her shoulders.

"I know you're working for the good of the family. Maybe you need a break? Away from the screen?"

"No, I—" Haleema muttered and leaned back. Maybe taking a break wasn't such a bad idea.

"I can't be long," Haleema said, standing up.

The three women drove in Haleema's car the few blocks to the market, a long series of stalls where almost anything was being sold. They mingled around the fruit and vegetable stalls, her mother haggling down with each vendor to get the best prices she could. Once her bag was almost full, they moved through the busy crowds to the meat market. A friend stopped her mother and asked about her husband and boys. She merely shook her head, indicating no further news. Eventually, they moved to the garments and trashy bric-a-brac; stalls selling trinkets of paste jewellery and gilded copper.

Kimiya tugged at her arm. "It's so exhilarating to be free," she said, running her hand down a batch of hanging silk. Haleema smiled, gazing at her. She had done one good thing, at least.

"Yes, and if you want anything, I'll buy it for you."

Kimiya laughed easily. "I want everything."

"Well, that could be expensive," Haleema replied, smirking.

They moved along, browsing the stalls. Haleema's eyes scanned a series of pictures in frames that seemed to animate as she walked past them. She looked again at one that morphed from an elephant to a monkey.

"Look at these!" said Kimiya picking one up excitedly. She reminded Haleema of a little girl. "It changes as you move them around." Kimiya waved it around and then placed it back, smiling.

Haleema's mother joined them, looking at them with mild interest. "Ah, don't waste your money. Just fancy gimmicks."

Haleema stopped, staring at the pictures, the realisation

appearing as if a fog had cleared.

Steganography!

"Only 10,000 Rial," said the stall owner, a young woman who eagerly stood up from her chair.

Haleema ignored her and turned to her mother. "I'll take some of the bags. I need to get back!" She rummaged around for her small purse in her jeans pocket and pulled out a note, handing it to Kimiya.

"And buy yourself one of those pictures."

As soon as she got home, Haleema rushed up the stairs and slid into the chair, slapping a hand on the keyboard to wake up the computer. She had been suspicious of the posts but unsure whether she was just chasing shadows.

Now, she was sure the thread was a digital dead letter drop, a way of passing information. Modern steganography was a method for hiding messages or data within images, video, audio or any file. Messages could be concealed within a single pixel on an image. Almost impossible to see with the human eye.

Yes. Hidden in plain sight, of course!

It wasn't Haleema's area of expertise. She would need help, and she knew exactly who to call.

Chapter 28

HAS22 Air Base, Iraq.

Zak Bowen walked down the ramp of the vast Hercules aircraft along with a handful of marines and officers. He had struggled to form a bond with any of them on the long flight from the States and was just happy to get off that crate. As he reached the tarmac, the heat hit him like a thick blanket, and he immediately felt the pools of sweat forming under his arms.

On the runway, a soldier parked in a jeep got out and snapped Zak a salute.

"Officer Bowen?"

"That's me," Zak replied, slowly saluting the marine back.

"Staff sergeant Franklin, sir. I'm to take you immediately to the briefing."

Zak inwardly groaned. He had hoped to get his head down on a fresh pillow for a few hours, maybe eat something that wasn't army-issue slop as had been the case on the aircraft.

"There'll be refreshments made available. Everything you need, sir," said Franklin, as if reading his mind.

Zak nodded and tossed his bag into the backseat of the jeep before climbing up.

They drove across the runway to a line of buildings, the

heat shimmering on the concert. They passed a makeshift basketball court, where soldiers pitched against each other, shouting for the ball. On the outside, several crates served as tables for the men to play cards on.

After ten minutes, the jeep pulled up outside the operations room—a block building surrounded by two-metre-high concrete walls. The structure looked like the whole design budget had been spent on functionality rather than aesthetics. Standing in the shade, just outside the solid metal doors, another guard saluted and let them through. All the windows were shuttered with metal, and Zak just hoped the aircon was working inside. Franklin led him down a series of windowless corridors to a steel door and pressed his palm against the keypad. The door shifted slightly with a click, and he pushed it open. To Zak's relief, the interior was fully air-conditioned, the cool air bringing him instant relief as he stepped into a large control centre. On the walls were a series of screens showing maps of the border spanning Iraq and Iran. In addition, there were satellite images that were hard to distinguish where the hell they had been taken.

Zak recognised Major General Dean Wexhall from the Colorado meeting as he stood up from a large interactive table.

"Welcome to base HAS22, Zak. Good to see you again. I trust your journey wasn't too uncomfortable?" he asked in a deep, authoritative voice.

Zak smiled and shook his hand. "It was fine, sir," he lied.

The Major General turned to Franklin.

"Staff sergeant. Get this man some refreshments." He faced Zak again.

"What would you like, Agent Bowen? Anything you need?"

"Right now, a Big Mac and Coke would be great." Both men

laughed. "Failing that, a sandwich and a bottle of water would be great—and coffee—I would love a coffee."

Franklin saluted and moved from the far side of the ops room to another exterior door before stepping out of the room.

"Zak, I appreciate this. You've heard some of it already, but you'll understand why this is so urgent when we brief you. There's very little time. Of course, this is a US military operation, but well, there's a very sensitive situation developing, and it will be handled by, let's just say a very competent team. But we'll get to that—"

Zak nodded slowly, unsure of where the Major General was heading with this and followed him to the table.

After ten minutes, Franklin returned with a tray and placed it down on a smaller table with a baguette sandwich, a mug of black coffee and a bottle of ice-cold water.

Zak downed half the bottle quickly, not realising how thirsty he was and took a bite of his baguette before looking up once more at the screens.

"Sir? He's here," said Franklin.

Wexhall jutted his head.

"Good. Then go get him and bring him here, sergeant."

Franklin saluted quickly and disappeared out of the same door they had entered.

"How's the homeland?" Wexhall asked, directing his attention back to Zak.

"Busy, we're always busy," replied Zak, taking a sip of the piping hot bitter coffee.

The Major General grinned and sat his huge frame down on a leather seat by the large table.

"Always good to be busy. Better get used to that, as I think it's going to get a lot busier."

A few minutes later, the door opened, and Franklin stepped through, behind him a tall black man in civilian clothes. The man looked briefly around the ops room before settling his eyes on Zak.

The Major General stood up along with Zak, and they exchanged salutes.

"This is Captain Kurt Coleman from special team 5 at Ghost 13," announced Wexhall

Zak walked up to him and held out his hand. Coleman looked him up and down briefly before holding out a massive hand.

"Zak Bowen, Chief Intelligence Officer—the agency," he said.

Coleman nodded, understanding.

"Take a seat, Kurt, Zak. We have a lot to cover."

The men took a seat each, facing the Major General, who handed them both PDAs with the briefing notes.

"So," the Major General began. "These Iranian scientists have disappeared from their relative facilities, and the common factor is that they are all related to the development of nuclear power." He tapped his fingers on the interactive table, bringing up their photographs.

"We have intel that UIS has been capturing scientists and engineers to help them with their cause. This itself is not that alarming, but we have recently received reports that they now captured a shipment of enriched uranium last week; the implications of this could cause a major problem, as I'm sure you'll agree. Most of the missing scientists are from the Iranian nuclear facilities, and this would give them the technical knowledge to at least start building dirty bombs or something more potent. We have tracked the missing scientists, thanks to data supplied by the NSA from the PRISM and ECHELON to this location in Ilam." The Major General paused and tapped on his hand device, revealing a satellite photograph of Iliam.

"Our HUMINT indicates they are due to be collected here," he double-tapped a warehouse on the outskirts of the town, and it enlarged to fill the whole screen, "by UIS at 0800 tomorrow morning. This is a thermal image of the area taken by one of our drones around an hour ago." He clicked again.

The image changed to show an overlay of the infrared signature of the warehouse. The heat signature of several groups of people inside was easily discernible.

"We estimate six hostages being held here with around eight Tangos. These hostages are some of the top minds in the country, and there will be dire consequences if they fall into the hands of the enemy."

"Wouldn't levelling the building be the easiest option to resolve this?" asked Coleman.

"That is, of course, an option," replied the Major General. "However, killing innocents is not the US way and, of course, would be a waste of such intelligence and resources. Our first objective is to rescue them and bring them back to the US for safeguarding until this conflict is over. If, however, your team fails, then our next priority is to stop them from falling into enemy hands at whatever cost. I have arranged transport for you at 0300 hours. Our staging point for this mission is here on the Iraq side of the border." He pointed at a spot on the map. "You will covertly cross the border here. Your team will have a very limited timeframe to secure the hostages. Once obtained, you will escort the hostages back to me at the staging site and hand them over to US Army regulars. Any questions?"

"Any info on what kind of firepower we can expect to be up

against?"

"Intel shows this is a local militia group. Expect basic firepower from poorly trained troops."

"Any more questions?"

There was a brief silence.

"OK then, you leave in eighty-five minutes."

Chapter 29

Ilam, Iran.

Karim took short breaths. He could smell the bucket in the far corner which the guards had left for the prisoners to defecate into. He pulled a blanket tighter around his shoulders as the night wore on and the temperature continued to drop. They were in an empty warehouse that had no facilities compared to their last location. The floors were bare, and all they had was a long bench to sit on. Several armed guards, dressed in civilian clothes, left them, deciding instead to smoke by the warehouse's front doors. Others came and went, and Karim could hear the occasional vehicle coming or going.

"How long have we been in here?" asked one of the other hostages. It was Garshasp, the small skinny man who had told Karim he was working in electromagnetic compatibility engineering. The other three in the room were also connected to secretive Iranian government projects, either high up in projects as highly skilled scientists or engineers.

Karim leaned his head back and closed his eyes. The edgy fear of not knowing what was happening or what their fate was, had been eating at them all. Since being thrown together in the previous days or weeks, they had all talked through the possibilities.

The probabilities of whether they would live out the week.

Karim figured they were being kidnapped to be used in some way. Or for a huge ransom to the Government. If so, the question was would they pay it? Let alone acknowledge their existence.

"I think two days, maybe more," replied Karim, his eyes still shut. "But they haven't fed us, so maybe they are waiting for something." Karim had his theories, and he could share them. Why not? But what good would that do? All the hand-wringing and fear were emotionally draining him, and now he was at the point of mental exhaustion.

He wondered if he would ever see his family again and reflected on the last few weeks.

Since he had been pulled from his car by gunmen, he had been relatively well treated, apart from the actual kidnapping itself. They had taken him, blindfolded to an initial holding area, stripped him of his clothes and personal possessions and given him a simple tunic to wear. He had then been locked inside a small room, fed and left to recover from the shock of all that was happening to him.

The next morning the gunmen blindfolded and bundled him and other prisoners back into the van for another long journey, lasting around six hours until they arrived at their destination. Karim, still blindfolded, had been led into a building, uncuffed and was then unmasked when he found himself in a big open plan, makeshift prison. Along with a handful of other prisoners, Karim counted five others besides himself, and they all cautiously examined their new surroundings. It was basic yet comfortable. In one corner, there was even a games section with chess boards and dominos. They were even supplied with towels and shown a shower and bathroom area.

It raised yet more questions in Karim's mind.

During the day, the prisoners were allowed to mingle in a common area, but at night they were confined to their individual windowless rooms, locked in again. There was no doubt that they were all captives, but so far, at least, there had been no brutality, and they received decent but straightforward meals. Karim felt some of his fears subside. After a few days, they were all moved again, another long drive, and once again were taken from the van into another building, this time an empty warehouse with barely any facilities. It was oven hot during the day and freezing cold at night. The more Karim thought about it, it seemed like they were in a location for a handover; apparently, they were commodities in some political game.

Then a shuddering thought occurred to him.

Were they being traded for the UIS? To build weapons for the Daesh at gunpoint? The other prisoners, like himself, were all highly skilled with a commonality in nuclear systems. That deep-rooted fear began gnawing at Karim. Part of him would rather die than work for them.

He pushed himself up from the floor and walked around to stretch his legs. One of the guards glanced over from the open doors to check and then turned back to his conversion. He wished they would close them and keep the warmth in.

Karim circled the large space, his hands behind his back. Feeling warmed, he went and re-wrapped the blanket around himself before curling up on the floor.

Suddenly there was the rapping sound of gunfire from outside—bullets started pinging off the metal planes in the building. Karim sat up and looked around at his fellow prisoners, who all looked as astonished as he did in the dim orange light.

The three guards inside the front doors all hit the ground as muffled cries came from outside.

Another burst of gunfire, this one much closer, made them jump, and one of the kidnappers began to shout orders to his comrades, who desperately tried to unsling their rifles from their backs. One of them managed to crawl into a defensive position and started firing back.

Karim gestured to the others to get down on the floor. He upturned the bench, and they all crawled behind it, covering their heads with their arms.

An explosion rocked the ground, scattering debris across the interior of the warehouse, and Karim pressed his arms tighter against his head, gasping in rapid breaths.

They were under attack. What was happening?

Cries of pain echoed out in the space.

Karim opened his eyes, his head still on the ground, and saw only one guard left inside. The others appeared to be dead. As the last remaining guard was firing into the darkness outside, shouting at the top of his voice, a plume of red sprayed out from the back of his head, and his body crumpled onto the ground. There was a moment of silence. Karim stared at the lifeless body, unable to move or close his eyes, shock gripping his entire body.

The Daesh was coming.

The ground began to smoke as if a fire burned underneath. Then he saw the billowing fog rushing in through the doors.

Another shout from outside that Karim could barely distinguish with the recent explosion and gunfire ringing in his ears. Then two dark figures, dressed in black fatigues with machine guns at the ready, appeared through the smoke and came towards him.

Chapter 30

Shiraz, Iran.

"So, did you have any luck with the steganalysis? Anything interesting?"

Haleema was on the phone with her friend Ko at the Cyber Army. He was breathing heavily, excitement in his voice.

"Oh Hal, I had so much fun with this one," he said, which to most people would have sounded like sarcasm, but Haleema could sense genuine excitement. "Yeah, there were messages in those images, but I had to do plenty of rooting around to find the algo they used."

"Right, the algorithm?"

"Yep. In this case, we need to know which pixels to read—a mathematical process. So, any steganographic message would be hidden in the bits, right inside the pixels. Either a 'zero' or a 'one.' Obviously, digital images have a lot of pixels, millions of them, in fact! Each pixel comprises consists of three bytes: red, green or blue—"

"Hmm, I know," Haleema sighed. She was familiar with the basics here. She also knew Ko liked this ritual of going through every detail. It was all worth remembering; however, she couldn't stop drumming her fingers on the desk as he explained.

Ko ignored her comment. "They might choose the least significant bit of each colour channel for the data. So hiding a message would be a case of storing three bits of info in every pixel without altering the makeup of the image too much: pretty hard to see with the human eye, I think you'd agree."

"Yes, it would be—"

"Once you've established there's data in those bits, you need to know which algorithm you're trying to decode. I had to run a shitload of queries to find the hard-coded byte key IDs. But they were there—"

There was a pause, and Haleema realised Ko had stopped talking.

"What did you find?" she asked urgently.

"Well, coded messages, yes. Had to spend a lot of time on that—"

"I'm hugely grateful," Haleema said, almost daring not to breathe. "And?" she added.

"I'll ping it over right now. It's all names, places. Maybe it means more to you than me."

"Ko, I owe you one. Thanks so much!"

Haleema watched his message appear on her Icarus message app.

"I have it!"

"No problem, so what is—"

"Got to go. Thanks again." Haleema killed the connection and opened the file.

The messages described deliveries of candidates in basic form.

All deliveries are to the same place: a depot warehouse named Khodro on the outskirts of Ilam, a small town around eighty kilometres away from the Iraqi border.

Haleema leant back and grinned.

***

Haleema got off the plane and passed through security without any issues. The four-hour flight from Shiraz to Ilam had gone by painfully slow—she was too excited about the idea of finding her father to be able to get any rest. Entering the arrivals lounge, she spotted Inspector Rahbar sitting with a coffee in one hand and a folded copy of the morning paper in the other.

"Good morning Inspector."

Rahbar looked up for what he was reading. "Well, it is morning. Come on; I've hired us a car for the drive."

Dawn was breaking over the distant mountains, casting the sky in an array of pink and orange.

"I hope this isn't a waste of my time," Rahbar said. "It's been a long journey."

Haleema didn't bother to reply, fixing her gaze out of the passenger window.

Five minutes later, his radio came to life. The sound of gunfire had been reported in the area they were headed to.

Haleema looked alarmed. "Shooting?"

Rahbar held up his hand. "Let us not assume anything," and then he added, "We'd better be careful."

Rahbar flicked off the lights as they approached the warehouse. Either side of them, outbuildings built from steel and wood were empty and devoid of any activity.

As they approached Haleema and Rahbar, both saw the first body strewn and twisted on the car park tarmac—a man dressed in jeans and a tunic, an Arabic headscarf still wrapped around his head.

"Oh my god," said Haleema, her hand covering her mouth.

They slowed at the man, and both looked down through the window at the body.

"There's another one!" Haleema said.

Rahbar pulled over, switched off the engine and picked up his radio to connect with the local police. Once through he gave them details of the scene and requested backup and medical support.

Then he pulled out his service SIG Sauer P220 pistol.

"Stay here. Do not leave the vehicle," he ordered.

Haleema gave him a look, one he recognised as growing defiance and strong will.

"It could still be dangerous," he added. She seemed to think for a moment and then reluctantly nodded.

Rahbar stepped cautiously out of the vehicle, his weapon held in front of him, and he trotted over to the wall of the warehouse. With his back to it, he sidled along towards the door and glanced into the space, a narrow field of vision. He edged around, his weapon still aimed ahead and pied the corner, his eyes darted left and right, taking in the scene.

A clump of clothes on the ground? He soon saw it was another body—a limp outstretched arm—two bodies. He stepped inside, keeping close to the wall and checked the vast space. At the far end, an upturned bench and a pile of blankets.

Whatever had happened here was over.

He placed his weapon back in his shoulder holster and leaned down to touch the arm of one of the bodies.

Still warm.

The body was of a young man in his early twenties who

looked to Rahbar like a classic criminal. Scarred face, unshaven. He'd encountered enough of them.

An AK-47 lay nearby. A pool of drying blood was soaking into the concrete floor around the bodies. He heard a noise behind him and turned.

"I thought I told you to stay in the car!" he hissed angrily.

Haleema ignored him; her wide eyes scanned the warehouse.

"My father. Is he here?"

Rahbar stood up and sighed. "No, he's not here," then he pointed at Haleema, "Don't touch anything!"

"Don't worry, I'm not as stupid as you imagine," she replied.

Rahbar headed back to the vehicle and opened the door, opened the glove compartment and took out a batch of evidence bags.

When he went back inside, Haleema was over by the bench and the blankets staring down at them.

"They were kept here," he shouted. His voice echoed up into the roof space. "I know it," she added.

Rahbar waved his hand at her. "Stay close to me, please, Haleema."

Haleema loitered for a moment and crouched down for a closer look at the blankets.

"Haleema!" he repeated loudly, irritation creeping into his voice.

She stood up and walked over, without a word, looking closely and then stopped.

She crouched down again.

"I've found a bullet casing."

"Don't touch it!" he barked, already walking towards her.

She looked up at him with an incredulous look on her face. "I told you I'm not an idiot!"

Rahbar pulled out an evidence bag as he crouched next to her.

"I certainly don't think that," he said quietly, catching her eye, his tone more considerate.

He looked at the bullet casing closely.

"Hmmm, looks like a 4.6x30mm casing. Not from an AK, the weapon of choice for every jihadist, bandit, and farmer in the entire middle east. No, This is…" He paused and seemed to think for a moment.

Haleema was staring at him, waiting for an answer.

"I'll have to confirm, but it looks like it's from an MP7."

"What is that? How do you know?"

He sighed as he pulled on forensic gloves and carefully plucked the bullet, and dropped it into the plastic bag.

"I had a lot of experience with ballistics, along with most police. It's standard knowledge." He stood up and stretched his back.

"Come on, keep looking."

***

After ten minutes or so, they heard several vehicles pull up outside, followed by a slight screech of tyres.

"The locals are here. Let me talk to them first," he said and went outside. Haleema glanced outside the door and watched as Rahbar flashed his ID at one of the policemen and spoke with him for a few minutes. One of the policemen looked at the bodies on the ground and shouted at his colleague that he recognised one.

Rahbar went back to Haleema.

"They are all known bandits, Haleema. All young, apparently," he said, trying to ease her anxiety.

A white van pulled up, and two men in white forensic gear jumped out, carrying equipment bags.

They strolled over to the warehouse doors, and spoke briefly to the policeman, who gestured inside. They glanced at Haleema and Rahbar before stepping into the warehouse.

Rahbar followed them inside.

"Inspector Rahbar from the Tehran Police," he said, introducing himself to one of the seniors of the forensic team.

"How long have you been here?" he asked.

"Not long," Rahbar replied.

"So, what did you find?" he asked.

"There seems to have been a short but intense firefight. We've seen eight dead male kidnappers, no wounded and no survivors. It appears that the scene has been cleaned. No signs of footprints or brass that's been left behind. Looking at the way the bodies are outside, it seems they were caught off guard. They fell back inside but were quickly overrun," said Rahbar.

"This doesn't have the feel of the usual gang-on-gang crime," the forensic said.

"No," Rahbar agreed, "maybe a military operation. This area here seems to be where some captives were being held. Are you going to need to test those blankets for fibres?" he asked, pointing at them.

He handed over the plastic bag with the bullet shell. "Also, I found this. This case involves the Criminal Investigation Department in Tehran, as you're aware, so all the results will need to be forwarded to me."

"If you say so," the forensic replied.

"As soon as you have them," Rahbar said, levelling his stare at the man.

"Certainly, Inspector. As soon as I have them."

Chapter 31

Sirjan, Kerman Province.

Al-Adel smiled eerily as he sat down opposite Amir, who was sitting on a chair in one of the offices in the recently cleared out council building. The fighters had arrived and pulled out undesirables onto the street. Al-Adel wanted public hangings as soon as possible to set the tone, but he needed victims.

The usual daily activity on the streets of the town had come to an abrupt halt, and the roads had cleared of residents. Only the black figures of UIS could be seen, breaking down doors and hunting for enemies.

The commander took out his cigarettes, shaking the soft pack until one slid out.

"Tell me, Amir Sheraz. What made you join our struggle?"

Amir looked at the commander blankly. For a moment he couldn't remember, the calm measured tone had surprised him.

"To rid the country of the corrupt Allaytolla—to take it back—" Amir dipped his head. "As you said at the recruitment—"

"And do you still believe that, Amir?"

"I—believe in the cause—" Amir said, hesitating. His

previous enthusiasm for joining up all but washed out.

"We have to struggle for that cause, do things that we are not always happy with or want to do, Amir. There is no room for weakness, no room for bystanders. This will be a bloody war, make no mistake. Our enemies must be eliminated quickly otherwise our greater caliphate will be unstable from the beginning—" He paused and took a drag on his cigarette before tossing it on the ground.

The commander stood up and went to the window, his hands behind his back as if he were a professor reciting in class.

"I need to know all my soldiers are with me. I need to know every single one of us is dedicated. You need to follow your brother's example—" He turned back to Amir.

"What is it that troubles you? Is the path that God has chosen for us not clear to you?"

Amir looked up at him with pleading eyes. "Yes, it is clear. I see things have to change; it's just—"

The commander began pacing again. "Look at our situation. They kill our people and insult our religion; burning the Koran or making cartoons of our holy prophet. If we don't defend Islam, then we are not Muslim. Do you understand, Amir?"

"I understand."

The commander continued, "This is all a test from God, our real lives start after doomsday. For now, this world is a paradise for the pagans and a hell for Muslims; we just need to be patient. Right now, you need to know that in the Crusader heartlands there is no protection for our blood and there is no room for so-called civilians. Those who do not stand up and take arms are as guilty of acting against God's will, as those who directly oppose it.

"We need martyrs to carry out God's will. All sacrifice their lives for their religion, for their brothers and sisters. Do you know what we do? We cry and pray for them, knowing they are now with our god in paradise."

The commander stood in front of Amir, close to him and put his hands on Amir's shoulders.

"Are you truly ready to represent the cause and make the ultimate sacrifice?" the commander asked, "for the protection of your family. Your loved ones, your brothers, and comrades?"

Amir had his head in his hands, sobbing. "Yes, commander. I am ready," he gasped.

Chapter 32

HAS22 Air Base, Iraq.

Karim stared at the palms of his hands, churning over the events of the previous twenty-four hours as if some clue to his fate might lay in those crinkly hands.

It had been soldiers, a US special forces team, who had come to the warehouse. Dressed in dark fatigues, balaclavas with what he assumed were night vision goggles strapped to their foreheads.

Karim's eyes had darted up from one of the soldiers' combat boots to his torso, where an assortment of pouches was attached.

Another tall figure had then come in, dressed identically, and pulled off his mask. He was a shaven-headed black man who stood and took a good look at each one of them. Then he took out a device from his jacket and proceeded to tap his finger on the screen.

In very clear Persian, he asked each of them their names and confirmed it on his screen. Then, he proceeded to tell them they were US special forces there to help. One of the others had given them water just as the distant sound of vehicles could be heard. The soldiers led them out, and there had been some kind of firefight behind them. Karim ran as fast as he could to the waiting helicopter and felt a huge relief when it had finally taken off and brought them to their current location.

Now, Karim looked up as the door to the windowless room swung open, and a US marine stepped inside. He stood straight against the wall, his weapon held vertically in front of him. A moment later, a man walked in, dressed casually in a dark green shirt with rolled-up sleeves and slacks, carrying a PDA. His ID card was slung around his neck, dangling by his chest. He was followed by a tall, thin middle eastern man with narrow glasses perched on his hooked nose.

"Gentleman. I am Zak Bowen from US special intelligence, and this is Raq Aleem, our translator."

Aleem repeated Zak's words in Persian.

Karim immediately half-raised his hand.

"We are all educated, Mr Bowen, and can speak English."

Zak hesitated and stared at Karim blankly.

"You can all speak English?"

Karim nodded slowly.

"Right. OK, I didn't realise. Sorry, Raq, you're dismissed. Go play basketball or something—"

The translator's eyes darted from Karim to Zak, and he began to open his mouth as if about to say something but decided against it. He turned and left the room, looking put out.

"Thank you for saving us!" another one of the scientists said.

"I, for one, thought we were all dead men!"

Some of the others murmured in agreement.

"We're looking forward to going home," another said.

Bowen pulled up a chair that was leaning against the wall and straddled it, his arms settling over the backrest. He sighed and peered at his PDA screen before putting it aside on the table.

"You were probably aware of the situation in Iran before you were taken. Well, it's gotten worse, a lot worse. The UIS has made considerable gains in the south of the country and is threatening a lot of central provinces."

"Shiraz?" Karim blurted out.

"I'm not going dwell on specifics, but—Shiraz is still currently under government control."

Karim nodded, relief evident on his face.

A chorus of voices began shouting at once.

"Mahan?"

"What about Fasar?"

Zak held up his hand.

"You will be given all the details by the case officer about specific information regarding your hometowns and families. I don't have the latest information on the ground here," he said, impatience creeping into his voice.

"So, when can we go home?" Karim asked, his arms crossed.

Zak lifted himself off the chair and put it back in its place.

"I'm going to come out with it straight. No one is going home right now. Did you all hear on the news about the UIS hijacking a convoy carrying enriched uranium?"

There were general nods of agreement around the room. "Until that uranium has been recovered," Zak continued, "the UIS will do anything to get their hands on any scientists for their expertise in that area. Unfortunately, that means you are all high-risk targets. What we will be doing is taking you back to the US until this all blows over."

Partash Ghasemi, the skinny engineer, stood up. "So, we're still prisoners? Is that what you're telling us?"

Zak looked at him if he had insulted him.

"You could all be dead by now. Those kidnappers were serious criminals intending to sell you to the Daesh. Would you rather be toiling for them now? Making weapons that they could use to unleash some kind of nuclear hell? Because that was your fate, all mapped out until we came along."

There was silence as the scientists in the room contemplated this scenario.

Zak held up a dismissive hand as if realising he was behaving being too harshly.

"Look, what we are offering you is far from the life of a prisoner. You will be free individuals. Your families will be taken care of and can be moved out of Iran if that's what you require. You will be provided with the most advanced facilities you can imagine, you will live in near-luxury and will want for nothing, and our compensation package is considered one of the best in the world for men of your calibre. When this whole situation with the UIS is resolved, and your country is no longer on the brink of civil war, you will all be free to return to Iran if you want to."

A murmur of low voices drifted through the room as the scientists and engineers discussed the possibilities of this offer.

"What if I don't want to leave my home right now? What if I want to return to my former life?" asked Karim, causing the room to fall silent again.

Zak gave the marine a sideways glance that Karim couldn't fail to notice and then shrugged and smiled.

"Sadly, this is not an option. Your government has done little to protect you. We can't risk the UIS gaining nuclear capabilities. Can you imagine what the civilian casualties would be like? For the safety of your country, all that you hold dear in this beautiful place, you will be coming with us."

Zak looked around the room, seeing the mixed emotions on their faces as the news sank in. "Now, gentlemen, if you have any further questions, Raq Aleem will be in shortly. There are facilities here for you to change, freshen up and get some food and sleep. We will be flying back to the US at 1300 hours tomorrow."

Then, the man from the CIA turned and left the room.

Karim stared at the door, realising that he was a political tool and, worse, still a prisoner.

Chapter 33

Sattar Khan Street Police Station, Tehran, Iran.

Papak Rahbar walked into his office, the sweat rolling down his back. The air hung heavily in the room. He threw his hat on the desk and placed his bag down before switching on the fan attached to the wall. The sudden breeze blew loose papers from his desk, and he leaned down with a groan to pick them up.

He peeked through the blinds and out the window down onto the street in front of the building. He could see the yard where police from all ranks were coming and going. A thick steel wall separated the station from the main street, and outside, a group of workers were constructing concrete pillars to prevent suicide bombers from ramming vehicles inside the police station.

There was a light knock at the door.

"Yes?" he said loudly, without turning.

"The forensic report from Ilam, Inspector."

Inspector Rahbar finally turned and took the report from the officer.

"Thank you, anything else?" asked the Inspector.

The officer shook his head. "No, Sir." He left the room as

Rahbar scanned over the report, slowly sitting down behind his desk. His phone rang, and Rahbar slowly picked it up, his eyes glued to the report. The bullet was a 4.6 mm x 30 cartridge from an MP7, as he suspected. The Heckler and Koch manufactured weapons preferred by special forces for close-quarter combat. There were also rimless bottlenecked cartridges from an AK 7.62×39mm round, and DNA samples were found.

"Inspector Rahbar."

"It's Massood. You can come up now." The line instantly went dead.

Rahbar grabbed his laptop bag and shoved the forensics report inside, and left his office. He headed past the investigation team, the rhythmic tapping of keys following him as he walked. A quick glance showed him rows of hunched shoulders behind monitors. He deliberately avoided the elevator and made his way up the steps to the fifth floor.

Massood gestured to the chair in front of his desk before steepling his hands together and focusing his eyes intently on Rahbar.

Rahbar looked at his superior as he fished out his PDA and the forensics report.

"So, where are we at with the Sheraz case?" asked Massood.

"The report from the local Ilam police and Haleema confirms her father, along with a number of other missing scientists, were at an empty warehouse on the outskirts of Ilam. The warehouse hadn't yet been leashed."

"What evidence?"

"DNA matches. We found a bucket that was being used as a toilet. We found the matches for several of the scientists there. The ground was also littered with blood and bodies. All of them are from a local gang. Some of them are known to the local police. Though two of them were from Tehran."

Massood had begun playing with his phone, although Rahbar had the feeling he was just acting as if he was mildly interested.

"There's another thing. A bullet cartridge was found from an MP7, commonly used by special forces, especially US."

Massood's green eyes refocused on Rahbar and blinked. After a moment, he nodded slowly as if taking in the information.

"What are you saying? That the US sent special forces over our border?"

"I'm not saying anything, just presenting the facts as I see them. Although it wouldn't be the first time it's happened."

Massood tossed down his phone onto a pile of papers and leaned back, waving a dismissive hand as if shooing away the suggestion.

"Could be anyone. The type of weapon doesn't prove much." Massood opened a drawer in his desk as if looking for something.

"You are right," said Rahbar, "but it also doesn't have the feel of a gang-on-gang attack. It was a well-executed procedure. Very few stray bullets, and no casualties from one side, and there seems to have been an attempt to clean the scene from the attacking side. Whoever they were, they were well trained and efficient."

"Well, it is interesting. Good work, Rahbar. Where is all the evidence now?"

"With the police in Ilam."

Massood sighed, bringing out a gold lighter and cigarettes, his eyes flicking back to the Inspector. "What about Haleema Sheraz? Where is she now?"

Rahbar noticed a gleam of concentration in the eye that belied the casual tone.

"Back in her apartment, here in Tehran. That's where I dropped her. She's determined to find her father, hence her being quite—" Rahbar leaned back, looking up at the ceiling fan, "—active in the investigation."

Massood considered that for a moment as he lit one of the cigarettes.

"And what are her plans?"

Rahbar shrugged.

"I don't know. But my guess is she will keep digging. She is very determined."

Massood stared at the swirling grey smoke as if it gave him solace, then levelled his stare at Rahbar. "That'll be all, Inspector. Thank you."

Chapter 34

Tehran, Iran.

With the blinds drawn, the room was dark, apart from a few flashing lights from her music system and a large screen on the wall. Haleema lay on her sofa covered with a blanket and stared at the patterned circular rug on the floor. She remembered her parents had bought it for her when she had first moved into the apartment, right after she had returned to Iran after finishing university in Cambridge, England.

Her eyes were bloodshot after crying for nearly an hour. Now it felt to her as if all the tears had been used up. Everything closed in, and the thought of her father in the hands of the Daesh made her fear the worst.

That he had been in Ilam, she was sure. No doubt.

They had missed him by hours. But what was going on? The more she thought about the scenario, the stranger it seemed. Local criminals had kidnapped him and other valuable government assets and taken them to Ilam.

Haleema sat up and pulled the blanket off her shoulders.

Close to the Iraq border. And what would that have to do with anything? Everything? Nothing?

She sighed and reached for her mobile phone. She needed to

tell Damir's partner, Omar, that he was no longer alive. Details would have to be spared. The police already knew about it. She rehearsed the conversation and dialled the number.

Ten minutes later, she ended the call and lay back down, emotionally drained. Omar had not taken it well and, at times, acted as though she were lying. When he finally accepted it, they talked about Damir for a while before ending the call.

The phone rang, and she looked at the unknown number on the screen.

It couldn't be Omar unless he were ringing from a different phone.

She answered.

"Haleema?"

She slapped her hand over her mouth on hearing the voice of her brother, Fadin.

***

"Fadin! Where are you?"

"In Sirjan."

Haleema gasped out loud. "Sirjan? Are you really there? Listen to me, Fadin I was imprisoned there..."

"Haleema. I haven't much time," he was whispering. "You say you were in Sirjan? How can that be?"

Haleema closed her eyes. "Never mind... I'm alright, I'm safe now, but I was captured when I was looking for our father. I think the Daesh took him. Anyway, I was taken to Sirjan and managed to escape."

"You were imprisoned? Did they hurt you?" Fadin demanded.

"I'm fine, but there has been a lot going on, Fadin. What is happening? Why the hell did you join them?"

"It's hard to explain on the phone. I wanted to look out for Amir. Now, you must listen to me." His tone was deadly serious.

"Amir is here too. Haleema and that's what I want to talk about. They are killing everyone; there are beheadings and hangings. They are training children to kill and be suicide bombers—and they are planning a big push north, across to Shiraz and then up to Tehran. They might succeed, Hal. They're armed to the teeth. Anyway, Amir—he has somehow been convinced to carry out a martyrdom operation."

There was a pause. Then Haleema stuttered, "W—what, Fadin?"

"Amir is going to carry out a suicide mission. Do you understand?"

Haleema felt the four walls around her pressing in as the words slowly sank in. What was happening? Her family was being torn apart; she felt her last bit of resolve slipping away. "Amir—no," she said so quietly Fadin could hardly hear her.

"Are you there, Haleema?" The voice snapped her back to the present.

"Yes, yes! Where are you, and where is Amir?"

The line crackled for a moment, and Amir's voice faded.

"Fadin! Where are you? The main barracks?"

"No, the north—along the—"

Then the line went dead.

"Shit!"

Haleema redialed the previously called number, but the tone was dead. She tried again, her hands shaking with desperation, but she couldn't connect.

Chapter 35

Liberatus Basecamp, Tennessee, USA.

Behind the main farmhouse, across a patch of unused land, came the sound of rapping gunfire. Joe observed from the side as several men lay on the ground firing at targets. Sandbags stacked three deep were set up at twenty-metre intervals towards the targets.

Joe watched Marty and Hodge crawl along the ground to a forward position and let off a few rounds at the cardboard target, and then Hugo followed suit from the opposite side.

Looking through binoculars, Joe kept a close eye on the targets. As expected, the ex-vets, Marty and Hodge, weren't bad; rusty, but nothing a bit of practice wouldn't fix. Joe noted Marty was slow at moving his ass and doing the actual assault course. Hugo, on the other hand, was going to need plenty of shooting practice, judging by his results, but he was keen to learn and evidently happy to be away from organising the building projects.

Hugo finished his exercise first and scurried to the edge of the range before walking over to where Joe was sitting at a table under a corrugated roof that was held up by four wood posts.

Hugo put his rifle down on the table.

"Not bad, bit rusty here and there," Joe said.

"Rusty, where?" Hugo looked down at himself, arms held out. "This is a well-oiled machine."

Joe smirked. "Better fun than managing this place?"

Hugo sighed. "Don't get me wrong, I like the idea of organising shit, but to be honest, well—I ain't very—"

"—good at it?"

Hugo made a mock face of being offended and stroked his rifle lying on the tabletop as if it were a cat.

"Hey, who's got the piece right now?"

Joe smiled and stared out at the other two, who continued to take potshots at their targets.

"They're not bad for old guys."

Hugo pulled up a rusty deckchair and slumped down into it. He took the rifle and began to take it apart.

"Yeah, well. For ex-military, they shouldn't be bad. Are you sure you don't want to have a run? Crawl around in the dust for a while, Joe?"

Joe sipped coffee from a tin mug, still staring at Marty and Hodge shredding the targets. "Yeah, I should. Maybe later, need to do some work, some things to look into." Joe turned to Hugo. "By the way, the guy you gave a flaming Sambuca last year—"

Hugo looked up at Joe.

"What about him?"

"Sirus came across something interesting. I'll show you later.."

There was a faint sound of a phone chirping. Joe rummaged around in his pocket and fished out a phone.

"Talk of the devil—it's Sirus calling now."

***

Joe shook his head and leaned back in the recliner. Hugo was sitting alongside as they looked up at Haleema's face on the screen inside a communications room set up in the farmhouse. It was the first time Joe and Haleema had talked this way in years, and both men had no illusion there wasn't a good reason.

She had explained the kidnapping of her father, her brothers joining the Daesh and then her own kidnapping and asked for help. That would mean going to a hostile country on the brink of all-out civil war and putting them directly in the firing line.

Haleema wiped a tear from her cheek and continued.

"All I know is that they are in Sirjan, in the north of the city. I haven't been able to get back in touch since Fadin called. As for my father, he could be anywhere; it looks like he was being sold to UIS, but then he was taken by someone else. Possible US special forces, as I've tracked communications originating in the US."

"Listen, I can't imagine what you're going through over there, but what you're asking is—extreme, don't you think?"

Haleema looked at Joe with imploring brown eyes.

"You have to help me, Joe. I've always done everything you asked and more. I know it isn't an easy thing that I'm asking you. I know that—" She paused and looked off-screen.

Joe sighed and looked to the floor, his hands clasped together.

"Your father. The message board—are there any more clues there?"

Haleema glanced down, and they heard her typing.

"I'm digging into that. They seem to have a system for

making deliveries. The comms all go back to Colorado, and Denver. But I need to do more work on this." She turned to look at Joe again. "I'm sending some files."

Joe nodded and took the wireless keyboard, tapped and brought up his Icarus window.

"Denver?"

Haleema shrugged.

"I did some reading and came across this, which rings some parallels with the kidnapping of my father. So, this guy, this Nazi, Reisser, and an American, Wes Helms. Helms ran Operation Paperclip to get the German scientists over to America. That's how NASA was created, right off the back of the German V2 rocket programme."

"Right? I don't follow," said Joe.

"He recruited Reisser, a high-level Nazi scientist, and together they worked to bring over lots of German brain power under 'Operation Paperclip,' working against the Russians who were trying the same thing. The point is they allegedly not only wanted to create a similar rocket programme for the US but other, more secret projects. They used various tactics to pull in the skills they needed. Well, it just sounds familiar. The rumour was they were responsible for constructing huge DUMBs. One is in Colorado, Denver to be exact."

"DUMBs?" Hugo said, looking at Joe and then back to Haleema.

Joe nodded knowingly. "Yeah, Deep Underground Military Bases, I've heard of them. Interesting historical lesson, Haleema. But what's your point?"

"It could mean nothing, but what if a paperclip-style op was still running? I've found numerous examples of other scientists and engineers, all high-level in their fields, missing.

A small number that I think were kidnapped, including my Dad, were held near the Iraq border. All the signs were of them being extracted by an elite professional team, not the Daesh."

Joe nodded slowly, not speaking for a moment, as he processed what Haleema had just told him.

"OK," he said, "That is interesting—"

There was a ping sound, and Joe saw Haleema had sent a file.

"What's this?"

A browser window displayed the picture of two Iranian men.

"This is Inspector Rahbar. He was reluctant at first but came with me to Ilam. His superior, the Chief of Police, is Massood Rajavil. I know for a fact he's in deep with a lot of stuff. I'm going to look into him. Heard he's a sadistic bastard." She laughed without humour. "It's ironic the work I did at the Cyber Army can be useful for these things.

"So, Massood is involved with this network," she continued, "I just don't how exactly how, but I just know he's up to his neck in all this."

Joe leaned back in his chair and exhaled slowly.

"Cabal?"

He turned to Hugo. "This goes a lot deeper than we first suspected."

Hugo nodded. "Sure does, bruh."

"Haleema. Can I call you back?" asked Joe.

She nodded slowly.

"Sure."

"Yeah, I need to look at all this. Speak to you in ten."

The video link screen went blank. Hugo turned to him.

"Well, what are we waiting for? Let's get over there."

Joe slapped his hands on the armrests and hauled himself

up.

"It's not as simple as that."

Hugo held his hands out, imploringly.

"Simple as what? All the shit she's done for your ass, for this—project."

Joe waved a hand back at Hugo.

"What she's asking is very dangerous—creeping around the Iranian border, going into Daesh territory. For what? To rescue her brothers, who signed up in the first place!"

"Ahh, c'mon."

Joe pointed out in the direction of the makeshift assault course. "—And with who? This crowd? Are you having a laugh?"

"What? They're not that bad! You're a harder bastard than I thought."

Joe stood at the window and stared out across the half-built wall, the branches of fruit trees creeping over it in the direction of the training ground. The cracking of distant gunfire continued to echo across the sky.

They weren't bad. Joe had lied. He needed space to think. Marty had an attitude problem, certainly.

The others? He had no idea, having never fought alongside them before. In the field, you had to trust the soldier next to you. Know they had your back. Otherwise, things could quickly go south. Joe had lost comrades before, good friends, and he knew if shit when wrong, they could find themselves in a major "fubar" situation a long way from home with no backup.

He thought about the big picture.

Massood, Daesh, the scientists. It was a puzzle and a mess. Did it all connect?

The more he resisted the idea of going to Iran, the more it beckoned to him. It was a big challenge, for sure. Yet, it could be the beginning of an operational force—a way to strengthen Liberatus. There had been many discussions with John Rhodes, the forefather of the Liberatus movement, around one central question: what if they'd need to defend themselves at some point in the future? Without battle-hardened crews, it was a fantasy.

Then another thought came to him, distant at first, and he cast it out of his head immediately as a non-starter.

Yet it wouldn't go away.

It would be challenging for sure, but not impossible. Perhaps more dangerous than the insane op he was considering now.

A deal for Haleema that would give them an edge, an advantage that might pay dividends in the month and years ahead.

After all, she was asking him to risk his life. Why shouldn't she risk hers?

Chapter 36

Tehran, Iran

Haleema decided to check how her little trojan had been doing. How long was it since she had sent it to Rahbar? A few weeks?

The programme gave her snapshots at any point of Rahbar's online activity since the virus had been deployed. She also had the option to connect in real-time and see his screen as well as access any browsing or emails. She pushed the feeling of guilt aside, clicking through the data. Initially, the man had been unhelpful, but she sensed him coming around to her way of thinking. She also needed him on her side more than ever.

From Rahbar's emails, she could see his correspondence with the police chief, Massood Rajavil. An email from Massood gave her his address. Somewhere to start.

She read through a few of the emails and then came across one about her father. She sat upright and began to go through them. Mostly short and to the point. Now she had the case number it was easy to find all the related emails. Massood seemed to be shooting down anything Rahbar put forward as a reason to continue the investigation.

Rahbar had passed on the CCTV footage. The location of his vehicle and his boss had been merely stonewalling him.

It was time to look more closely into Massood.

Ideally, she wanted to get physical access to Massood's computer, even just for a few minutes; it would be all she'd need.

But how?

The Police Chief seemed to have built himself a kind of enclave, a castle that had who knows what kind of security measures. Breaking in was a dangerous option, maybe out of her league. If she got caught, she'd get shot or just be made to disappear for sure.

Could she access it remotely using the same method she used to tap into Rahbar's online activities?

Possibly.

But Massood had not accessed his work emails from any-where but his work PC, and he hadn't left any trail of his personal email or anything that could get her into his personal network.

It would need something else.

***

She found out Massood's home address easily enough as all top figures in Iranian society were kept on a highly secure database that the Cyber Army and Haleema had direct access to. His house was situated in the affluent area of Elahieh, an area with mansions and expensive real estate against the backdrop of the towering Alborz mountains. She turned down into the palm-lined street and slowly drove past the high walls of his property. She passed a high gate that was firmly shut. At a glance, she saw a camera pointing at the road. Continuing around the corner, she followed the wall until she had gone around the block, the wall surrounding it like a fortress.

The property must be enormous, she thought. According to the map, it was a vast, sprawling house with plenty of outside grounds. The canopies of palm trees peeked over the top of the wall, swaying in the light breeze, and Haleema wondered what lay over the other side.

As she pulled in at the top of the road, two middle-aged women were leaving via the side gate; they turned, walking in her direction. Haleema waited and watched as they passed by, laughing and talking.

A line of vehicles beeped horns as they negotiated the narrow streets. Her eyes drifted to graffiti scrawled over a metal cable box on the street, and an idea came to her.

Within minutes she was driving again, her eyes glued to the walls. The traffic crawled along at a snail's pace, giving her a chance to look closely.

She turned and continued along the road, following the wall again, and spotted the cable box for the house a few metres from the front gates.

If she could access it, there might be a way of causing a problem with Massood's internet.

An idea formed.

Not without problems, though. She spotted a CCTV on one side of the gate, turning slowly to scan the street. Then a large man in a suit and sunglasses appeared and put a cigarette to his lips.

Haleema looked at the cable box once more as she drove past.

Once she was home, Haleema put a frozen pizza in the oven and searched for information on cable boxes for the Datak telecom company. It wasn't long before she had a printout of what all the different wires and cables were for in the most common ones. Then she loaded up her 3D printer with a small cotton label and grabbed the Datak Telecoms logo from their website. The printer went to work, instantly lasering the logo in an embroidered style onto the material with a low rumbling noise.

She quickly showered, put on a dressing gown and plated her pizza, studying the printouts as she ate. She rummaged around under the sink, pulling out a variety of screwdrivers and a wire cutter as a last resort. The printer noise changed, and a beep indicated it was finished. She inspected the logo and went to her bedroom cupboard, and got to work.

After an hour, she was ready, but it was way too early. She set her phone alarm for three hours' time (2 am) and slipped under the sheets. When she awoke, Haleema felt alert and ready to go. She dressed in dark jeans, a black T-shirt, and a dark navy training top, grabbed her tools and drove to Massood's district. She took another pass of the house. All seemed quiet. She parked up around the corner and slipped three screwdrivers and the small wire cutter into her trainer's top zip-up pocket.

With a deep breath, she got out and walked around the corner towards the cable box, keeping to the unlit side of the road, her eyes focused on the CCTV camera that rotated on the far side of the gate. When it turned away from her, Haleema moved quickly across to the box and crouched down. She began unscrewing the top of the cover panel, keeping an eye on the camera as it slowly turned again. As the camera came back to face her, she ducked behind the far side of the box, hands wrapped around her knees, keeping still as a rock. She counted the seconds in her head, coming back out to continue each time the camera passed back around. After three rounds, the whole cover was removed.

She stared at the jungle of wires and cables, reciting the diagram she had printed out earlier. Six thick internet cables fed the immediate area, housed in a smaller box. But which one was Massood's?

She could disable them all, but that might screw up her plan. The last thing she wanted was genuine telecom engineers crawling all over the neighbourhood in the morning.

She put the cover back and stepped into the shadows. Pulling out her phone, she swiped up to get to the list of available wifi networks; four, then five, connections were active. When the camera had turned away again, Haleema crept along the wall towards the gate of Massood's house. Heart pounding, and trying not to imagine someone stepping out at that moment. She kept looking at her phone, watching the signal strengths change as she moved closer. She identified "datak_01897" as the only network signal getting stronger. Happy she had found the right one, she U-turned and ran back behind the shelter of the box, hiding while the camera did its pass.

Then she heard a car around the corner and froze, seeing the headlamps light up the street. If it turned, she'd be exposed like a deer on a motorway. It was too late to move or hide.

The car slowed, then moved passed without turning. Haleema exhaled, checked the camera then got back to work. She checked the coaxial cable markings; there was no easy way to identify them, so she began unscrewing the coupling that kept the first one in place and pulled it out. She checked her phone and saw "datak_01897" was still up, but one of the other networks had dropped off. She put the cable back and started on the next, keeping half an eye out for the camera. As she pulled out the third cable, she finally saw the "datak_01897" wifi signal had dropped off.

Relieved, she started screwing the cover back on, not bothering to do them all. Happy her job was done, and at a quick inspection, no-one would notice, she took off down the road back to her car. If all went as she hoped, the household would be waking up to no internet, and they'd put a call into the telecoms company to send someone out. Right now, there was nothing she could do except go home.

First thing in the morning, Haleema drank coffee and then waited for as long as she could bear to before making the call. She figured they'd discover it in the morning, around seven. Spend an hour trying to reconnect and play around with their machines before making the call.

After a few minutes, she got through to a service rep.

"How may I help?"

"Good morning. I'm from the Rajavil household at 1, Shahad, Elahieh. We had an Internet problem and called out an engineer this morning?"

Haleema waited, listening to a tapping keyboard.

"Yes, an engineer will be with you at 10.30. Was there another problem?"

"No, not at all. That's the point," Haleema let out a laugh. "It's all back on now. Must have been some glitch in the matrix. Can you cancel that?"

"Of course. Thanks for letting us know," more clicks from the keyboard, then, "That's now cancelled for you. Is there anything else Datak can help you with today?"

"No, thanks again."

Haleema disconnected the line. She smiled to herself; trust an engineer to be sent out the same day to one of the wealthiest neighbourhoods. How long would she have to wait if her connection went down? She checked to time, 9:15, enough time to get ready and enjoy another cup of coffee. She pulled on the dark blue jacket with the Datak logo she had sewn on the lapel. She took out some dark jeans and flat shoes to complete her uniform. Sitting down on her sofa, she went over the plan in her mind. She had done this sort of thing before, but now the stakes were higher. If she was caught, there was no doubt that Massood could make her disappear after some hellish interrogation. She heard some stories of what went on to those classed as enemies of the state. Haleema shivered at the thought. She finished the last of her coffee, covered her head and grabbed her toolbox on the way to the door.

At the gate she stood, looking up at the camera after ringing the bell, making herself look nonchalant and bored, despite the heightened anxiety inside her stomach.

A guard opened the gate and looked her up and down. She gave him a winning smile.

"Datak Telecoms. 10.30 appointment?"

The guard grunted and stood aside before shutting the gate behind her. He escorted her up the broad path, lush gardens on either side, with a clump of palms on the left and water sprayed fed the lawn. Haleema's heart raced as she approached the house. She took a sideways glance at the automatic rifle hanging at the guard's side. It was highly unlikely Massood was at home, but it grated at the back of her mind. If so, would he recognise her? Would he have seen photos of her? Almost certainly.

At the front door, they were met by a middle-aged woman that Haleema assumed was a housekeeper of some kind.

"She's here to fix the internet," he said, turning to return to his post without waiting for a response. The housekeeper smiled and gestured for her to come in.

"I'll need to check your line in and the main router first," Haleema said. The housekeeper nodded and started leading the way. They walked across a grand reception area with antique furniture and polished marble floor towards a wide hallway. Children's laughter echoed down from a room on the upper-level and voices.

Such luxury for a monster, Haleema thought.

"This way," the woman chirped, and they stepped into one of the downstairs rooms that looked like a junk room. A row of tables had piles of boxes stacked high.

"This is where we keep the router, but it is completely dead," she said, gesturing to the box that, indeed, had no flickering lights. Haleema immediately knew this was not Massood's office. Where she needed to be, she walked over to the router and picked it up, scrutinizing it before replacing it.

Haleema nodded, looking concerned. "And what other equipment, computers, and laptops do you have in the house?" The woman paused, thinking. "Well, there's a wifi booster on the top floor for phones and laptops. But down here, just a PC in the main office. His wife and kids also have tablets, but that's all I think."

"OK, I'll need to check the ones in the office?" Haleema.

"Yes, follow me."

They walked back toward the front door, then turned into a study. It was plush with panelled wood walls and huge bookshelves with a large oak-style desk, behind which were French doors leading outside.

Haleema put her toolbox down and began to look busy, rummaging through the box for tools she didn't need.

"It's good to see a woman doing technical jobs," the housekeeper said. Haleema smiled to herself. If only she realised what she had been up to; hacking for the Cyber Army while moonlighting for a libertarian movement in the West.

"Thanks. There aren't many of us." Haleema walked around the desk and switched on the main PC, but the woman didn't make any attempt to leave. Haleema took off her jacket, indicating she wasn't going anywhere soon. "This might take a while," she said.

The woman shifted her weight from one leg to another, looking around the office nervously.

"Yes, of course. Well, I'll leave you to it."

When she was gone, Haleema took out a USB drive and plugged it in, booting the computer from it. She started the installation of her baby, the monitoring virus.

It should only be a couple of minutes.

But that seemed like an eternity now.

As she waited for the installation to complete, her eyes were drawn to a laptop, and she quickly opened it up. When the process finally finished on the PC, she inserted the USB. Then she powered down the PC into sleep mode, took a cloth from her bag and gently wiped down the keyboard and anywhere else she might have touched. She repeated the process for the laptop, carefully returning it to its original position.

Looking around for a final check, she took a deep breath and went to the door. As she opened it, Massood was coming down the stairwell.

Shit!

Haleema ducked back inside and looked around for somewhere to hide. Behind his desk were French doors leading outside, but if she went out, it would look suspicious if a guard was nearby. A mobile phone rang outside, and Massood immediately answered it. He stopped walking and said a few words, then began walking away back to the rear of the house. Haleema took her chance and left, turning to the front door. The housekeeper came out of the room opposite at that moment.

"Any luck?" she asked, looking down at Haleema's toolbox.

Haleema forced a smile, wishing her heart would calm down. "There seems to be an issue with signal strength; I need to check the cable box on the road. See if we can find the problem."

"Right. The guard will let you out." The woman returned to the room.

Haleema forced herself not to run down the pathway as she approached the guard.

"I'm going to check the cable box," she said.

He opened the gate and followed her out onto the road, pulling a pack of cigarettes from his jacket pocket and lighting one, watching Haleema, who walked down to the cable box. She unscrewed the panel, taking her time and reconnected the cable housing that she'd undone the night before. The guard threw his cigarette now, gave her one more glance and returned inside. Haleema checked her phone, saw the wifi connection had returned and quickly replaced the panel.

Haleema walked back to her car. The connection was back up, so they wouldn't bother calling the telecoms company with any luck. She felt light-footed with relief and grinned to herself as she popped open the car door.

***

Once home, Haleema brewed tea, grabbed some food, and

immediately scanned her downloaded mirror copy of Massood's drive, starting with his browser history. There were plenty of visits to official news sites, especially the UIS news, it seemed, luxury property; he certainly seemed to have money to burn, judging by his house. Then there was a recruitment website; had he decided to change careers? Haleema clicked through and landed on a jobs board website, listing a long feed of international jobs for a wide range of sectors.

She then accessed Massood's emails and searched for any correspondence from the GreyFire recruitment company. There was a list of alerts that appeared to email him every time a job was posted in "procurements". She jumped back to the job site and navigated to the category, and clicked on one of the jobs. A message appeared asking her to log in.

She paused for a moment and sipped her tea. With a few clicks, she accessed his computer remotely.

Good, he wasn't currently on it, judging by the lack of activity. She watched for a few minutes to make sure and then went to his email inbox. She jumped back to the site and clicked the password reset button, and entered Massood's email address. She waited for the link to arrive, hovering in his inbox so she could intercept the message as it arrived. Once she had created a new password, she deleted the emails so he wouldn't see them.

Now, finally, she logged in and checked out one of the adverts, displaying a list of qualifications.

What was it about this job that interested Massood? Something was nagging at the back of her mind, and she tried to put her finger on it. She opened the folder that had the details of the missing scientists.

She scanned each one and read one that jumped out at her.

Nuclear fission engineer. $250K.

The same job role as her father. Except she knew he didn't earn nearly a third of that amount. It had been posted two weeks before he had gone missing. Working faster, she checked the other job posts against the other missing scientists and engineers.

Systems Engineer. Experience in nuclear power design, operations, or equivalent.

Computational Electromagnetics Systems Engineer. Advanced degree in EE or Physics.

A match with another one of the missing scientists.

They began to match up, one by one. But what did this all mean?

Haleema pushed back her chair and stared at the screen. Was this for real? A recruitment site as a front for a human trafficking site?

Who was posting the jobs? She looked at the details of who had made the posts, GreyFire Consulting, all the same company. They were apparently an American firm based in Colorado. She jumped onto the web and started to look for more information about the company. However, when she began to look into their details, she was unable to find any information about them at all.

So it was a pure front?

Massood's computer? She looked thoroughly for around fifteen minutes and found nothing there either.

Haleema felt her stomach rumbling and decided to take a break. She reheated some Ash–e Reshteh, a noodle and bean soup from the previous evening, and made more tea.

Should she go to Papak? It seemed to confirm her thoughts that a third party, possibly some secretive group high up in the

US, could be involved. One thing, though, it proved Massood was playing a dirty game.

After finishing up, she went back to her laptop and carefully searched Massood's emails for any reference to Ilam. A message popped up from Massood to Natan Helms concerning a procurement post with an invitation to lunch concerning some skill fulfilment that Massood said he could help with.

She looked for other messages that had been sent to Helms. The most recent was a reference to a change in time. Was this a warning that she and Rahbar were en route to Ilam?

There were other coded messages with dates and locations, but she couldn't work out what they referred to.

She made a decision. It was time to speak to Rahbar with the evidence she already had.

Chapter 37

5.15 AM
Kandahar, Afghanistan.

A taxi van sped through the narrow, cluttered streets; street vendors milled around setting up their stalls for the day.

The city had been on the map since Alexander the Great founded it as Alexandria Arachosia in 329 BC. Having been fought over by many empires for its strategic location, with its tall stone structures, it felt like you had travelled back in time. More recently, it had become known as the epicentre of the continuous war that had dragged on since 2001.

Joe knew the city and its dusty streets well from his time based there. It felt strange to him to come back—a country where friends and comrades had been made and lost.

Joe, Hugo, Marty, and Hodge were squeezed into the vehicle. Collecting supplies, weapons, and everything else had been complicated at best.

Joe had wanted to check how these guys operated together as a team and work on any weaknesses, so he had set up a series of paintball games with the objective of "capturing the flag."

From the small group of volunteers with military experience

at the camp, Joe wanted to make sure he had a small, reliable and agile team. What they were embarking on was dangerous, and Joe had no doubt the potential for close contact was very high, so everyone needed to be "battle ready" if possible. The last thing he needed was someone who might panic. Everyone had that experience except Diane Yu, who was young but had completed two years of military service in South Korea but hadn't been in a real war scenario.

Joe had divided them up into two teams: red and blue, with Marty, Hodge, and Hugo as red and Josh, Billy and Diane as blue, defending the flag.

Joe wandered around the edges of the game, watching it play out as the reds closed in, creeping through the small woodland on the far side of the training course. After a few games, Joe quickly realised who he wanted to take.

They had then travelled to Europe as a group and then switched to separate flights for the onward journey to Kabul and then south to Kandahar. In the south old city, Joe got his team booked into a hotel and slipped out to make a series of phone calls from a booth in a continental café several blocks away.

His first call was to a contact known merely as Mr Wallis. Joe knew him from his military days. A midwestern voice answered the call with a gruff tone as if he had just woken.

"Mr Wallis here," he said.

"It's Mr Donovan in regards to our meeting later today regarding the import opportunity."

"Ahh yeah, I have been expecting your call. Meet me at the Royal Afghan Hotel. No more than two of you, and don't be late—otherwise, I walk."

"Be assured—I'm serious about doing business," Joe

replied.

"Alright. 1400 hours it is then."

Mr Wallis proceeded to hang up the phone.

Joe then called Haleema, updating her very briefly that he was in Kandahar and that he would call again when inside Iran.

Several hours later, Joe, Hugo, and Marty were in one of the vehicles, parked up in a hotel car park watching the comings and goings of the hotel staff and guests through the arched entrance. Standing outside, several armed guards milled around, casting glances over people passing by.

"Marty, stay in the vehicle. We'll go in and talk to this guy," said Joe.

Marty was about to say something and then thought better of it and just nodded.

Hugo and Joe got out of the vehicle and walked through the parking lot before stepping into the air-conditioned hotel. They headed through the reception area, across a polished marble floor towards the bar area. Large ornate wooden fans turned slowly on the high ceilings overhead. On the far side, the bar and café area was set on the edge of an inner courtyard garden with a small decorative fountain bordered with carefully arranged flowers and plants. A handful of hotel guests, who looked like they had originated from every far corner of the world, were enjoying the tranquil setting.

Joe and Hugo eased themselves down onto wicker chairs that were arranged around a glass table. A waiter dressed head to toe in white, including his turban, appeared almost instantly and attentively took their order before gracefully heading away.

"Classy joint," said Hugo, jerking his head back and forth as if giving the place his approval. "Why aren't we staying here?"

he added.

Joe feigned a smile. "If you stayed here, you'd get accustomed to it and slack off. Then start demanding peeled grapes."

Hugo gave a derisive snort of laughter, still taking in the scene, his gaze focusing on the reception area. After five minutes, the waiter brought their drinks, and they sat in silence, watching the scene before them.

"This might be your guy," he said. Joe turned his head slightly to expand his field of peripheral vision.

"Yeah, it is."

A dark-set man, smartly dressed, moved towards them and stopped at their table.

"Mr Donovan," he said with a smile. Joe stood up and shook his hand, and gestured to Hugo. "My associate, Mr Lopez." He sat down, crossed his legs and looked at Joe. Although American, he had a middle eastern look about him that, Joe surmised, must be a significant benefit for blending in.

"So, Mr Donovan, how can I help?"

"We need some equipment. Basic stuff and a good robust vehicle, with Afghan and spare Iranian plates." Joe handed him a typed-out list. Wallis took and cast an eye over it for under a second.

"This shouldn't be a problem."

"Great. Then we just need to know the costs," Joe said.

Wallis thought for a moment, making calculations in his head.

"The weapons and gear are going to be four grand, US. Paid upfront. As for the vehicle, there are a few options I'll have to look into, but that'll be a lot more. Probably around five."

Joe and Hugo exchanged glances.

"OK, well, how about we give you two up front and the rest on delivery?"

The waiter appeared, and Wallis dismissed him with a wave of his hand. "I'm good."

Wallis thought for a moment, then gave a curt nod. "Not ideal, but, well, as we go back to the old days."

Joe leaned forward and drained his coffee. "Give me a minute, would you?"

He stood up from the wicker chair without waiting for a reply and headed for the toilets, picking up a copy of the daily paper en route. Inside the bathroom, he locked himself inside one of the cubicles, counted out the money, and then placed it in an envelope which he slid inside the newspaper.

He returned to the table and placed the paper on the table. "When can we expect delivery?"

"Tomorrow morning, around ten. I'll need to confirm the location."

***

After collecting all the gear, they headed off in a navy blue 6-door Ford Excursion model that Wallis had arranged for the long journey. It was a fourteen-hour drive from Kandahar, along mountainous roads, before they crossed a deserted border point into Iran and on towards Sirjan. After a few hours driving along a rarely used track, the Ford headed off through some rocky terrain, then pulled into a disused farmstead on the outskirts of Bardsir. It was well hidden from the main track and had come recommended by Haleema as a good forwarding ops location with Sirjan only one hundred kilometres away.

Joe jumped out first and looked around. It was quiet enough, that was for sure.

He looked across the valley to the far hillside, where a few goats seemed to be their only company.

The driver unlocked the chained padlock that secured the front entrance. Joe looked around inside, checking all the rooms, which appeared basic but clean. The stone walls kept the house cool. He went back outside to help the others with the equipment and supplies.

Once they had the two large boxes inside, Joe opened them up and pulled out three US army issue rifles, pistols and a handful of grenades. The rest was ammo, night gogs and dark clothing for each of them, as well as local garb to help them blend in as much as possible, considering they were white Westerners. They also had plenty of food rations and ten twenty-litre water bottles.

When working on the planning, Joe had estimated they would need enough supplies for three days as a maximum. He didn't intend to hang around for very long if possible.

"Headlights!"

It was Hodge from the rear of the house. Joe went to join him and saw the vehicle moving up and down as it traversed the terrain of the track.

"This should be Haleema," Joe said. The vehicle got closer as Hodge raised his weapon and aimed at the possible threat. Then, the car stopped, and the lights flashed three times in quick succession, then twice and finally, once, then stayed off.

"It is," he added, then looked around at their storage containers, rummaging around inside. He pulled out a flashlight and returned the signal. The headlamps came back on, and the car drove up to the house driveway.

Joe went out to greet her, hugging her. She had her hair

tied back into a ponytail and was dressed in jeans with a zip-up jacket. Probably to make herself appear more male at a distance, thought Joe.

"How was the journey?" he asked. Haleema opened the boot and pulled out a backpack.

Haleema sighed. "Long, but it was fine. Thanks, Joe." She slammed the boot shut and caught his eye. "Listen, I saw Iranian army units on the way here. They were transporting a lot of big guns and artillery? I don't know exactly."

"How many? And where exactly?"

"Well," she thought for a moment, "at least ten, and there were trucks, a few other armoured vehicles. Plenty of soldiers...."

"Where was this?"

"They were all stopped at the Anar crossroads, about two hours' drive?"

Joe nodded, his face set in grim acceptance. "Alright."

She looked at the house. "Who have you got here?"

"C'mon. I'll introduce you, and then we'd better get down to business."

"Fadin contacted me again. We're in touch via an encrypted app, so we have a location," Haleema added.

Joe nodded. "Great."

They walked to the house, and Hugo appeared in the doorway against a subdued light.

"Ah, you may never have actually met, but this is Hugo."

"Hey, Haleema. Once again, thanks for helping me out in Spain last year," said Hugo, who gave her a brief, polite hug.

"That's no problem," she smiled. "It must have been scary for you."

"Yeah, a bit rough," he replied, "for sure."

They went inside, where the other men all turned and looked at him. Joe then introduced her to the two others in the team.

"This is Hodge Balfour, a fellow Englishman." Hodge gave her a cheeky grin, putting on an upper-class British accent. "Charmed, I'm sure." Then he added in his more London twang, "Don't worry, love, I only speak like that to impress the ladies." Haleema smiled politely and turned to the older, shaven-headed one.

"This is Marty Faulkner," said Joe. Marty almost grimaced as he shook her hand and merely grunted. Haleema took out a map of Sirjan and spread it open on one of the tables. The team gathered around.

"We're currently here," she said, pointing at the empty plains outside Sirjan. "Fadin and Amir are housed in one of the smaller barracks on the outskirts of the city here." She pointed to a section of housing blocks near the Sirjan Eastern Bypass road. "Fadin also mentioned there is an abandoned shop here. It overlooks the smaller barracks, so it should be ideal for us to set up in," she added, looking around. "I hope it works for you?" Most of the men nodded except Marty.

"Can we trust this Fadin?" he asked, looking at Joe.

"I'll bet my life on it. He's my brother," Haleema interjected.

"I'm asking Joe," Marty said sharply.

"I can vouch for Haleema. I've personally not met Fadin or Amir, but if she says it's good, I'm happy," said Joe.

Marty looked away with a hint of disgust but said nothing.

"It's a fair question," Joe added before focusing on the map again. "At 0400 hours, we'll find a spot around here," he circled an area of the outlying desert across from the bypass on the outskirts of the city. "We can give our entrance point a recon before going in." Joe continued to outline the details as well as their extraction plan, then looked up at the team.

"We all know why we're here. Fadin and Amir joined up with the Daesh. That was their call and, obviously, not one we all agree with. Amir has been coerced into a suicide mission, and Fadin wants them both out." Joe turned to Haleema. "That's all we know, right Hal?"

"Right," she replied, "and their location. I can contact Fadin at any point."

"Maybe Fadin and the other guy should be left to stew in their own shit," Marty rasped. There was silence as Joe stared him down.

"While you're here, you're under my command. This is the operation. You're getting paid. If you don't like it, you can go home, or if you have concerns, talk to me privately.

"There's something else," Joe added, glancing at Haleema. "Haleema mentioned seeing Iranian artillery guns, at least ten and other hardware amassing at Anar. That's two hundred kilometres away. No doubt getting ready for an offensive on Sirjan."

"Great," Marty said. "This gig is getting better by the minute."

Joe ignored him. "OK, that's it. Dismissed."

Marty turned and walked away, disappearing into the other room.

Joe looked around at the remaining team.

"Any other concerns?"

The men shook their heads. "We're fine with it, Joe. I'll talk to Marty—he'll be fine. Besides, he won't give up the chance to kill some of those bastards," Hodge said.

"Hopefully, it won't come to that." Joe folded up the map.

"Let's eat something and get a few hours of sleep. Hugo. Can you get some food together?"

"Sure, vato," Hugo replied and turned to the supplies.

Joe turned to Haleema. "You should stay here. It'll be dangerous."

Haleema's eyes widened with surprise. "No way. I need to come—you need me there."

Joe shook his head. "It's not a good idea. You just tell Fadin who we are. We'll set up a signal and—"

"Joe! I'm coming with you. There's no way Fadin and Amir will just jump in your truck. I have to be there to see them, so they know it's cool. Besides, they're my blood. They need to see my face."

Joe paused. He knew she was right, but the idea grated on him.

"Alright. Your call."

He went to one of the supply boxes and pulled out a Glock 13, and handed it to Haleema.

"No, I don't actually like guns," she said. "I'm a hacker, remember?"

"Well, we're gonna have a lesson right now. Real basics. Otherwise, you're not coming," Joe said sharply, giving her the eye. "I'm in charge here," he added. Haleema went to say something, then hesitated.

"Right, boss," she replied with a wry smile.

Chapter 38

Sirjan, Iran.

Dark skies over the Sirjan cityscape were slowly turning into an orange hue as Joe and Hodge scanned the outskirts of the town through binoculars. Joe quickly identified the Sirjan Eastern Bypass road and the blocks of housing beyond it, well away from the main routes that Haleema advised as the better entry point to the city. Very close to that patch was a barracks for UIS fighters that Fadin had identified as their location. In front of sections of the road were half-built anti-tank defences; star-shaped "hedgehog" metal beams jutted up from the ground, and barbed wire set along a line of metal posts stood a few metres behind.

The defence effort must be a recent one, Joe thought, as they were nowhere near finished—still, plenty of options to get in.

"Alright," he whispered and rolled onto his side, moving in a crouch back to a facade of rocks in the endless brown desert, well away from the main road. Hodge followed him around to where the Ford was parked up. Marty, Hugo, and Haleema milled around, waiting for them.

"OK, I'll take point with Hodge, go take a look and radio you when we're happy. Hopefully, you can just drive across."

Joe and Hodge began walking and were enveloped by the darkness in seconds as they headed towards the amber lights of Sirjan in their loose civilian clothing and backpacks. After five minutes, they had crossed the bypass and arrived at the first of the buildings and began to crouch, keeping to the deep shadows. Joe took point, and Hodge followed him in.

The sound of the morning prayer drifted across from the central mosque from the city, the insertion time carefully chosen to coincide with it. Almost everyone would be attending the Fajr prayer apart from a few guards at the main roadblocks.

They came to a street, and Joe checked both ways, and they scurried across, slipping down side streets, stopping only occasionally to check their location on the GPS. Each stage of their journey had been carefully planned.

After five minutes, they came to a crossroads, their target location, a disused store, just ahead of them on the far side.

Joe signalled with his hand for the others to stay hidden and then moved across to the building. He disappeared among the ruins of the neighbouring building, carefully stepping around slabs of concrete and loose masonry.

He checked out the interior. There were three levels, but the staircase to the top had collapsed entirely. The only spot they could use as a base was the second floor above the store, which had a good view of the barracks where Fadin and Amir were based as well as keeping an eye on the immediate area, especially below them. The streets would become busy as the morning kicked in but they would be well out of sight. Joe checked a stretch of wasteland behind them that gave them three options to escape should they be discovered.

Joe returned to the street and flashed a light across to Hugo and Marty, who then moved across one by one. Happy the location would be suitable, Joe radioed the others to join them.

"We need eyes on that barracks at all times. We have to confirm they are in there," said Joe, unpacking some of the surveillance equipment. "I'll take first watch, then at 07:30, you take over Marty and then at 09:30, Hugo, Hodge, you're on at 11:30. We'll keep rotating after that. Everyone keep notes on everything, and I mean everything: the time anyone comes and goes, any deliveries—anything. Understood?"

Marty and Hugo both nodded.

"How are we going to spot these guys? When they're wearing that garb, they all look the same to me, vato?" asked Hugo.

Joe pulled out a PDA and began tapping the screen. "We'll just have to hope they show their faces, though they don't normally mask up unless they are heading out for an operation. Only for their propaganda marches and videos. Also, Fadin should be contacting Haleema with more info."

The window had old shuttered blinds that gave just enough of a view of the street below and the scattered buildings where Amir and Fadin were supposedly based.

Joe got himself into a comfortable position, scanned the street briefly and turned back to the others.

"We're gonna be here for a while, so stay disciplined and keep alert."

The streets began to get busier as the morning wore on, the fruit and veg sellers hauling their carts of produce to the market three blocks away.

The afternoon turned to evening, and Joe's team had been in the same location for ten hours, taking turns to watch the barracks. There had been plenty of Daesh loitering around the outside of the barracks building, but so far, there had been no contact from Fadin.

***

There was a distant buzz, and Haleema pulled out a phone from her pocket.

"It's Fadin," she said, then paused as she read the message.

"Dammit, they've moved Amir to another location."

All eyes turned to Haleema, aware that this meant a change in their plan.

"Great, we'll have to abort," Marty said, barely hiding the relief on his face.

"He knows the location, though. It's in the Najaf Shahr area. About three kilometres away." She looked up at Joe, who pulled out his PDA and began searching on the map app.

"This might be good. At least we don't have to storm into a barracks," Joe said.

"Unless the other place is a fortress filled with even more Daesh," counted Marty.

"Nip it, will ya, Marty? We're getting paid, aren't we?" said Hodge with a scowl.

Marty tapped his boot on the floor and merely stared back at him.

"Well, as it's close by, I'll take a look and see if there's a place to park the Ford." Joe was putting his device away in his pack.

"Joe, this requires a complete re-plan. Where's our extraction point? Our RV point?" Marty asked.

"I don't know yet. But we have a job to do. I'll go and recce, see what the situ is and then make a decision," Joe stated.

"A decision?" Haleema asked, looking concerned. "On

whether to continue, you mean?"

Joe held his palm up, "I always made it clear that if the situation looked too dangerous, we had the right to abort."

"Damned right," muttered Marty.

Joe stood up and began pulling his Arabic headscarf over his head.

Hugo stood up as well. "Joe, you look too foreign, too English. I'll go, bruh,"

Joe shook his head. "No, you look too Latino, mate. I'll be fine—I'll keep low."

With his dark beard and complexion, Joe didn't think he'd have a problem.

"Y'sure?" said Hugo.

Haleema cleared her throat. "I will go. No one will look twice."

Joe had already begun to head through the arched doorway onto the stairs. "Forget it, see you in an hour. Any longer than that, and assume I'm dead. Then, you're in charge, Hugo."

"Fuck," said Marty under his breath.

Joe silently disappeared, and they barely heard him leave the building.

"So, your brothers worth it?" asked Marty.

Haleema looked up, trying to read his face. "Yeah, they're worth it. They're good men. Just misled, I don't know—"

"I'm only doing this for the money," Marty cut in. "Just so you know, I have no sympathy for your brothers joining that bunch of losers."

Haleema sighed, looking back at her phone. "Well, I hope you enjoy the money," she said under her breath. Hugo glanced around at them both from his position at the window while Hodge continued cleaning and dismantling an MP9.

Fifty-three minutes later, Hugo heard a noise on the stairs and pulled his weapon around to the doorway.

"Flight," came a voice.

Hugo relaxed and breathed again—it was Joe.

"Fight," he replied. Joe appeared in the doorway, pulling off his keffiyeh from his head.

"Well, how is it looking?" asked Haleema eagerly.

Joe took a long gulp from his water bottle and leaned against the wall.

"Better for us. It's a big house, with a wall and gates. There's a guard outside. I hung around for a while, didn't see much activity, though."

"There could be a whole army in there," said Marty.

"Not according to Fadin. A few guards at most," Haleema interjected, staring at her phone screen.

"Well, I don't know your brother from shit, so—" Marty said, staring at her.

"What did I say earlier, mate? For fuck's sake." Hodge was chewing gum that made his craggy face look like he was chowing down on a wasp.

"Shut it! Everyone!" hissed Joe. He wondered about his decision to bring Marty. The bloke was a negative tidal wave, but his shooting skills were needed if things got messy.

"Here's what we'll do."

Chapter 39

UIS Safehouse, Sirjan, Iran.

Amir hauled himself to his feet after his evening Isha'a prayer and carefully folded up the matt, then sat down on the hard bed. The room was sparse, a chair, an empty wooden bookshelf that had been cleared of its contents; books deemed unworthy and against the ideology of the UIS. According to one of his comrades, the house had belonged to a wealthy family, infidels connected to the university, who had disappeared when the town had been liberated. Now it acted as a luxury, albeit a basic stepping stone away from the barracks for the "Martyrs".

On the wall, a large print of the supreme leader of UIS, Abu al-Adnani, dominated the room, as they did in every room where the mostly young men prepared for their last days.

Amir thought about his family. They were misguided for the most part, except for Fadin of course, who had seemed to rally to the cause. He suppressed his jealousy, but it simmered away so quietly Amir was almost consciously unaware of it. And it shamed him that his father and sister had worked for the oppressors, the "infidel" government.

Then there was the mission. The final one he would ever take.

The prize waiting for him in the afterlife. In paradise. A matter of weeks now? Or days?

His handler, Hassan Akhtar, hadn't told him yet, but the preparation had been ongoing since Amir was "chosen". No details had been revealed of the target or location; instead, a rigorous run-through of the technical specification.

It will be quick for you, they said. But for them, suffering, pain and straight to hell.

Amir placed two sleeping pills in his mouth and swallowed them with a gulp of water. He lay down on the bed.

To keep the demons from his nightmares at bay for just a little longer.

***

1.38 AM

Hodge moved quickly over a small wall and into the garden with everything he needed to start a little fire in the stone outhouse. A small can of petrol was syphoned from a car and a lighter. When he got inside the shed, everything was as Fadin had told them it would be; filled with old tyres, stacked wood planks, and old furniture.

Plenty of kindling to get things going.

Fire.

Always attracted attention.

Hodge carefully dosed the contents and poured a line back to the door, then took out his lighter.

***

Joe, Hugo, and Marty were sitting in the last two rows of the 4X4, their rifles facing upwards, while Haleema sat in the driver's seat. Their vehicle, tucked in behind other parked cars, had just enough space for them to keep an eye on the guard outside the gate. The guard, who was now slumped on a stool, was glued to his mobile phone.

Ahead, a car passed by. The moon had disappeared behind a bank of clouds, darkening the street.

"Where's Fadin now?" asked Joe.

Haleema glanced at her phone. "Just around the corner, waiting out of sight."

"Skyred to Night Owl. Firestarter in effect. Am in new position now, over." The voice came through their earpieces, low and clear.

"Roger that, Skyred. Standby."

Joe leant forward and gently touched Haleema on the shoulder. "Keep an eye on the road. When we appear at the gates, be ready to drive up—and fast," Joe whispered.

Haleema turned and smiled. "Roger that."

They waited in silence for a few minutes, and then all saw the flames licking the window of the outhouse, a gentle orange hue lighting the dark trees and the wall of the main house. The guard seemed oblivious at first, still transfixed on his phone, then his head turned slightly as he sensed the changing light. He turned around, then jumped to his feet and rushed inside the gate.

"Right, let's rock 'n' roll," said Joe. The men left the vehicle quickly, adjusting their weapons before moving along the wall. Joe reached the corner, checked the road both ways and scurried across and slipped inside the gate. He peered across to the gatehouse and saw the figure of the guard speaking into his radio. Joe signalled with a hand to Marty, who followed Joe's path and joined him inside the house grounds. They moved amongst a group of small trees and crouched down. Hugo joined them seconds later, just as the front door opened.

Another guard rushed out, turned the far corner and disappeared in the direction of the fire.

Joe and Hugo moved in silence up the steps to the open door while Marty stayed put, his rifle aimed in the direction of the outhouse.

***

Hodge had pounced on the first guard from behind after he finished his rant on the radio. Hand over mouth, knee in the small of his back and expertly slashed his blade across the jugular. A wet gurgling sound emitted from the open throat as blood gushed down the guard's front. Hodge pulled the body slowly to the ground, hand still covering his mouth and waited for the man to die before dragging him out of sight. He wiped the blade on the dead guard's tunic and crouched down in the dark, feeling the heat of the growing fire, which hissed and crackled, its shadows dancing across the house, trees, and lawn.

Come on then, you bastards.

***

Inside, Joe and Hugo took positions on either side of the door, assessing the situation. The house seemed quiet. They were in a spacious reception devoid of any furniture; carpeted stairs circled up to another floor. Marks on the wall suggested there had been grand paintings that had been taken away. The house must have been seized from a wealthy family, thought Joe. He briefly wondered what might have become of them as he led the way up the stairs, pistol aimed directly in front, to Amir's room.

Let's hope Fadin got his info right.

On the next floor, Joe came to the first door on the left and slowly turned the handle. Not wanting to take any chances, Joe stood against the wall, aiming his pistol straight inside, pieing the gap in segments until the door was wide enough for him to get inside. He glanced at Hugo, who waited at the top of the stairs, also crouched, looking down behind the stairs they had just climbed.

Joe crouched down on his haunches and moved just inside to make himself less of a target. In the low light, he could make out the figure lying on their side on the bed. Satisfied there were no other threats, Joe stood up and went over to the bed. He grabbed the shoulder and pulled back. The man opened his eyes suddenly, jolted from a deep sleep and stared at Joe in confusion.

He knew it was Amir straight away, having studied the photos Haleema had shown him. Joe quickly slapped his palm over his mouth and showed him his weapon.

"Keep your mouth shut and do as I say. Haleema sent me. I'm a friend of hers, and I know you speak English. We're getting out of here. Shake your head if you understand," said Joe.

Amir shook his head.

"I'm going to take my hand off now. If you make any loud noises or say anything, I will have to knock you out. For both our sakes. Nod, if you understand?"

Amir nodded vigorously once more.

Joe slowly took his hand away, leaning his face closer to Amir with a devilish grin as if to underline his point. He stood straight suddenly and waved his pistol at Amir. "Get dressed. Make it quick."

Amir hauled his feet onto the carpet and went to his clothes, draped over a nearby chair.

"My friend is outside, he'll lead us out, and I'll be right behind you. Needless to say, don't make a single sound." Amir nodded, apparently scared, as he pulled on a shirt.

Joe depressed his ear radio.

"This is Night Owl. We're coming out. Stand by."

***

Haleema watched the house and the growing fire next to it with increasing nervousness. She looked at her watch, feeling utterly helpless. A figure turned the corner, adding to her anxiety, and she watched as a man walked down the street opposite her and crossed over. Slowly she recognised her brother.

"Fadin!"

She went to get out, but he held his hand up, looking behind him.

"Stay in the car," he said quietly and slipped into the row behind her. He leaned over, kissed her on the cheek and gave her a warm smile.

"Imagine meeting you here, sister."

***

Within a minute, Amir followed Hugo down the stairs. As Hugo rounded the bend, he stopped dead and held up a fist. A Daesh guard stepped into the hallway, looked up and saw Hugo straight away. He went for his rifle, but Hugo was ready and fired two shots that hit him straight in the chest, dropping him like a ninepin. Another one had been following him out and dived back into the room and began firing blindly.

"Back!" Hugo pushed at Amir's chest. Joe came alongside and fired at the door, but the angle was too sharp to get a good aim. He took a smoke grenade from his belt and tossed into down into the reception. Above them, they could hear footsteps from one of the rooms.

Hugo fired another volley and turned to Joe with an anxious look. "Guess it's shitshow time."

"Yep," Joe grunted, looking down at the expanding smoke.

"BlueMagic, we're coming down the stairs. One AK in the front room first left."

"Affirm got it."

"Let's go. I'll lead," said Joe.

Before Hugo could protest, Joe was halfway down the steps, aiming in the direction of the side door. A gap in the smoke revealed Marty holding his M4, tucked into his shoulder. He moved to the parted door and smashed a boot into it, crashing it open. The Daesh man came rushing out, and all Marty needed to do was pepper bullets into him. Marty then moved to the bottom of the stairs and aimed upwards, covering their backs.

"Go!" he shouted.

Joe, Amir, and Hugo emerged from the smoke and rushed down the steps to the gate. There was a rapid burst of gunfire from the house, like crackling wood. Haleema had parked a few metres down the road with the engine running, and the men rushed to it.

***

Marty appeared at the gates, turned and fired a round at the house doors, then waited behind the wall on the street side, his weapon aimed at the gate entrance.

Joe peered through the window and waved his hand, "Get into the next seat, Haleema. I'll drive." He clambered in as Haleema shuffled over to the passenger side and placed her pistol on the top of the dashboard.

"Where the hell is Hodge," Joe muttered, then depressed his radio. "Skyred, where the hell are you? We're leaving."

"There he is," said Hugo, pointing ahead of them. They watched Hodge clamber over the wall, jump down to the sidewalk and then join Marty at the other side of the gate. Marty looked around the edge of the gate and gestured him across. Hodge ran to the vehicle and clambered inside next to Amir and Fadin.

Haleema was turned around in her seat, trying to hug Amir, who looked confused. He kissed her on the cheek and smiled weakly. "Haleema. What are you doing here?" Amir looked at his brother, nodded and then briefly turned around to look at Hugo.

"We're getting out of here, brother."

Just then, Marty jumped in the back seat next to Hugo, shouting, "Let's go!"

Joe slammed on the gas, and the SUV spun off into the road, away from the house.

"Any pursuers?"

Marty and Hugo were both turned, looking behind them. "We're good," said Hugo.

"For now," Marty added.

"What is happening here?" Amir asked.

Marty slapped Amir on the shoulder. "Savin' your ass is what, buddy,"

Amir ignored him, focusing on Haleema.

"Did you arrange this?" asked Amir in a stern tone of voice.

Haleema looked confused now. "Well, yes. To save you from," she hesitated and spat with contempt, "martyrdom."

"This madness ends tonight, Amir," Fadin cut in.

Amir began to look flustered, jerking his head around as if looking for a way out of the vehicle.

"I don't want any part of this. I had my destiny—my path is set—you've messed up everything. You don't understand—"

Haleema frowned. "Amir, we're getting you out of here. You should be thanking us. We just saved your life!"

A series of booms reverberated across the entire sky, followed by flashes that turned the night to day in an instant. The arguing stopped as all in the car looked out—then another three, then four thunderous booms somewhere in the city behind them.

"They're attacking—" Haleema said.

The vehicle sped through the empty road. Trash carts lined the side, one upturned spewing debris onto the street. They came to traffic lights, and Joe slowed slightly, assessing whether to go straight or turn. He caught movement—an object hurtling towards them. A Toyota pickup truck came smashing into their front bonnet from the right-hand side, pushing their 4x4 into a tailspin on the road. A loud deafening crash. When it came to a standstill, there was a second of silence as steam rose from the engine.

Haleema heard shouts from behind her.

"Company!"

A Daesh soldier leapt from the Toyota passenger seat, pulling up his AK 47 as he ran at Haleema's side of the car, a mask of hatred across his face.

Haleema didn't think. She grabbed the MP7 from the dashboard as the soldier brought round his weapon to aim at her. She pointed at his body mass through the open window and fired.

The man shouted and fell to his knees.

An intense, loud burst of bullets deafened her from behind as one of the men finished him off.

"This way!" The shout was muffled.

A hand grabbed her arm and pulled her toward the passenger door. Joe was gesturing to her, still shouting.

Pok! Pok! Pok!

The windshield was taking a battering, filling with holes. Before she knew what was happening, Haleema was on the ground next to the vehicle. Marty and Hodge had clambered out of the doors on the same side. Gunfire seemed to be erupting all around them.

She saw a flash of Marty getting hit in the shoulder and falling to the ground, seemingly shouting in anger more than pain.

Hodge had positioned himself at the back of the vehicle, firing rounds while Joe took cover behind the front bonnet.

She shouted for her brothers but barely heard herself. "Fadin! Amir!"

Fadin crawled out of the middle doors, keeping his head low and fell onto the road. Their eyes met for the briefest of moments, and Haleema began to crawl over to him, looking across at their assailants and bodies littering the ground. Another flash, like a fast-moving film; Joe casually gestured with a flick of his MP7 to Hodge and disappeared to pincher the enemy vehicle.

There was a single shot from Joe's weapon, and then it went quiet except for the sound of a distant siren alarm drifting over the city.

"Clear!" Joe shouted. He was soon back, crouching down over Haleema.

"It's over. You OK?"

Haleema looked back at him like a rabbit in headlights and then brought herself out of it.

"Deafened but OK," she shouted. Joe checked the others.

"I'm hit," groaned Marty, holding his shoulder. Hugo, who had been crouching by the rear wheel, shuffled over to him. "I can look at it."

Joe roared to everyone, "Stay in cover, eyes peeled. We need to get out of here sharpish! Hodge, try the vehicle. It might still go." Hodge looked sceptically at the steam coming from the bonnet.

"I'll try," he said, already moving toward the driver's door.

The artillery fire opened up once more overhead; a shell hit one of the buildings they had driven past, and a plume of ash and debris showered the road. There were distant shouts, and a family of five with children came out of a house further down the road. They began to run in the opposite direction, perhaps heading to safety.

"Make it quick!" someone shouted.

There was a sound of the engine turning but no spark of life.

Haleema hauled herself to her feet, helped by Fadin.

"Try their pick up," Joe shouted to Hodge. He gestured to Haleema and Fadin. "Help me move the bodies out of the vehicle, Hodge. Keep your eyes out for hostiles." Joe glanced at him, still being tended by Hugo, then ran across to the pickup. Hodge hauled out the dead driver, dragging him out of the way and jumped into the driver's seat. He turned the engine, and it started up.

Fadin and Haleema pulled another dead gunman from the back and put him on the side of the road.

"Alright—Hugo, Marty, get in the back. We're leaving."

Haleema looked around. "Where's Amir?" Then she caught a glimpse of him staggering back along the road they had come.

"Hey, Amir!" she shouted again and began to move before Fadin grabbed her.

"Leave him—we've done all we can."

All eyes turned to the distant figure as it turned a corner, disappearing from view.

"No, we haven't!"

"We can't go back. It's too dangerous!" Fadin said angrily.

Haleema continued to stare down the road, then screwed up her face and turned back, realising now that he had made his decision, the anger dispersing from her body as she understood she probably would never see him again.

***

The commander, Yafir Al-Adel, and his handler, Hassan Akhtar, had been immediately alerted and rushed to the scene of the insertion and gunfight. They inspected the burned-out house, then ordered the removal of the dead bodies of their men from the attack and now stood in Amir's room, as he explained once again.

"I think they were Americans, but I didn't see them as I was blindfolded," he lied.

"So, Americans. Why would they want you, do you think?" asked the commander in his rasping voice.

Amir shook his head, acting perplexed. "I do not know. My guess is something to do with the mission or to get information about our positions elsewhere."

The commander held his hands behind his back, gently rocking on his feet, then turned and began walking around the room, pausing at the window as he spoke. "So, we think they were Americans. They accessed the house, killed two guards near the outhouse and grabbed you, taking you out to a waiting vehicle. You heard a firefight, and then the vehicle drove away. You managed to escape when our pursuit team crashed into them." He turned to face Amir. "How did you escape with a blindfold?"

Amir shrugged nonchalantly. "I wasn't cuffed. I just pulled it off."

The commander considered this for a moment before continuing, "And you heard no talk about where they might be headed?"

Amir shook his head. "No, they hardly spoke. They pushed a gun barrel at my head and told me to be quiet or get shot."

Then, Akhtar's radio broke into a rapid static noise, and he answered. It was one of the officers from the city's defensive positions. Amir and the commander waited, looking at Akhtar, catching only snippets of the panicked conversation—a series of booms in the distance. Akhtar ended the communication and looked at the commander with a mixture of surprise and trepidation.

"Commander Al-Adel, we're under attack from artillery from the West and the North."

Al-Adel looked at him for a moment, another sound of an explosion nearby making his subordinate's statement redundant. He nodded. "The devil is at the gates. Alright, I will go to the command centre and deal with this. Get four or five men and check if the Americans are still in the area."

Akhtar nodded and jerked a thumb at Amir. "What about him?" The commander turned to Amir. "Nothing changes, Amir. Except for the timing. We need to bring the operation forward. Prepare to leave early as soon as possible."

Chapter 40

Rafsanjan, Kerman Province, Iran.

It was mid-afternoon the following day, and the heat seemed to suck out all the oxygen from the air. Amir was sitting in the back seat of an old Subaru, a man called Rabbi in the driving seat chain-smoking and flicking his butts onto the road. They sat waiting in front of the makeshift stores, several old garages that were converted into a kind of marketplace where traders sold everything from food to motorcycle parts. Outside one, plastic crates were stacked high, and an old man shifted through them, rubbing off the dirt from engine parts and sorting. Amir stared at him blankly, lost in his thoughts.

Normal life. It seemed so long ago since Amir had experienced anything close. It may as well have been a dream. Going through the days that turned into weeks and months. He reflected blankly on his life achievements so far. What were they exactly? There were happy times, although fleeting, but the commander was right. Nothing in his life had been significant until now. How naïve he had been, so compliant of the state, tolerant of their crimes, choosing to bury his head and tune out what was happening. Just like most of the Iranian people.

Sacrifice, his and many others, was necessary to realise the dream of the caliph, the dream of forging a new future for his beloved country.

Akhtar came into view, walking along the road, glancing around before slipping into the back seat next to Amir.

"Everything is ready, drive, brother," he said to the Rabbi before turning to Amir, nodding reassuringly. Just fifty metres along the road, Akhtar gestured to a large detached building with large metal shutters that were firmly pulled down to the ground. In the frame of a side door stood another man dressed in dark overalls.

Rabbi pulled over, and Akhtar and Amir got out and walked across. Inside came a strong smell of oil and sweat. A black Toyota was placed over a pit where another mechanic toiled with an unseen problem underneath. At the far end, a small room with glass partitions exposed a messy office, with a desk almost submerged under piles of paper and other crap.

The man at the door turned and hugged Akhtar, slapping his back.

"God is great," they both proclaimed. Akhtar turned to Amir. "This is our comrade, Amir," then he gestured to the man from the garage, "Our brother, Ekram."

Both men shook hands. "Amir is the one taking the road to martyrdom for our cause," Akhtar added.

"Ahh, yes!" Ekram hugged Amir, grinning devilishly, revealing crooked teeth, then turned, holding out his hand to a large military truck behind them.

"This, packed with three hundred kilos of explosives, will deliver a massive blow to the enemy. More than we could achieve fighting them head-on! A stake right into their heart! You are a great man, Amir. Tomorrow they will be singing your praises across this great country of ours!"

Chapter 41

New CIA Headquarters, Denver, Colorado, USA.

Zak stepped into the spacious office that was set on the fourth floor, overlooking the green hills. In the distance, an aeroplane took off from the Buckley Air Force Base, where Zak had arrived from the middle east twelve hours earlier. He had travelled with the Iranians back on a transporter, and thankfully this time, he was fully rested.

Merlin Jackson, the Associate Deputy Director, a large man with swept-back dark hair and oversized glasses, stood up, shook hands with Zak, and then offered him a seat.

"Great job in Iran, Zak. Great job."

Zak had only met Jackson a few times but had taken a liking to the man. He held a "no-nonsense" demeanour and had a way of cutting to the chase.

"My pleasure," replied Zak.

"We have successfully thwarted a major UIS op. They don't have the skills to do anything with that highly enriched uranium they grabbed, thank god. But the problem remains," he wiped his forehead with a handkerchief, "that they still have it."

He straightened his tie. "Still, the Director has had the good news—duly noted."

"Can I ask a question, Deputy Director?"

Jackson waved his hand. "Merlin, please—by all means."

"The Ghost 13 option. I'm still not sure why we couldn't use—I mean, our company use Special Operations Group for paramilitary ops, recruited directly from JSOC, so—"

Jackson nodded vigorously. "Yes, yes, I know. It's a fair question. There's a lot of upheavals right now within the intel community, changes and so forth.

"It's all been coming from the top. Of course, we've argued that we have the resources and teams, together with the military, all perfectly capable of carrying out these kinds of operations, but they increasingly prefer to use Ghost 13."

"How big an operation is it?" Zak asked tentatively, wondering if he was pushing his luck.

"I don't even know the full details. Thirteen groups, around the globe, all organised into an intelligence and military-led hybrid."

Zak remembered something about that, something to do with his father, in the early days.

"Started in the UK, right?" said Zak.

The Associate Deputy Director looked up at Zak and smiled. "Yeah, that's true. The original setup was between MI6 and GCHQ back in '99. Then it expanded aggressively. Glad you know your stuff." He looked serious again. "They have the backing of some serious players, so we just have to roll with it for now."

He took off his glasses and placed them on his desk as if closing the subject. "Seriously, great job out there. The Director is happy with the way it played out. But it's not over. Time to get back to work as that shit show in Iran doesn't look like it's gonna blow over anytime soon."

Chapter 42

Rafsanjan, Kerman Province, Iran.

The three men were standing around the desk in the garage office, studying a folded-out map.

"Is that clear, Amir?" Akhtar asked, looking up at him with pride in his eyes.

"Yes. I understand," he replied without emotion.

Akhtar looked at his watch. "We need to leave. It is time."

Ekram gave Amir and Akhtar another hug, then walked over to the garage doors.

The two men followed him out of the office, Amir climbing up into the driver's seat of the army truck. Akhtar spoke to Ekram briefly and then joined him in the passenger seats. The doors slammed shut, and Amir started the engine as Ekram pressed a button next to the main garage door, which began to slide upwards.

He turned, patting the side of the vehicle as it drove past him onto the road.

"It won't let you down! I've been working on it for over a month!" he shouted. Amir barely acknowledged him.

All senses had evaporated into the still, humid air. Akhtar was speaking, but Amir barely heard him. He drove at a steady pace along the road to the intersection they had shown him on the map.

"Amir! The commander." Akhtar handed him a mobile phone.

Amir took it and held it against his ear.

"Commander?"

"Comrade Sheraz. Allah is great and will reward you. Your brothers await in heaven. We will all see you there."

The line went dead. Amir handed the phone back to Akhtar, placing his sweaty palm back on the wheel. The intersection lay ahead. Traffic was light.

"Straight across," Akhtar instructed.

Once across, they could see the high wire fence of the army barracks that was built alongside the road. Fifty metres away, the low buildings and other army vehicles could be seen inside the perimeter—the green specs of soldiers moving around. A pole hoisted the Iranian flag that fluttered in the breeze.

Although he had already been briefed, Amir was surprised at how lightly guarded it was. A wire fence, a security barrier with a few guards. It had been carefully chosen, and the Iranians apparently were not expecting any major problems this far north.

"Pull over here," his passenger and handler said sharply. Amir did as instructed. Akhtar slapped him on the shoulder. "I'll see you on the other side, brother," he said, opening the door and jumping down. He peered back up at Amir and handed him the detonator, a small plastic box on a lanyard. In his pocket, Akhtar gently held his hand over the hidden detonator. Either way, Amir would ascend to martyrdom today.

"Hang it around your neck and hit the button when you're

near the building or a good target. Remember, drive hard and fast. They won't realise anything is wrong until it's too late. Good luck, comrade." With that, he slammed the passenger door shut and began walking back along the road. Amir saw in his door mirror that a white sedan that had been following them had pulled over behind. His handler got inside. Then, he and the driver waited as if they were keeping an eye on him.

Amir barely noticed the sweat covering his entire body, soaking his green shirt as he started driving again. Looking ahead, he could see the turning that led to the entrance of the barracks. He changed down a gear and edged out into the middle of the road.

Use the momentum of speed, Akhtar had told him.

Through the wire fence, he saw a soldier step out of the booth; weapon holstered onto his back. Heart pumping, Amir, swung the wheel and turned into the barracks entrance road, directly ahead of the barrier. The soldier held his hand up to stop, but Amir slammed his foot on the accelerator.

Steel plates welded onto the front grills should smash the barrier without any trouble, the man from the garage had said.

The soldier, a fixed look of surprise, just managed to jump out of the way as Amir smashed through the barrier with a loud grating crash, debris from the fittings showering the side of the vehicle. Then, gunfire raked the back of the truck—a bullet cracked Amir's side mirror.

Ahead, a group of soldiers who were by the main building looked in Amir's direction, alerted by the gunfire. Some raised their weapons. Amir focused on the main building behind them, driving at top speed now, the engine screaming in protest from under his feet, his hands vibrating on the steering wheel as the whole cabin shook.

Amir swallowed hard. Now, it was happening. It seemed like a dream, except he knew very well it wasn't.

Words of prayer uttered under his breath came quickly.

His sweaty hand grabbed the detonator switch hanging around his neck. Blankness shrouded his mind; only the thought of his mother's face appeared as he pressed down on the switch.

Soldiers began firing directly at him, shouting out, and cracks peppered the windshield.

The button clicked.

Amir's final moment was the smothering blinding white light scorching his eyeballs. There was an intense heat burning into his back, followed by a loud whoop that burst through his eardrums.

Chapter 43

Shiraz, Iran.

As soon as Joe stopped the vehicle, Fadin bolted out the rear door and through the gate of his house. Haleema quickly followed him in.

"Guess he's happy to be home," said Hugo, pulling his backpack up from the footwell and opening his door.

"Yeah, and got a bit of explaining to do, I imagine," Joe added.

The team had got out of Sirjan in the nick of time as a general alarm bellowed over the city through loudspeakers. They had already cleaned up the RV point, the house they had stayed at, but the plan had been to return to the house and split up from there. That plan was now out of the window. They raced for the frontier until they were well out of Daesh territory and headed for the relative safety of Haleema's city, Shiraz.

Marty and Hodge dispensed their clothes and gear, took their cover identities, and got separate flights from Shiraz airport.

The vehicle with Joe, Haleema, and Hugo pulled up outside Haleema's house. They slowly walked into the courtyard, hearing the sound of laughter from his mother, who was naturally overjoyed at seeing her son alive, as well as her daughter again.

They stepped through the door into the fresh interior of the house. Fadin's mother came to them, tears rolling down her cheeks.

"Thank you, thank you," she said in broken English.

Joe waved a hand, indicating no problem.

"Amir? Amir?" she said, her eyes darting between Joe and Hugo.

Fadin spoke for them rapidly in Farsi. She turned to him and spoke, asking a question, and when Fadin shrugged, she slowly slumped down into one of the chairs in the kitchen; her joy now turned to sorrow. With her head buried in her hands, she jerked as fits of sobs reverberated throughout her body.

Joe silently gestured with a hand at Hugo, and they both moved out of the kitchen to an adjourning living room.

There was nothing they could say or add. Best to let Fadin and Haleema deal with it, Joe thought. They placed their bags on the floor, the conversation continuing in the kitchen, and sat on the cushioned chairs.

"What's our plan?" asked Hugo.

"I need to get back to Spain. There's business to sort out over there. We've done all we can for Haleema." They both leaned back and rested in silence, looking over the detailed Arabic wall hangings.

After twenty minutes, Fadin entered the room, and Hugo and Joe stood up. "Mother is distraught. She has gone to rest. You are welcome to stay here as long as you like."

"Thanks, Fadin. We will rest tonight, if that's OK, and take off in the morning." Fadin nodded his agreement.

"Thanks for all your help, by the way. I don't know what

is going to become of my country, but it seems to be getting worse," said Fadin.

"Your sister has been a valuable friend," Joe said. "And you need to be careful. You'll be on a list after this."

Fadin said, "Yes. I will make a plan and work something out. Come on, let's eat."

Chapter 44

Tehran, Iran.

The stretch of wasteland, set behind a playing field in the East Tehransar area, served as a convenient place for locals to park vehicles. There were no buildings overlooking it, just a long concrete wall that ran alongside the road. This was why Haleema chose to meet Rahbar there.

He had been reluctant at first, but she had insisted that the information was too sensitive to risk bringing it to the station or even her house.

"You must see it with your own eyes, away from places where surveillance might be a risk," she had said. This had piqued the Inspector's interest, and he had finally agreed.

Haleema waited in her car, fidgeting with her hands and changing radio stations every few minutes. It seemed the more she dug, the more worms she found, and the circumstances around her father's disappearance were revealing themselves to be only a part of a bigger conspiracy. She rubbed her eyes. The tiredness from the last few days had caught up with her now. She had returned alone to Tehran on a flight from Shiraz the previous evening and barely slept thinking about Amir; a mix of anger and remorse stirred in her like a nasty potion.

God only knew what was in store for him now.

You've done all you can, Haleema, she kept telling herself over and over, but it felt like a hollow mantra—a lie.

Then she wondered when she would be able to sleep again, a deep sleep, knowing everything was alright with her world and waking up with excitement and joy for a new day. Would she ever have that feeling again?

She watched Rahbar's white Toyota pull into the waste ground, throwing up a cloud of dust as it navigated the sections that had no tarmac and headed in her direction. For a second, she wondered why she should trust him. He was the police, after all, and slowly it dawned on her what a huge risk she was taking.

He pulled up alongside, peering out of the dirty window, and nodded before slowly getting out of the vehicle. He took his time, mopping his forehead with a white handkerchief, looking across the waste ground both ways before getting into the passenger seat next to Haleema.

She took a deep breath and handed him a folder.

"This is proof Massood has been in contact with Natan Helms, someone high up in the US Government. He's also been communicating with one of the military leaders of UIS."

Rahbar took the document and read it for a while. Haleema saw the initial shock on his face as he turned the pages.

"This is my boss, the Chief—" he started but stopped to read something. Rahbar looked at Haleema as if an enormous burden had suddenly been dropped on his shoulders.

"There's a judge on the Revolutionary Tribunal I know who I can go to with this. We grew up together." Rahbar paused.

"Can you trust him?" asked Haleema.

Rahbar nodded. "Yes, yes. Absolutely, without a doubt."

Haleema looked at him carefully. "And if you could find a way to trust me, perhaps with his name—in case."

Rahbar turned to meet her eye for a moment, then nodded his understanding.

"Yes, of course. His name is Judge Ervand Neyestani. He certainly has the necessary powers to be able to act quickly on this."

"I hope so. Otherwise, it might put our lives in danger."

Rahbar nodded. "Leave it with me, and I will contact you as soon as I can."

He stepped out of the car, and Haleema watched him drive back across the potholed tarmac back onto the street.

Chapter 45

Tehran, Iran.

Haleema's phone buzzed, illuminating the dark room. She had just switched off the light to try to get some much-needed sleep. It was a message from Rahbar.

"I have important information. It would be best for you to come to my house as soon as you can."

Haleema jumped up in bed and reread the message. She began typing her reply:

"When is good?"

She stared at the screen, and the typing in progress animated across the bottom of the message thread.

"It would be best to come quickly. Now, if you can."

Haleema hit reply. "OK, I'll get a taxi now. Send me your location card."

She lept out of bed, dressed and called a taxi, pacing anxiously as she waited.

What was happening? Had they found her father?

She stood by the door, her eyes closed, praying it was good news.

***

Haleema stood outside the large house, checking on her phone that the address was correct before stepping through the gate. When she stepped up to the front door, she noticed it was ajar. She buzzed the bell and waited, wondering if he had left it open for her. She stepped inside into a lit hallway.

"Inspector Rahbar?"

Silence.

She moved along the hallway and glanced through to the darkened kitchen directly ahead.

"Inspector Rahbar?"

Something was wrong, and the feeling that she should leave right there and then was overwhelming.

To her right was an open the door to a living room. The lights were off, but she could just make out her reflection in a long mirror on the wall. Towards the bottom of the mirror, a dark shape caught her eye. She moved into the room and opened the door wider, letting in more light from the hallway.

Looking down, she gasped in shock at the body of Rahbar, lying on his side with his ankles and hands tied.

Eyes wide with shock, Haleema took an unsteady step toward the body and saw that a thin cord had been wrapped around his throat. She leaned closer, barely believing what she was seeing.

As if her senses had accelerated into overdrive, she sensed a hushed footfall from the front door that woke her from the shock. She stepped back from the body and turned around towards the door to see a shadow move across the wall.

The figure moved into the room and flipped on the lights. A policeman stood in the doorway frame. He looked at Haleema and then down to the body and swiftly reached for his sidearm.

Haleema threw her hands up.

"Wait! I just found him like this!"

The sound of some others coming through the front door, voices and a crackling radio. Another policeman entered the room, his eyes widening as he saw the dead body.

"Get your hands above your head and turn around."

Haleema moved her hands skyward. The second policeman approached cautiously, grabbing her wrists and slapping on handcuffs before frisking her roughly.

"He was helping me out, and I found him dead! Do you seriously think I had something to do with this?"

He ignored her, and she was led outside into one of the police vehicles that were lined up outside.

Chapter 46

Haleema was bundled into the back of a van with the hood obscuring her vision. She shouted in protest but soon gave up. Her futile attempts at struggling led nowhere, and she soon slumped onto the cold metal floor, listening to the sound of the engine change through the gears. Outside, the passing sounds of the late-night city. Persian house beats grew louder before fading, snippets of conversations from the street. The music reminded her of Damir, and once again, she thought of everyone she had lost; Damir, her brother, and her father. She ran through the events in her mind, the snapshot of Rahbar's corpse returning to her in a flash.

Now, she was in police hands. Perhaps her status as a government employee would help her. Then, the hope faded. She had been set up for this. No connections or vague strings to secretive state departments were going to save her now.

After twenty minutes, she felt the van slow down and turn, moving down a slope. The engine sound echoed off nearby walls, adding to her claustrophobia.

The van stopped, and almost immediately, the rear doors swung open. Hands grabbed her ankles, and she was dragged out of the vehicle. Another pair of hands grabbed her legs, standing her up. The hood was removed, and she gratefully sucked in the air.

"Please, I didn't kill anyone," she protested. The two policemen continued to ignore her and led her through a series of doors, scanning their passes as they went. Then, she was being led down spiralling steps. Harsh lights on the concrete walls flickered into life as they descended, their footfall echoing up into the tubular space.

Several levels down, they broke off from the stairwell through a door where a guard waited, staring at her with fierce green eyes. He turned to one of the cells and opened it with a swipe of a card, and pushed her inside. The automatic door closed with a clank behind her.

Inside the four concrete walls of the windowless cell were a single dirty mattress and a bucket in the corner. The smell told her what that was for.

She crouched down on the mattress and massaged her arm that had been gripped hard by one of the policemen. She thought about Rahbar. He wasn't perfect but he didn't deserve to die like that. She had lost her only ally in the police force. The twisted politics. All the deaths.

And she still hadn't found her father.

Was he even still alive?

Now, she felt herself slipping towards despair, even questioning her sanity. She lay down in the fetal position, letting the darkness elope her, hoping it would chase off the doubt and looming fear.

Whether it was an hour or more after falling asleep, she couldn't tell, but the main ceiling light woke her up. She squinted up at a tall figure in the doorway and recognised him immediately.

Massood.

He appeared to be just watching her as he enjoyed a cigarette, blowing a plume of smoke in her direction. Haleema sat up quickly, suddenly alert and awake.

"Why am I here? I haven't done anything!" she said, raising her voice. Her anger was overlapping her senses.

Massood smiled eerily. Smiling didn't suit him.

"Perhaps you're missing the fact you were discovered with Inspector Rahbar's body. The murder of a high-ranking police official almost certainly will require you to be hanged. I could, in fact, have you killed right here, right now. No one would question me." Massood paused, drifting off in thought as if remembering something. "You wouldn't be missed."

Haleema looked up at him, defiance blazing in her eyes. "If you're going to kill me, then just do it!" She looked away and clasped her arms around herself. "If you could just tell me where my father is," she added.

Massood crushed the cigarette under his shoe, letting out of laugh. "Your father? Yes, that's what this is all about, I suppose. That's what made you such a thorn in my side." He looked back at her, assessing her with his dark eyes. "He is an important man, of course. Not only to Iran but to other countries as well."

"So the Americans are involved?"

Massood smirked. "I didn't say that. This isn't about America or Iran. It's about something greater. Not only is your father important, but you are too. Perhaps your talents in the art of hacking and the work you've done for the Cyber Defence Command will help save you. You're too valuable to be killed or to rot in prison."

Haleema nodded slowly. "So, he's alive?"

Massood began to step out of the cell.

"I didn't say that either."

Chapter 47

Haleema, dressed in an orange jumpsuit, shuffled along with dozens of other "detainees" inside the tube-shaped tunnel. Instructions droned out from a loudspeaker to keep moving forward, to keep a straight line and watch their step.

She had endured a six-hour interrogation by Massood and then was taken, blindfolded, from the police station and put into the back of a boiling hot van for what seemed like hours without a break. Then she had been handed over to other authorities, who spoke English, and she began to suspect she was heading west, perhaps to Europe.

There was a huge relief to get out of the vehicles and into a more refreshing environment. Her blindfold was removed, and she looked around at what looked like a major transportation centre. The walls were made from metal, and vents and pipes sprawled overhead, leading off in all directions. She was surrounded by dozens of other people, all dressed in the same orange overalls. All were looking afraid and uncertain.

They were separated into different gender lines, stripped, X-rayed and then showered before been made to put on new overalls. Yellow, this time. Then given food, basic rice and stew, with water and then, after an hour told they were moving again.

Then, they were blindfolded and put into vehicles once again. It was a short ten-minute drive this time, and when they got out, she heard the clanking of equipment and the rush of aircraft engines and felt the sharp desert winds whipping against her overalls.

An airfield? The transportation hub was close by. A CIA black site?

After shuffling up a sloping ramp and being made to take a seat, her blindfold was removed, and she found herself huddled together with the other detainees in moulded plastic chairs in a large transport aircraft.

Then, after a ten-minute wait, the engines roared into life, and the aircraft took off to their unknown destination. Haleema wondered again at what lay in store and clasped her fingers together in a vain attempt to keep her fear in check.

She whispered to the woman next to her without moving her head, keeping her lips tight. She didn't respond.

"What's your name?" Haleema repeated.

"Just call me Amy," the girl hissed back. "What does it matter?"

"We all need friends in a situation like this. I'm Haleema—just trying to figure out what is going on. What did you do?"

The girl closed her eyes as if wanting her internal nightmare to evaporate, along with Haleema.

"Nothing. I don't know why I'm here. No one's told me anything. I was taken over a month ago."

"What do you do for a living?"

"I'm just a structural engineer. My family have no idea where I am." The girl's voice wobbled, and Haleema sensed she was beginning to sob. "They have no idea—"

"I know, I understand," Haleema tried to reassure her.

A guard fired a hard stare in their direction and began to walk down the column of detainees towards them. They stopped talking, and the guard sat down nearby.

Talking was strictly forbidden, and there was nothing to do but try to sleep, which, as she was sitting up with her ankles and wrists tied, was not easy.

How long had she been in transport for now? It seemed like an age. She couldn't wait for it to end, but what was at the end? That question prevented her from sleeping at all. So she merely kept her eyes closed.

The six-hour journey passed by without incident, except for the uncuffing and shuffling of various detainees being led to the toilet and fed with a tasteless mush that Haleema imagined was the standard fare on space flights or third-world armies.

She had no idea what time it might be when the shuddering aircraft touched down. She watched in despair as everyone in yellow suits was, once again, hooded by the guards.

She heard the automated clicking releasing their ankles from the locks, and they were led off the aircraft, down the slope and back onto solid ground. A bitter wind cut through her body, making her shiver; she put her head down and hunched up, trying to keep warm. The cycle of being transported, eating tasteless slop, attempting to sleep, all seemingly never-ending and Haleema had numbed to it all now. She felt less than human, a machine going through the motions, the cog repeatedly turning.

Back into another vehicle, a jeep this time, and Haleema listened to the engines without fear or anticipation.

Now she felt helpless like a leaf being blown in a storm, destined to disappear, probably forever. She was so sleep deprived and disoriented she didn't know what was going on. She couldn't even help herself now, let alone her family.

Outside the vehicle, the engine noise seemed to have muffled as if they were now underground or in a tunnel system. She felt the van slow and turn corners, one after the other, before finally, it slowed down and came to a complete halt. Through the thin material, Haleema sensed the back doors opening, and a bright artificial light flooded the vehicle interior.

A figure ordered them to stand up and step toward the rear of the vehicle. A hand helped her down the steps, and then the hood was taken off. She blinked at the light and gradually focused on the figure in front of her. He was a young, hard-looking man dressed in black and grey military fatigues who was gesturing for her to hurry up.

"Come on, out."

She stepped into what seemed to be an underground station, the tiled walls all leading in one direction. Ahead was a platform, and when they all shuffled onto it, everyone looked up in awe at the vastness of the space. It seemed to be a massive transport hub, the biggest she had ever seen, like a giant aircraft hangar. In front of them was a round-shaped train that had three levels like some long worm-like aircraft, with thick portholes for windows.

"My God." Haleema turned to see it was Amy. "What do you think this is?" the girl asked, her eyes looking ahead in wonder, her fear seemingly evaporated.

Haleema exhaled. "No idea, but I guess we'll find out."

The yellow suits were herded on board through the doors. Inside was a series of individual reclining seats with headrests. They were all facing in different directions as if they rotated on their own axis. Each detainee was shown to a place by the guards until everyone had been buckled in. Haleema, positioned next to a porthole, glanced out across the station and watched the continuing construction of a far platform with dozens of workmen.

Where the hell am I? What is this place?

After twenty minutes, the doors closed, and the interior lights dimmed. The train began to move, picking up speed with apparent ease and yet Haleema could detect no engine noise, just a quiet swish as they entered a dark tunnel. The seats pivoted slowly, and Haleema caught the eye of the next detainee, a young man, for just a second, as astonished as she was. After ten seconds, they were moving much faster, a blur of lights passing them by and then through her window, she saw the outside wall with transparent sections and realised they were travelling under the ocean. A faint light from above radiated the grey water with the clear vision of the darkest blue.

The transatlantic! But how? It was a project in the early stages, something she had read about but never really believed was possible. One of those crazy ideas only really exists in old novels from a different era.

The train was continuing its increase in speed. Every fibre of her body felt it.

Now, she knew they must have completed the project but must have kept it under wraps. For what? She cast back into her memory of what she knew. The tunnel itself, 150 feet below the ocean surface, tethered it to the seabed like anchors, the same principle as a clock pendulum. The technology already existed in advanced offshore oil rigs, they had said. The cable itself had enough flex to deal with strong currents.

Haleema held onto her seat as she felt an immense force

against her body. They were gaining speed, getting faster.

A Geopositioning system that tracked volcanic seabed fluc-tuations and, all along the tunnel system, sensors would track any other hazards.

Her hands gripped tight, and she felt she could no longer breathe.

Then, there was the tunnel system itself.

Based on maglev technology that was capable of speeds up to five thousand mph. To achieve that, they used magnetic fields that meant no air resistance.

Shit!

She felt nauseous and breathed in slowly, closing her eyes to fend it off, but that only made her feel worse. For a second, Haleema saw herself propelled through the ocean in a translucent tube, and then blackness took her.

Visions of men hauling her up, then darkness.

A bright light kept taunting her, and she wanted to shout and punch to make it go away. To leave her in peace.

Pain stung her cheek.

A glimpse of a man's face, his eyes looking at her carefully.

"She's coming round—"

Haleema felt nauseous again and gripped her stomach while trying to turn her head.

She vomited hard, hearing it slosh into a metal can that had been placed beside her.

A voice reassured her.

"The nausea will pass. Here, drink this when you're ready."

She slowly looked up and saw the water container being held out to her. She could barely move, managing only a nod, and the hand lifted the bottle to her lips. She glugged water and then pulled away.

She looked up to see two men in grey fatigues standing over her.

"Right, she's fine," said one, who walked off.

Looking around, Haleema could see she was no longer on that train. The other detainees were lined up in front of an arched tunnel with an empty road that stretched off into the distance. The soldier, or whoever he was, hauled her up so she was standing.

"Can you stand on your own?" he asked with mild irritation.

Haleema nodded and wiped her lip. "Yes."

He stepped away.

"Just stand with the others," he said, pointing at the line of detainees.

Haleema walked over and joined them. A hand took her arm; it was Amy.

"Are you alright?" she asked.

"Never better," Haleema mumbled. "How long was I out?"

"The whole journey. I was too far back and couldn't see. I'm sure they used us as guinea pigs on that thing. It was two hours, then another long truck ride to here."

Looking around at her surroundings, Haleema could see they were on a vast concourse, as wide as an eight-lane highway that stretched in both directions, set in a vast arched space. The ceiling looked to be at least three or four hundred metres high, with large vents, cables and a piping system built into them halfway up.

Opposite them were arched doorways, big enough to let large vehicles through, leading off the concourse, with white numbers painted on the concrete walls next to each one. They were in sequence; 045, 046 and 047 and so on, disappearing into the distance.

Other large military vehicles, as well as transport trucks, screamed past them at high speed onto unknown destinations. Up ahead, what looked to Haleema like a fleet of black SUVs slowly came into focus as they got nearer.

Haleema did not doubt that they were deep underground in some off-the-grid military base.

She had come across references to DUMBs or "Deep Underground Military Bases" when snooping around files and documents related to Cryostone, the secretive military tech corporation. On paper, they had looked impressive, but now the vastness and reality of what lay before her almost knocked her against the wall.

The SUVs slowed and pulled into the layby track where everyone was congregated before stopping. A tall man in his fifties with combed back jet black hair and a white suit slowly got out of the first car and made his way towards the young military man who pulled out a PDA device. While they exchanged words, the man with black hair casts his eyes across the detainees, glancing down at the screen.

The military man then walked along the line and pulled out a few of the detainees. He came to Haleema and looked her in the eyes. "You too," he said. Three of them, including Haleema, were taken with the man in the white suit to the first vehicles. He gestured for them to get into the back seats, which were spacious.

The man got into the front passenger seat and nodded to the driver, another dark-fatigued military man. There was a glass screen separating them, so when the man in white turned to speak to them, they heard him through a speaker.

"Good afternoon. Yes, it is the afternoon, but down here, that can be hard to fathom sometimes. Welcome to Station

12. I understand you may have had a traumatic journey, and I'm truly sorry, but things will become a lot more comfortable for you now." He looked at each of them in the eye before continuing. "I'm Doctor Black, and I'm here to impress upon you the importance of your work here. Everything will become clear soon enough." He faced the road for a few seconds and then turned back and looked directly at Haleema.

"Ms Sheraz. I hope you're looking forward to seeing your father again?"

Chapter 48

Haleema felt the tears well up as she held her father, refusing to let him go.

"I always believed you were alive! I searched for you everywhere, and you wouldn't believe what I went through."

Karim held her equally hard and stroked her back. "We've found each other now; that's the main thing, Haleema. Always remember that."

He held her back and looked at her with smiling eyes. The crow's feet crinkled up just as she remembered, the greying beard neatly trimmed.

"You look well." Haleema wiped her eye and rubbed his arm gently before moving back to the seat on the white table. She glanced at the guard by the door, who looked impassively ahead, and sat down. Karim eased himself down opposite her and poured her more water from the bottle. They were in a white holding room that had a dark glass interior window on one end and a cream sofa at the other. In the corner, a plant that looked plastic.

"So you were brought here," Haleema's eyes darted to her side, "some time ago then, I guess?"

"Yes, yes," he replied, apparently waving away recent memories as if to discard them quickly, his eyes glancing at the guard, "but it's all fine. I'm working, doing well. We have a lot to catch up on. So, how are your mother and brothers?" His eyes fell on her in the following silence. Haleema felt herself shrink as if she were a little girl again, admitting something terrible to her dad.

"Ma is fine, anxious, of course," she said quietly. Karim slowly dropped his head a fraction and blinked slowly. "Amir—" she paused. "Amir is—well, he was caught up with them, the Daesh. Fadin, too but he's back home now."

Karim looked at her, puzzled, as if failing to comprehend.

"Daesh? How can that be?"

Haleema shook her head.

"Two minutes left," the guard said, "Then I have to take your daughter for her briefing."

Karim and Haleema held hands across the table.

"Look, Haleema. We'll talk. They will be asking you questions; it's like a debrief, nothing to worry about, I'm sure."

Haleema looked at him wide-eyed. "You promise? I'll see you again, won't I?"

Karim laughed easily. "Why, yes. We're both here because they want to use our talents. I have a nice little place to live here, as you will. There is even a good comprehensive package, very generous."

Haleema shook her head.

"I don't understand. What is going on here?"

He patted her hand and smiled at her.

"I'm sure you'll be briefed, and everything will become clear."

The door opened, and Haleema turned to see a man in a dark blue suit casting his eye in her direction, a thin tablet device in his hand.

"Miss Sheraz? If you will."

***

Three weeks later.

The screen on the wall displayed a tranquil view of Colorado scenery; the distant trees gently buffeted by the wind, the fluffy clouds moving overhead. The apartment was ultra modern with an open plan kitchen and dining area finished in metallic. A low sofa and chairs, with a large media screen built into the wall, completed the compact but smart habitat with a double bedroom with an en-suite bathroom off the living area.

It was an identical layout to Haleema's living quarters, except she had put her stamp on her place already. She had acquired equipment, a laptop, as well as some useful bits and pieces, like the external drives, USBs and an assortment of cables—all for the good of her new employers, of course.

Haleema sipped her tea from the kitchen bar as her father cleaned up the kitchen after their meal.

"When your mother gets here, we'll almost be a family again," he said.

"Do you believe they'll bring her here?"

Karim turned and frowned at her but said nothing. Haleema shrugged, instantly regretting her remark. She wanted to believe that as well. Somehow, the bubble they were now living in seemed much safer than the outside world.

He stepped over to the dining table and slowly eased himself into the leather and steel chair, sighed and leant back.

"Well, it's not a bad life, really, and we're doing something good here. Look at the transatlantic tunnel. What an achievement by the human race. They said it couldn't be done, but great engineering proved otherwise."

Haleema stared into her tea. They'd had this discussion so many times. The fact that her father believed he was doing work that was beneficial to the populace was understandable. But he couldn't discuss it, of course. Not in detail, and they were almost definitely listening.

"Yes, of course," she replied.

And her project? The disaster projection model was supposed to be working out how to save lives in a nuclear war. All the different scenarios were complex and exact calculations were needed to be accurate what with the different variables; weather, strike locations, casualties and the fallout calculations that included the radius of the airburst, fireball, radiation, and the spread of thermal radiation. Each type of warhead and kiloton yield created different offshoots of calculations.

War seemed more and more likely. At least that was the line in the "bunker". And it made her feel depressed—the inevitability of it all. The tone of the officials, her managers, seemed to accept that war was upon them. Russia, China, North Korea and her own Iran were all poised to strike.

And they were "safe" down in the vast underground complex that had eight levels, spanned sixty square kilometres, the size of Manhattan and was linked by a complex tunnel system linking all the other stations that had been relentlessly built in secret since the 1960s.

Right bang underneath Denver airport.

That was what she'd heard.

Snippets of rumours, hearsay, the occasional word and her father seemed to know things more than he was letting on.

Chapter 49

Station 12, Denver, Colorado, USA.

Haleema walked towards her quarters, her footfall clanging on the metallic lattice walkway that connected the whole living section for the fourth level. She passed arched doorways on either side and, for a second, felt like she was in an industrially styled hotel. She was restricted to the east wing and two levels; the fourth level that she lived on and the fifth where she worked. She had never seen any other part of the enormous underground base and had been given scant information on her arrival, except that it was a haven for the upper echelons of the US government and military to enable it to continue operating in any disaster.

That much was true, thought Haleema, but her experience and the dirt she had seen over the years taught her that there had to be a more sinister agenda. For the past three weeks, she had kept her mouth shut and eyes open, focused on the work assigned to her and made mental notes.

Now, it was time.

She slipped her card reader across the pad outside her door and walked into her quarters; the lights flickered on at her command. The door closed behind her, and she stepped into the kitchen area and snapped shut the laptop console where she had left it, casually slipping it into a holder. She walked back out and headed down the walkway until she came to a staircase. To her left was a view of a central hub where several walkways intertwined, connecting the other sections of the east wing. Ascending quickly, Haleema was soon on the upper floor and continued until she reached a corner and an unlocked door. She opened it and slipped inside a long narrow service conduit. Vents hissed overhead, and opposite the wall was a bank of servers humming quietly. These she knew were running an unimportant low-level network for the east wing communications.

She moved out of sight from the door and crouched down, pulling out a thin PDA from her laptop bag, leaving the laptop itself in place. Logging in, she accessed the network and then, carefully disguising her location and IP, tapped into the exterior internet. After five minutes, she was on Icarus and virtually tapping Joe Bowen on the shoulder with a series of encrypted messages.

The plan, such as it was, had worked, and Haleema was now on the inside, but the process and implementation had been a lot more complicated.

She knew Massood was getting large payments for every "asset" he grabbed and handed over to the Cabal. The dark web message board she had delved into had revealed that. When she had placed herself on the "shopping list" it had pretty much guaranteed her safety. Someone like Massood wasn't going to let 150 grand go unclaimed. She also had another card up her sleeve. A card that would sink Massood and one she fully intended to use with extreme prejudice.

Rahbar's death had been a significant blow, and she hadn't

seen it coming. He was a useful ally, and despite his flaws, the Inspector had come around to her way of thinking.

For a moment, as she waited for Joe to respond, a feeling that nothing would be the same again hung heavy over her. That she would have to get used to death. Get used to losing people around her.

Nothing will be the same. Just get used to it, Haleema.

A message popped up on the screen.

"Sirus! Happy days. Glad you made it. I was getting worried."

"Copy that," Haleema typed, "family member is here." She was careful not to name anyone in case it led back to her. She continued typing: "I'm sending you co-ords. Still making slow progress on the reccy. It may take time. You still in my homeland?"

"Still here wrapping up loose ends. Plans or maps of where your facility would be good—but stay safe and keep your head down."

"I'll try. Got to go, I will check in with you in a few days. Over and out."

"Take care, Sirus. Out."

Chapter 50

Revolutionary Tribunal, Tehran, Iran.

The anonymous package had been treated with suspicion. With the increasing UIS attacks, there could be no half measures or chances taken, but the officer of security had given it the all clear and indicated it only contained paper documents.

The tribunal officer carefully opened the package addressed to Judge Ervand Neyestani and pulled out the papers. He nodded to the security officer, indicating him to leave, and the middle-aged man gladly did so, barely hiding the relief on his chubby face.

The officer's eyes widened as he scanned over the top page. The document laid out detailed evidence incriminating the highest, most powerful Police Chief in Iran, Massood Rajavil.

Evidence of collaboration with the UIS. Evidence of bribes, torture, and disappearance of prisoners. The latter didn't surprise him. In fact, those methods were necessary for upholding the Iranian state. The treachery of dealing directly with the enemy, though, was something else. He flipped through the pages quickly and, after a minute, leant back in his chair.

Where had this come from? Did it matter? The Revolutionary Tribunal might want to consider this, but ultimately it was not that important.

This was more than enough to action his immediate arrest.

Got you, Massood, he thought.

He returned the papers inside the package, stood up and walked down the marble-tiled hallway to the office of Judge Ervand Neyestani with urgent speed.

***

Unable to sleep, Massood made his way down to the ground floor; the night was just beginning to turn to dawn. He poured himself a Scotch whisky in his expansive living room. The burning liquid warming his throat felt good, and he took a second one before sitting down on an ornate Versailles settee.

The Chief of Police tapped through his tablet, reading the headlines of the local news website, but he was barely taking in the reports of UIS gains in the south and increased bombings across the country. The fact that the current regime was becoming unstable had not been lost on him. His mind had been drifting on how best to use the funds he had made from all the asset transactions.

It might be prudent to begin moving his money out of the country. If, or rather when, the Daesh gained control, who knew what chaos would ensue? Yes, he had been assured that a commanding position in the regime would be made available to him, but what other unknown factors might occur? Sudden changes in their laws, some crazy wealth tax or a land grab? A new leader not so keen to be his ally? He had been happy to supply information to the Daesh but didn't trust them an inch.

A bark from somewhere outside the garden wall interrupted

his thoughts. It sounded like it was beyond the property walls, but he couldn't be sure. He went to grab one of the radios that he kept in every room from inside the drinks cabinet and depressed the responder.

"Eagle to ravens. What is happening out there?"

Silence.

He moved to the window and repeated the message. Alerted now, he realised something was wrong and glanced outside.

He immediately saw movement through the trees: a quiet swishing sound, one of his armed guards slumping to the ground. Khaki-green figures moved expertly across the gardens, hunched low with their weapons poised.

He needed a gun, fast. He ran across the hallway to his office and quickly opened a desk drawer, pulled out a Glock 13 and slammed in a magazine.

Who could they be? It must be a rogue group. Criminals.

A crash of glass, followed by a loud bang as something hit the front door like an explosion.

The French doors behind his desk erupted with shards of glass blown across the room, followed by armed military police, all aiming machine guns in his direction. Massood knew he was a dead man if he lifted his weapon and dropped it to the floor.

Keep alive. They won't get away with this.

"Kick your weapon away carefully and turn around with your hands on your head," one of the men shouted in Farsi. Massood looked carefully at one of the men's uniforms and badge—NAJA Special Units Command.

"What's going on here? Do you know who I am? Do you want to see your families again?"

"Shut up! Do as I say," the leader replied, moving closer,

his MPT-9 submachine gun pointing directly at Massood's forehead.

"You're under arrest for treason, espionage and terrorism offences. It's over, Mr Rajavil."

Massood looked puzzled for a short moment, then reluctantly kicked his pistol across the floor. He turned around, hands on head, anger simmering along with dark thoughts of what he would do to those responsible.

Chapter 51

Station 12, Denver, Colorado, USA.

The focus of the vast arc-shaped room was a curved screen that dominated the entire wall space, ever-changing images of maps and crisp satellite images of different regions of the world continually changing from one to the next. Tiny red dots with a pink exterior circular band calculated the fallout radius.

Haleema was focused on her project on her own screen, re-checking calculations and fallout scenarios which varied considerably according to weather patterns. At the back of her mind was Massood. She wondered if he was wallowing in prison. She hoped so. The package of evidence she had assembled, the same material she gave Inspector Rahbar, had been placed with an anonymous and very useful time capsule service that posted it all to Judge Ervand Neyestani on a certain date that Haleema had specified. She had sent an identical package to the Liberatus media headquarters in London as well. It had all been a backup plan in case Rahbar somehow was compromised, which, unfortunately, he had been. The tall, lean figure of her supervisor, Leone Kaine, moved across the walkway towards her station, his head turning towards the main screen before facing her.

Haleema had built a rapport with him, working hard to get on his good side. Haleema was under no illusion that she would have to work hard to survive in this new world. She and all the others were prisoners, albeit with very comfortable living quarters and modest salaries, forced to work for their unknown masters who had not yet revealed their faces.

How would all this end?

Haleema had no idea but was under no illusion they were not going to let anyone leave, knowing what they knew.

Would they dispose of her and the others once their work was complete? What were they planning and preparing for exactly?

Kaine stopped in front of her, holding out an entry card and a scribbled note.

"Hal, can you do me a favour? I'm stacked. I need these files from the vault. Now I don't need to tell you the sensitivity of that area, so don't hang around or cause me any shit."

Haleema looked at the card, forcing her face to remain impassive. Access to the vault, a highly restricted area which had piqued her interest when she'd heard about it.

"No problem," she replied. She took the items from him and remained in her seat, looking back at her screen.

Kaine raised his eyebrows and held his palms together as if he were praying. "I kinda need them now," he said with a smile.

"Oh, sorry, sure." She stood up, returning his smile before heading along the raised walkway to the exit. She passed by the pale figure of Kacper Fagan, one of the Chief Technology Officers who she rarely spoke to. He turned his head slightly and nodded curtly, unsmiling, at meeting her eye.

She moved quickly along the harshly lit corridor and turned at the main stairwell, passing several other workers, descending down a level, and returning to the service conduit room. Once inside, she closed the door behind her and walked right up to the end and around the L-shaped corner, past the quietly humming servers and leant down, rummaging her fingers under one of the machines until she felt what she was looking for and pulled out a small machine with a card slot, a data cable, and a blank entry card. It had been her little side project. Plans are easily found on the net with weeks of searching around the workshops on the fourth level and then finding the storeroom for access cards.

She attached it to her tablet and connected the other end of the cable to the card machine, and booted up a software application on her screen. Next, she inserted the entry card that Kaine had given her and activated the copying of the data. It took less than ten seconds. She quickly removed the card, picked up the tablet sleeve and slotted in a blank card before copying the data onto it.

When it had completed, Haleema stashed the gear back in its hiding place and left the room, heading back to the stairwell and then taking an elevator down several levels to the crypt. The doors opened, and Haleema stepped onto another metal lattice walkway. Directly opposite the elevator were steel doors with a security console next to them. She inserted the cloned card and watched, with relief, as the doors parted.

She paused for a moment before stepping into the cool darkness. Lights faded on as she moved, revealing a vast warehouse-like space with a maze of twenty-metre-high shelving. A space that was seemingly devoid of any other people.

Directly in front of her was a long desk on top of which lay a thick book titled "Index". Next to it was a touchscreen built into the flat wood with a low blue screen displaying the words "Station 12 crypt". The chair behind the desk lay empty, as if they hadn't deemed the area worth having a security guard yet.

Looking around, it appeared she was alone.

On her right-hand side, on the floor, a pile of metal sheets, tins of bolts, with boxes of drilling equipment lay scattered as if they had been thrown down. Obviously, they were still building some of the crypt interiors.

She tapped the screen and read down the list of entries that indicated the rows from A–Z and sections for the file subjects. Next to the list was a wireframe map of the vault.

Was it Kaine she had overheard? Something about a huge server centre elsewhere in the station?

That was something she needed to look into.

The index gave her the location of Kaine's files, and she quickly retrieved them from one of the storage boxes. Giving it a quick glance, she could see it related to the simulations that they were carrying out. She placed it on the front desk and browsed through the index, flipping the pages.

There were countless lists: Genesis, Xyla, and Monarch. What could any of these be? There were also sections about station personnel and technical information about the base structure. Alongside them in a column were dates of entry, some reaching back to the 1960s.

The amount of information was overwhelming, and Haleema had no clue as to how to start finding what might shed light on what this place was or how it fit into her and her father's virtual abduction.

She would be able to come back with the cloned card. But for how long? When would security tighten?

Monarch.

She ran her finger down the entries and took note of the location: E213. She made her way along the narrow path between shelves looming like dark towers until she reached row E and found the correct place. She pulled up a narrow ten-step ladder attached to rails along each row and climbed up to the top. The box wasn't heavy, but it took a while to find the right files. When she fished it out, she returned to sit on the floor and browsed through it, making mental notes of everything she read.

The details of the Monarch programme made her wince in disgust, yet now she understood so much more.

Chapter 52

Tehran, Iran.

The clanking of metal doors echoed down the wide grimy corridor behind them. The white-painted walls long turned grey, were peeled and blistered like a skin disease. The air was thick with the smell of urine and death. Massood was familiar with this from his cell. Now he shuffled along, flanked by two guards, his entire body covered in bruises and cuts from the interrogation.

Enemies in the police departments had all crawled out like worms from the ground, and Massood was certain his initial beating was just the beginning, a warming up entrée before the main brutal main course of torture so beloved of the Iranian state.

Hisses and whistles at Massood followed his direction from the other prisoners. They came to an empty cell, the doors clanking open automatically, and the guard shoved Massood inside. The doors slammed closed behind him.

"Welcome to your new home, Chief."

Epilogue

Station 12, Denver, Colorado, USA.

Haleema walked along the highest terrace walkway that was layered on eight levels overlooking what appeared to be a park set in the centre circle of the vast space. She was not close enough to see if those trees and bushes were real. Probably not. Above, a large artificial light beamed down as if it were the sun itself, casting an unnatural hue and stark shadows. Workers and operatives walked along the pathways through the park, as if this place were now the new normal, the way of things to come.

She turned into one of the tunnel walkways and took an escalator back up to the fifth level and headed to the service cupboard. She logged on, and Joe picked up, his face appearing on the small screen.

"Haleema, there's something we found out. The suicide bombing at Rafsanjan, it was Amir."

There was a shocked pause. Hal stared into the mid-distance off screen, an expression of resigned dismay. To Joe, she looked as fragile as he'd ever seen her.

"I'm sorry," Joe added, unsure of what else to say.

"How many were killed?" she asked, flatly.

"I think it was fifteen Iranian soldiers and—Amir."

She closed her eyes.

"If you need some time," said Joe. She shook her head immediately.

"No, there's work to do. I'll work through this in my own way."

"Sure, Hal, but we can do this another time."

She sighed, wiping her eye. "I don't think we have time." She inhaled as if to compose herself and continued in a more systematic tone. "Alright. Well, they've moved entire databanks of top secret information. There's a vault with huge archives moved from the underground facility underneath Washington DC," said Haleema, leaning towards the screen, sitting cross legged on the floor in her spot by the servers. "The secrets down there must be phenomenal," she continued. "It can't be a coincidence they're also moving all the alphabet agencies out here; the CIA, NSA, and others." Haleema paused for a moment before adding, "Joe, I think something big is happening."

"Is this about nuclear war? Is that the endgame?" wondered Joe aloud.

"They have us doing projection plans, fallout figures. I can't see what else it could be," she said. "But that's an assumption. I haven't heard anything else." She paused for a moment. "I just don't know, Joe."

"OK. Anything else?"

"Yes, lots. There's a man known as 'Doctor Black.' His real name is Doctor Klaus Klasfeld and is the overall head of several shady projects. There's the 'Monarch project', headed up by Otto Bielek who's also known as 'Doctor Red.' It's some kind of mind control programme, probably the same one your friends, Jamall Salazar and Zara Zimmermann, came out of." Haleema paused and looked at her notes. "Then we have a

Major General Dean Wexhall whose cover legend is 'Doctor Blue.' He runs 'Red Horse' and is a Major General in the US Army."

"Jesus. What's Red Horse exactly?" Joe asked, leaning forward to the screen.

"Military and secret weapons technology, the people who really run Cryostone. Another interesting fact is it was originally set up by the head of the American secret service, Wes Helms at the end of World War Two, together with a Nazi engineer, Doctor Wernher Reisser."

"Yes, I remember. Helms was mentioned in the Batchman documents we looked through last year. The biological programme and the creation of the Spanish Flu we read about—"

"Yes. 'White Horse' was originally headed up in 1918 by a young Helms, of course. It's now run by Doctor David Gertner, that's Doctor Green to you," she said, with a smirk.

Joe paused, thinking, staring off the screen into the mid-distance as he contemplated the increasingly large web they were uncovering. "That's mind blowing. Everything is connected—and this Reisser?"

"All I know is he was scooped up in 'Operation Paperclip' in 1945, connected to secret Nazi technologies and weapons. I think he was the architect of this place I'm stuck in now."

"OK, I'll look into all this."

"Look, Joe, I'll send over what I can. Don't know how long I can feed information out this way, though."

"That's great work, Haleema. Keep busy but be careful."

"Yes, I know. I can't thank you enough for saving my mother and Fadin," she said, her voice filled with regret.

"Least I could do. We're all so sorry about Amir, Hal."

"It's OK, it's OK." Grief catching her throat, unmistakable

through the light static. She held up her hand and gave a quick wave.

"Speak soon, Hal."

The monitor pinged as the call ended. Joe stared at the blank screen for a few moments and hung his head.

We have to learn from this.

Yet, he knew, hoped, they'd done their best. They'd risked their own lives and killed men to bring her brothers back to her. And now, he felt bad, a twinge of guilt for what he'd asked her to do.

Joe opened up the files Haleema had sent. He stared at the black and white image of Doctor Wernher Reisser, in SS uniform looking earnestly into the camera lens. Next to him was Klaus Klasfeld aka Doctor Black and the shorter Wes Helms, both looking off camera. He began skimming through the other documents and felt his heart pounding.

The more he read, the grander and more complex the puzzle became.

Now he knew all his deepest fears, and those of his Liberatus comrades, were true.

***

May 18th 1962. Denver, Colorado.
Station 12 construction site.

The jeep threw up red dust in its wake, zooming past a line of diggers and workmen on the sloping road that led to a huge tunnel entrance that spanned around thirty metres across. Large trucks filled with mountains of soil passed them heading back out. Temporary tracks had also been laid down, and a row of skip train cars sat idle. As they entered the tunnel daylight turned to an artificial hue in an instant.

Helms, in the front seat of the jeep, turned to Reisser who was sitting in the back, arms spread across the chair arms, his long dark coat flapping in the breeze that buffeted the vehicle.

"How long until Station 12 is operational?"

Reisser looked pained for a moment. "You know very well the endless setbacks have caused problems. Stage one will be complete on time, I assure you, but the next stages are planned over the next few decades as you know."

"Yes, including the airport on top. That will come in time." Helms turned back to face ahead as the driver slowed the jeep and turned off onto a slip road that continued their descent further down into the earth.

Reisser had spent fifteen years working on this project following Helm's request to head up one of the most ambitious and secretive projects in US government history. It had consumed his entire life where he would spend months underground in the "new city" they were building for themselves. It was a grand project, and Station 12 was just the start. Helms was pushing for a network of them across the entire country and Reisser had no doubt he would make it happen.

The jeep pulled up inside a large circular space that had a series of other tunnels leading from it. In the middle what appeared to be a park, with bushes and lines of trees. Above them, the curved ceiling was at least sixty metres high with steel beams crisscrossing the full length of the space with powerful lights pointing down.

Helms looked across at the park and turned to Reisser.

"What is this?"

"This is the exact centre of the entire structure, a common space for inhabitants. Psychology is important, to manufacture a closeness to nature if there is a lockdown situation. Home comforts. Don't you agree, Mr Helms?"

Wes Helms placed his hands on his hips and considered the space.

"If you say so, Doctor. Now, let's look at the rest of the facility."

***

Present Day
Station 12, Denver, Colorado

Doctor Black stepped off the tubular vac train onto a tiled empty platform, situated at the far south of the vast underground network in one of many restricted zones. The trains connected with the far reaches of the base as well as connecting with the main tunnel highway that was known as the trans-Atlantic line. As he walked across a concourse area to the row of elevators to take him to the upper levels, the Doctor mulled over the wonder of the hidden technologies that they were able to harness. Although the trans-Atlantic had been a public project, revealing the vacuum transportation system as a marvel of cutting edge technology, the expanded underground lines around it had not. Those were the veins leading to the Cabal's beating heart.

The Doctor came to a large rounded steel door set back through a maze of corridors from the station and held his eye to a scanner. He stepped through, the door shutting automatically behind him and briskly walked along a tunnel, a tube of light above fading on as he moved before dissipating as he passed. The tunnel curved, forming a semi-circle, and connected a series of chambers inside. Doctor Black came to another circular door and repeated the eye scan. He still marvelled at what trillions of black budget dollars could buy, shoehorned in from their friends in the financial system that had access to the money machine.

He stepped into a room where a rack of black hooded capes hung on a stone wall and removed his watch, radio for base comms and other personal effects. He slipped on one of the capes and continued on, through a grand arched entrance, grounded with marbled floor. Ahead, a subdued light lead the way through the darkness. On either side of him were doorways to the staircase that spiralled out of sight.

He entered a wide open space that formed a huge circular arena, resembling a Roman colosseum. Thousands of seats spanned the upper levels, looking down at the arena.

He pictured gladiators fighting to the death and slaves being ripped apart by lions and smiled to himself, amused at the thought.

At one end of the chamber, was a dominating thirty foot high altar, moulded from iron and gold of the Baphomet, the Sabbatic Goat, symbol for the occult, serving as a centrepiece at the head of the temple. The monument stood like a great Egyptian statue, horns glinting from spotlights above. The right hand pointed up, while the left pointed down to hell.

As above, so below.

In the middle of the circle a figure, hooded in black, was kneeling in front of the altar. Doctor Black slipped into a seat on the edge of the arena and waited, admiring the spectacle before him.

The figure stood up and turned and began walking towards the doctor, black robe brushing along the ceramic floor. He pulled off the hood from his head, revealing combed back white hair and the deeply tanned face as he approached.

"Doctor, it's good to see you again," he said, loudly across the space. Doctor Black stood up and descended the few steps to greet him.

"Natan! Making full use of the sanctum, I see? It's a magnificent space."

The two dark figures shook hands, Natan Helms looking around from where he had just walked. "Yes, yes, magnificent." He turned back and gestured to nearby seats. They sat down, Natan clasping his hands together while the doctor leaned forward, elbows on his thighs.

"It's a worthy temple for all of us, a fine place of worship. We'll need all our spiritual strength, guided by the light of Lucifer for the massive conflict ahead."

The doctor nodded, his jaw set in grim determination. "I cannot wait for that day."

"When my grandfather first saw those German underground facilities, it inspired his vision of how a similar undertaking could work for us. To think the Nazis paved the way for all this..." He gestured at vast space around them.

"Yes, incredible."

They were both well versed in the knowledge that both world wars had served their purpose, serving their own higher power. An ambitious vision of three world wars originally set out by Confederate General and high level 33rd degree freemason, Albert Pike in a letter in 1871 to Italian politician and fellow freemason Giuseppe Mazzini, founder of the Mafia.

In the letter Pike wrote that a first Great War was to "permit the Cabal to overthrow the power of the Czars in Russia and of making that country a fortress of atheistic Communism. The divergences caused by the Cabal agents between the British and Germanic Empires will be used to foment this war. At then at the end of this war, Communism would be built and used in order to destroy the other governments and in order to weaken the religions."

Then a Second World War would be fomented by taking advantage of the differences between the Fascists and the political Zionists. This war must be brought about so that Nazism is destroyed and that political Zionism becomes strong enough to institute a sovereign state of Israel in Palestine. During the Second World War, International Communism must become strong enough in order to balance Christendom, which would be then restrained and held in check until the time when they would need it for the final social cataclysm.

A Third World War would take advantage of the differences caused by the agents of the Cabal, pitting the political Zionists against the leaders of Islamic World. The war would be conducted in such a way that Islam and political Zionism mutually destroy each other. Meanwhile, the other nations, once more divided on this issue would be brought to physical, moral, spiritual and economical exhaustion after which they would unleash a formidable social cataclysm which in all its horror demonstrate clearly to the nations the effect of savagery and bloody turmoil.

Then everywhere, the citizens, obliged to defend themselves without knowing where to render its adoration, will receive the true light through the universal manifestation of the pure doctrine of Lucifer, brought finally out in the public view.

All financed by the trusts and banks in service to the Cabal brotherhood.

Helms turned to Doctor Black. "I wanted to cover our projects briefly before the big 'council of thirteen' meeting, so we're both in sync."

"Yes, yes, of course."

"So what progress? Let's start with 'White Horse.'"

"Doctor Green and his people need more time on the virus, specifically the vaccine. It could be another year at least before any bio operations can be considered," the Doctor said, a flicker of disappointment on his face. "I'll keep you posted. I have to update the 'council' anyway, and hopefully, there'll be better news at that time."

Helms nodded, a craggy frown forming across his tanned forehead.

"These things take time. What about Project Monarch?"

Doctor Black's expression eased, a more successful subject; the mind control project that had brought in a conveyer belt of new controlled "talent" in the form of trafficked children. Then, the seamless process of breaking their minds and training them to become their assassins, political pawns, agents and other assets.

Monarch: originally inspired from the discovery of Josef Mengele's child subjects at that Sowie mountain complex in 1945. The infamous German SS officer and physician, the "Angel of Death" as he became known, had disappeared to South America after the fall of Nazi Germany, never to be found or captured until his reported death in 1979.

Mengele.

The original "Doctor Black" who helped implement Project Monarch after the war, despite the fact he still pursued his genetic research in Brazil.

"Very well, Doctor Red has a handle on things, and I drop in regularly to co-ordinate the use of these assets. As you're well aware, we have them placed in every facet of power; government, military and intelligence and the network of trafficking groups keep us well supplied."

"Very good."

Doctor Black turned to the Senator.

"Can I ask how the Middle East situation is going?"

Helms pursed his lips as if the question was inappropriate, then his features relaxed. "Not a problem. Major General Wexhall and I felt there was an opportunity in Iran with the uprisings. An ideal situation to play our hand, to push it along a bit. Create another Syria—"

The Doctor smiled, knowingly. "Ghost 13?"

Helms rubbed his hands as if he were feeling cold. "—Our very own.

"Other than that, I cannot say too much about Red Horse, I'm afraid, Klaus," Helms stated with finality, slapping both palms on his legs and standing up. "War is a complex thing. Creating and nurturing it is like a bringing up a lion; small and harmless until it becomes a fully grown beast," he added.

"Yet, the world needs beasts—monsters to maintain the balance," replied the Doctor, standing up with him.

Helms smiled at his protégé. "Let the day 'cometh' and the rain of destruction fall, leaving the world to our worthy bloodlines." He turned and faced the statue of Baphomet across the great hall of worship. "Bring the monsters—"

Free Thriller

Exclusive offer. To grab your FREE Novella eBook, head to:

www.jaytinsiano.com/secret-access/

PLUS, you'll get access to the VIP Jay Tinsiano reading group
for:
Free Books and stories
Previews and Sneak Peeks
Exclusive material

Also Available

For updates and a full list of retailers for each book, visit:
www.jaytinsiano.com

Black Horse (Dark Paradigm #3)

ISBN:978-1-9162397-6-0

As the clock ticks down to a devastating world event, Zoe Bowen's investigation into her partner's apparent suicide takes her down a dark, dangerous path.

Zoe Bowen, part of the banking elite in London, is thrown into a conspiracy when her partner throws himself off his Canary Wharf balcony.

But nothing points to suicide apart from the official verdict.

As Zoe investigates further, she unravels a string of similar suicides that equally make no sense and a global plot to devastate the food supply. As the investigation pulls her onto a threatening course, Zoe confides with her brother, Joe Bowen, and together they enlist the help of hacker Haleema Shiraz to infiltrate one of the front financial corporations of the cabal to uncover the truth.

What they discover is even more terrifying than anything they could have imagined; they stand at the edge of an apocalyptic event that will change the world forever.

As the clock ticks down to the cabal's devastating endgame, Zoe and her allies race against time to stop them before it's too late.

Pale Horse (Dark Paradigm #4) Coming in 2024.

ISBN: 978-1-9162397-7-7

As the world hurtles toward the brink of collapse, the key figures of the freedom-fighting faction known as Liberatus find themselves thrust into the very apocalyptic future they both anticipated and dreaded.

In the heart of London, Zoe Bowen, still grappling with the scars of her past encounters and her climactic battle against Dr. White, embarks on a desperate quest to locate John Rhodes amidst the escalating chaos gripping the British capital.

Meanwhile, Joe Bowen, far removed from his Spanish stronghold, faces a perilous journey to reunite with his comrades.

Within the Tennessee Liberatus enclave, Hugo Reese gains a tenuous grip on their dire predicament, unaware of the treacherous betrayal brewing within his own ranks.

Deep beneath the surface in Station 12, Denver, Zak Bowen finds himself at the epicentre of a massive emergency simulation that, to his horror, transforms into a chilling reality.

As the shadowy cabal executes its devastating agenda, the world teeters on the brink of collapse. Hold tight as this pulse-pounding apocalyptic conspiracy thriller hurtles toward its electrifying climax.

White Horse (Dark Paradigm #1)

ISBN: 978-1-9162397-4-6

Half a world away in Spain and running from his past, a Los Angeles gangster unwittingly takes a train that's headed straight into a terrorist attack. He survives only to face an even deadlier threat.

On that same train: a virologist with clues to a deadly epidemic. Did his secrets die with him in the strike?

Raging in the aftermath, a foul-tempered police chief with a daughter caught in the attack thirsts for revenge. But against whom?

An orphan child without a name disappears down a dark, illegal CIA mind-control programme. Now trained in the ways of death, he prepares to do his master's twisted bidding.

From its first pages, the relentless techno-thriller White Horse drops you with a thunderclap in the middle of these colliding worlds. This tale of a global conspiracy that threatens humanity itself will keep you guessing whether anyone can survive.

False Flag by Jay Tinsiano. (Frank Bowen #1)

ISBN: 978-1-9997232-2-4

1991: A plan to destabilise Hong Kong is emerging; the key players are being put into place, the wheels are in motion, and innocent people will die.
Frank Bowen is a Londoner on holiday in tropical Thailand. Half drunk and strapped for cash, he's the perfect bait for a political plot that will leave him running for his life with nowhere to turn.

Pandora Red by Jay Tinsiano. (Frank Bowen #2)

ISBN: 978-1-9997232-3-1

Frank Bowen's mission is to find a GCHQ whistleblower, but in doing so unwittingly risks everything, including his own family's safety.
As part of a covert team assigned to dangerous missions, Bowen believes he knows what he's up against until a team of Russian mercenaries are thrown into the mix, leaving everyone and everything hanging in the balance.
It's a race against the clock to save all that he holds dear and uncover the dark truths behind his mission.

Ghost Order by Jay Tinsiano. (Frank Bowen #3)

ISBN: 978-1-9162397-0-8

Frank Bowen attempts to piece together a fractured life at

home but finds himself pulled back into the dark state once again. Only, this time, he's playing both sides.

Blood Tide by Jay Tinsiano.

ISBN: 978-1-9997232-6-2

Detective Douglas Brown transferred to Hong Kong to forget his past and the dark memory that still haunts him—Richard Blythe.
Blythe, an explosives expert gone rogue, had terrorised London and outwitted Brown, leading to the deaths of countless innocents.
Now the detective's worst fear has come true. Blythe is free from prison to wreak havoc and lead Brown on a deadly cat and mouse game in the city of Hong Kong.
Blood Tide is a gripping terrorism thriller from Jay Tinsiano.

Blood Cull by Jay Tinsiano & Jay Newton

ISBN: 978-1-9162397-2-2

A series of ritualistic killings.
A retired detective inspector desperate to save his wife.
A horrifying secret.
Detective Inspector Doug Brown has retired to Scotland, but when his wife falls ill, there is no choice but to take on a private contract offered by an old acquaintance.
Soon he finds himself on a dark path, tracking down a ritualist killer of affluent men who has so far eluded the police.
But as the merciless killings continue, Doug is unknowingly

getting closer to unveiling a sickening conspiracy.

About the Authors

Jay Tinsiano

Jay was born in Ireland but grew up on the flat plains of Lincolnshire surrounded by cows and haystacks before moving to the city of Bristol, where he has lived, apart from far-flung nomadic excursions, ever since.

He is the author of the Frank Bowen thriller series and, in collaboration with Jay Newton, the Dark Paradigm Apocalyptic thriller series, Doug Brown and the shorter Dark Ops stories.

Jay is an avid reader, specifically of crime, sci-fi and thrillers, with occasional non-fiction thrown in. He can be occasionally found in a Waterstones bookshop café or perhaps a quiet pub, furiously scribbling notes and whispering to himself.

Jay Newton

Jay Newton practices and teaches martial arts, is a keen cyclist, manages a band and is an avid fiction reader.

He is currently working on the Dark Paradigm and Dark Ops series with Jay Tinsiano and lives in Bristol, UK, with his family.